LIFE NATURE LIBRARY

THE
INSECTS

TIME
LIFE
BOOKS
®

LIFE WORLD LIBRARY

LIFE NATURE LIBRARY

TIME READING PROGRAM

THE LIFE HISTORY OF THE UNITED STATES

LIFE SCIENCE LIBRARY

GREAT AGES OF MAN

TIME-LIFE LIBRARY OF ART

TIME-LIFE LIBRARY OF AMERICA

FOODS OF THE WORLD

THIS FABULOUS CENTURY

LIFE LIBRARY OF PHOTOGRAPHY

LIFE NATURE LIBRARY

THE INSECTS

by Peter Farb
and the Editors of
TIME-LIFE BOOKS

TIME-LIFE BOOKS NEW YORK

Peter Farb, an eminent author and naturalist, has written several best-selling books, among them *Face of North America* and *Man's Rise to Civilization as Shown by the Indians of North America*. He is also the author of *Ecology*, *The Forest* and *The Land and Wildlife of North America* in the LIFE Nature Library. His sensitive concern with the relationships among living things is the product of a study that began in his boyhood and has continued with unabated enthusiasm through years of writing and traveling. A member of the Ecological Society, former secretary of the New York Entomological Society and a Fellow of the American Association for the Advancement of Science, Mr. Farb has written widely on nature subjects for various publications and has served as a consultant to the Smithsonian Institution.

On the Cover

A blue darner, a dragonfly common in Europe, rests on a slender reed. Dragonflies are among the strongest fliers in the insect world. Three hundred and thirty-two different species are recorded in North America.

Contents

TIME-LIFE BOOKS

EDITOR
Jerry Korn
EXECUTIVE EDITOR
A. B. C. Whipple
PLANNING
Oliver E. Allen

TEXT DIRECTOR   ART DIRECTOR
Martin Mann   Sheldon Cotler

CHIEF OF RESEARCH
Beatrice T. Dobie
PICTURE EDITOR
Robert G. Mason

Assistant Text Directors:
Ogden Tanner, Diana Hirsh
Assistant Art Director: Arnold C. Holeywell
Assistant Chief of Research: Martha T. Goolrick
Assistant Picture Editor: Melvin L. Scott

•

PUBLISHER
Walter C. Rohrer
General Manager: John D. McSweeney
Business Manager: John Steven Maxwell
Production Manager: Louis Bronzo

•

Sales Director: Joan D. Manley
Promotion Director: Beatrice K. Tolleris
Public Relations Director: Nicholas Benton

LIFE NATURE LIBRARY

EDITOR: Maitland A. Edey
Assistant to the Editor: John Purcell
Designer: Paul Jensen
Staff Writers: David Bergamini, George McCue,
Robert McClung, John MacDonald, Peter Meyerson
Chief Researcher: Martha T. Goolrick
Researchers: Gerald A. Bair, Doris Bry, Peggy Bushong,
Joan Chasin, Eleanor Feltser, Susan Freudenheim,
Le Clair G. Lambert, Paula Norworth, Roxanna Sayre,
Paul W. Schwartz, Phyllis M. Williamson, Sybil Wong

EDITORIAL PRODUCTION
Production Editor: Douglas B. Graham
Color Director: Robert L. Young
Assistant: James J. Cox
Copy Staff: Rosalind Stubenberg, Suzanne Seixas,
Florence Keith
Picture Department: Dolores A. Littles, Sue Bond
Traffic: Arthur A. Goldberger
Art Assistants: James D. Smith, Mark A. Binn

The text for this book was written by Peter Farb, the picture essays by the editorial staff. The following individuals and departments of Time Inc. were helpful in producing the book: LIFE staff photographers Alfred Eisenstaedt, Fritz Goro, Dmitri Kessel and Howard Sochurek; Editorial Production, Robert W. Boyd Jr.; Editorial Reference, Peter Draz; Picture Collection, Doris O'Neil; Photographic Laboratory, George Karas; TIME-LIFE News Service, Murray J. Gart.

Introduction

FOR some 300 million years the insects have consistently been the world's foremost opportunists. We can only speculate on what potentialities ancestral insects must have possessed that enabled their descendants to populate the land and fresh waters with the greatest assemblage of species of any group of organisms. Whatever the mechanism, the insects pushed in everywhere, invading and monopolizing every possible niche and exploiting nearly every possible source of food. As they did this, each group and species evolved many distinctive characteristics that adapted it for its particular environment and way of life, and for survival despite many enemies. This massive insect evolution continually and profoundly affected the evolution of associated plants and animals, practically every one of which is what it is today in large measure because of the all-pervading influence of insects on its ancestors.

Insect diversification, however, extended far beyond the primary invasions of the land and fresh-water environments, for a great many insects soon began to feed on other insects, sometimes on close relatives. This has progressed to such an extent that today perhaps half of the insects are parasites or predators of other insects; and it is not uncommon to find parasites of parasites, or even parasites of parasites of parasites—each, in typical insect fashion, narrowly specialized for its own particular niche. In addition, the characteristic highly organized insect societies (perfect communisms, based on almost automatic sterilization of the proletariat) evolved in at least four major groups and in a number of minor ones. As with the insects themselves, insect societies are enormously diversified; some are small, simple and primitive; others are highly organized and integrated; and still others have degenerated and evolved habits of parasitism on other societies.

As a result of all this, there are now so many different insects that even today not more than half or two thirds of them have been named; and we are vastly ignorant about the details of the lives and ecology of the great majority. Relatively few species (chiefly those of economic importance to man) are really well known. It is for this reason that the only safe generalization about insects is that there is an exception to every generalization. So I know that the author and editors of this book must have had many difficult moments deciding how far it was possible to generalize without error or oversimplification on the one hand, or prolixity on the other. I think they have been remarkably successful and have produced a book, with a most interesting text and a wealth of illustrations, that effectively presents the major features of insect natural history.

ALEXANDER B. KLOTS
Research Associate, The American Museum of Natural History

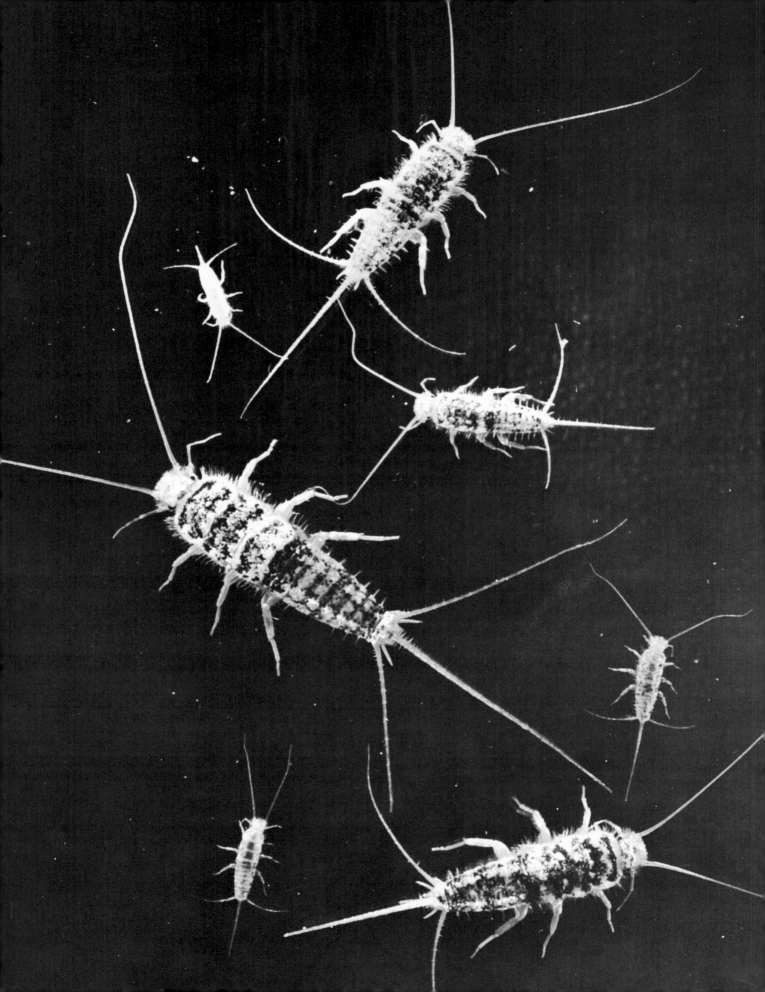

1

The Realm
of the Insect

WERE a naturalist to announce to the world the discovery of an animal which first existed in the form of a serpent; which then penetrated into the earth, and weaving a shroud of pure silk of the finest texture, contracted itself within this covering into a body without external mouth or limbs, and resembling, more than anything else, an Egyptian mummy; and which, lastly after remaining in this state without food and without motion . . . should at the end of that period burst its silken cerements, struggle through its earthly covering and start into day a winged bird—what think you would be the sensation excited by this strange piece of intelligence? After the first doubts of its truth were dispelled, what astonishment would succeed!"

This is no excerpt from a medieval bestiary that describes some fanciful companion of dragons and unicorns. Rather these words were written in the last century by two pioneer entomologists, William Kirby and William Spence, to describe the commonplace metamorphosis of a caterpillar into a moth. It is not only moths, but the buzzing, humming, leaping legions of other insects as well that have fascinated men for centuries. Man shares the planet with these little creatures, yet there is much in their lives that remains an enigma.

The lowly insects impress man by apparently possessing an uncanny wisdom out of proportion to their size. They do many things that man does, often with seemingly greater efficiency. There are insects that raise crops and herd insect "cattle" that they "milk" of a sweet liquid. There are insect architects that construct living quarters so intricately engineered that they achieve year-round weather control. There are insect carpenters, papermakers, slave raiders and undertakers. Some insects—ants, bees, wasps and termites—live in social organizations considerably more complex than those of human societies.

Watch a commonplace solitary wasp for half an hour. This wasp never knew its parents, nor did it ever trouble to observe other wasps in order to develop its hunting methods. Nevertheless, when it matures, it "knows" how to find a certain kind of site in which to excavate a nest that is a duplicate of the engineering design its species has been using for countless generations. This done, it sets off in search of prey—not any insect, but usually the caterpillar or spider that its ancestors have always hunted. It ignores all other possible prey. Eventually it finds one of the favored kinds. It inserts its sting in the precise spot that is anatomically the best to paralyze, but not kill, the victim—for the prey must remain alive. Then the victim is carried unerringly back to the nest, often many yards distant, and placed inside. Following this, the wasp lays a single egg in the nest, seals it, camouflages it and flies off to repeat the exact sequence with another nest. Later the egg hatches and the tiny larva sets about dining on its paralyzed victim, growing fat before it, in turn, becomes an equally adept adult hunter.

The complex sequence of steps carried out by the wasp in propagating its species, without instruction by the previous generation or the benefit of imitation, seems incredible and contrary to all the experience of a human observer. And well it might, for the realm in which the insect exists is foreign to man. "Something in the insect," wrote Maurice Maeterlinck, "seems to be alien to the habits, morals and psychology of this world, as if it has come from some other planet, more monstrous, more energetic, more insensate, more atrocious, more infernal than our own."

THE whole physical and sensory plan of these creatures differs markedly from that of man and the higher animals. Man's skeleton is internal, but an insect wears its skeleton on the outside of its body. If it can hear at all, it may have its "ears" on the legs or abdomen. It detects odors by means of long feelers, or antennae. It has neither lungs nor larynx, but can still make noises. Many species can produce sounds that can be heard a mile away by rubbing parts of their bodies together. The salivary glands of some insects produce silk or venom. Instead of always having two eyes, some insects have none. Others may have as many as five, but they do not focus like human eyes, or even distinguish the same colors.

Yet even such differences in perception do not explain the abilities of the solitary wasp. These must be sought in the complexities of the insect nervous system. Nor is insect intelligence superior to man's. It is of a different kind. Man depends to some extent on things he has learned to govern his behavior, the insect almost never. It is bombarded by sensory impressions that serve to push buttons, stimulating automatic behavior which, for want of a better name, is often called instinct. The sequence of steps undertaken by the solitary wasp is largely the outcome of a complex interaction between stimuli and reflexes. The wasp is locked into its behavior pattern; it is completely unable to alter the

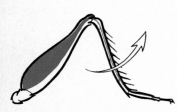

The supporting structure of man and insect is entirely different. Man, being large and heavy, must have strong bones, surrounded by flesh and muscle. For a tiny insect, a tubular construction is the strongest for its weight; tissues and muscles are inside. But in each, muscles act the same way. Shown here in green, they are anchored at each end to a structural segment, and when contracted, move the lower leg in the direction indicated by the arrow.

order of its behavioral steps, to omit a step, or even to repeat a step. Should a human experimenter interfere, say by removing the victim from the nest, the wasp will nevertheless go on to the next step and seal up its egg in an empty larder. The wasp, like all but an exceptional few insects, is completely unable to exercise the kind of judgment man would use, and restock the nest.

Despite this rigidity, the nervous systems of insects are highly complicated and serve their owners well. They have developed during roughly a third of a billion years of evolution and, combined with an incredible variety of physical adaptations, have made these animals enormously successful. There are some 800,000 species of insects known today and many thousand new ones are described each year. Some authorities believe that the total number of insect species on the planet, when all are known, will reach upward of one million, and one authority believes the number may be as high as 10 million. But even the total already known is about three times the number of all the other animal species on the earth combined.

INSECTS are all around man, living in his house, puncturing his skin, consuming his food and clothing, contesting the harvest of his fields, or simply filling the summer air like dancing motes. There is scarcely a place on the planet that is not home to at least one kind of insect. Insects have been found deep underground in caves, and a termite was recently captured in a trap attached to an airplane flying at 19,000 feet. Some 40 kinds of insects live in the bleak Antarctic. Bumble bees, beetles, moths and butterflies live as far beyond the Arctic Circle as flowering plants grow; mosquitoes and biting insects penetrate the polar regions as far as the warm-blooded animals they feed on. Insects are abundant in the driest of deserts and in rushing rivers; a few even live on the surface of the ocean beyond sight of land. In the Himalayas insects are found amid rock and snow 20,000 feet above sea level.

Wherever they live, insects seem to endure with a unique kind of indestructibility. Some of them have been frozen solid at temperatures more than 30° below zero F. and still lived; other kinds inhabit hot springs where temperatures reach 120° F. Still others survive in as great a vacuum as man has the power to create. Brine-fly young live in almost pure salt; their relatives, the petroleum flies, spend their immature stages in the pools of crude oil around the wellheads in southern California and are not found living anywhere else. A grain weevil may live for hours in pure carbon dioxide; this gas, immediately poisonous to man and most animals, acts as an anesthetic to the weevil and the inactive insect can survive on the reserve oxygen in its breathing tubes. Many insects can endure long periods without water; they possess fuel reserves and can get the water they need by burning these reserves. This is so-called metabolic water: it is produced by the burning of carbohydrates in the body, where they are broken down into water and carbon dioxide. The carbon dioxide is eliminated, but the water is retained.

Insects have a tremendous range in size, probably greater than that of any other major group of animals. The smallest insects are smaller than some single-celled protozoa; the largest ones are larger than such mammals as mice and shrews. The smallest North American insect is a beetle about one hundredth of an inch long; it could easily creep through the eye of a needle. The fairyflies, parasitic insects so tiny that they can deposit their young to develop inside the minute eggs of other insects, are as small or smaller. Among the largest insects in the world today is the Atlas moth of India. It measures fully 12 inches from wing tip to wing tip—a span nearly as great as that of an oriole. Insects in past ages were even larger: the fossil of one primitive dragonfly ancestor shows a wingspan of 30 inches. But such huge insects were and are the exceptions. Most are less than a quarter of an inch in length, which makes them small enough to inhabit many places free from the competition of larger animals.

Insects seem endowed with physical strength out of all proportion to their size. An ant can pick up a stone some 50 times its own weight. By putting small loads on wheels so they can be pulled, experimenters have found that a bee can haul a burden 300 times its own weight—roughly equivalent to a human pulling three 10-ton trailer trucks at the same time. Similarly, if a human had the same jumping ability as a grasshopper, he could vault one third the length of a football field.

But these seeming feats are actually illusions. Just as insects inhabit a different sensory realm from man's, so there is no basis for such power comparison between the two. For one thing, insects possess a remarkable musculature. Man has fewer than 800 distinct muscles, but grasshoppers have about 900 and some caterpillars more than 4,000. Furthermore, the insect muscle is extremely resistant to fatigue; a fruit fly can be made to fly continuously for as long as six and a half hours, and the desert locust for nine hours. But it is actually the insect's small size that makes it appear to possess prodigious strength. As any animal increases in size, it does not increase in strength in the same proportion. Also, as size increases, weight increases, but at a far more rapid rate. A man is only about four or five times as long as a giant walking-stick insect of the tropics, which may measure 15 inches from end to end. But the man's weight is many hundred thousand times as much. If insects could grow as large as humans, they probably would be no stronger.

THE success of the insects as a group is due to their having at least six major assets in the endless struggle for survival: flight, adaptability, external skeleton, small size, metamorphosis and a specialized system of reproduction. The most obvious endowment that sets insects apart from all other living things except birds and bats is flight. With wings, insects were able to spread over the globe; if conditions became unfavorable at one place, they simply took to the air to find another. Flight has given them an advantage over landbound animals in being able to search actively for their mates, forage widely for food and make good their escape from enemies.

Second, no other form of animal life has been able to adapt to such extremes of living conditions. The things insects feed upon provide just one example of their endless adaptability. In addition to eating every kind of higher plant, some also feed on paintbrushes, corks of wine bottles, mummies, stuffed museum specimens, tobacco, pepper, opium, and other apparently unappetizing and unnutritious substances. Their feeding tools, too, are as varied as their appetites. What began as pairs of jointed legs in primitive insects have evolved into the

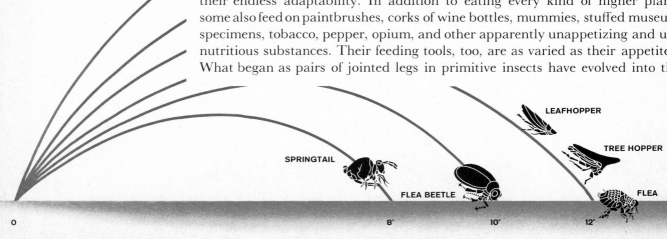

SPRINGTAIL

FLEA BEETLE

LEAFHOPPER

TREE HOPPER

FLEA

0

8"

10"

12"

retractable soda straw of the butterfly, the skin-piercing and bloodsucking tools of the mosquito, the vise of the beetle, the hypodermic syringe of the aphid, the extensible grappling hook of the immature dragonfly.

Third, the insect wears its skeleton on the outside of its body in the form of a cylinder—the strongest possible construction for a given amount of material. The external skeleton is formed by the hardening of secretions from the animal's true outer skin, and it is a remarkable protective armor. Its essential ingredient is chitin, which is flexible, lightweight, tough and very resistant to most chemicals. Sections that have no need for flexibility are further strengthened by a complex substance called sclerotin or cuticulin, somewhat similar in composition to man's fingernails. In addition the entire skeleton is coated with waxes that provide two-way waterproofing, not only keeping wetness out but also preventing the inside of the insect from drying up. This skeletal overcoat has become modified into a startling variety of bodily forms: jaws, spines, camouflaging projections, lacy wings and needlelike stings.

Fourth, the small size of insects is of great advantage in survival. Their demands from the environment are meager. The speck of food that is a feast for an insect is usually much too small to be noticed by a larger animal; a dewdrop quenches its thirst, a pebble in the desert provides shade. Many insects are thus able to occupy tiny niches in the environment where they can find both food and protection from enemies at the same time. Certain weevils spend their lives inside seeds; tiny leaf miners inhabit the paper-thin zone between a leaf's upper and lower surfaces.

Science fantasy sometimes depicts insects grown as large as a human, but that is an impossibility. The engineering of an insect's body is very efficient for its small size, but there are obvious limitations. One is the strength of its skeleton: as a hollow cylinder increases in size, it grows progressively weaker. More important, insects breathe through a maze of microscopic air tubes that bring oxygen to all parts of their bodies. Air seeps into these tubes by the diffusion of individual molecules of gas, a method that works only over short distances. That is the reason very few insects have bodies more than three quarters of an inch thick; much thicker than that, and the insect would suffer from oxygen starvation and become too lethargic to survive. Nearly all exceptionally large insects are tropical species, possibly because a gas diffuses more rapidly at high than at low temperatures.

Fifth, most insects receive survival benefits from the life pattern known as complete metamorphosis—the multiple changes that lead from a caterpillar via a cocoon to a moth, for example, or from grub to beetle and from maggot to fly. With this sort of pattern, the immature insect can exploit one food supply while the winged adult is nourishing itself on something completely different. Compared to man, who spends only about a fifth of his life span in developing to maturity, a typical insect spends most of its life as an inconspicuous larva,

CHAMPION JUMPERS

For their size and weight, insects are the strongest jumpers in the entire animal world. The champion flea's 12-inch leap may appear modest by man's standards. But the flea actually jumps 200 times the length of its own body—the equivalent of a six-foot man bounding the length of five city blocks. Shown below are some well-known jumpers and the distance they cover.

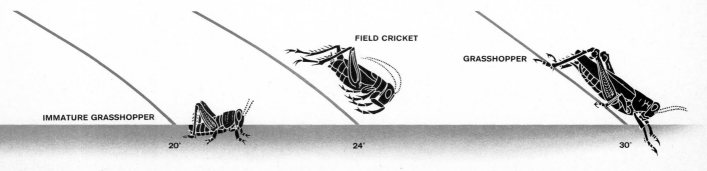

IMMATURE GRASSHOPPER 20"

FIELD CRICKET 24"

GRASSHOPPER 30"

during which time it develops a multitude of adaptations for coping with the problems of survival. One wood-boring beetle, the old-house borer, passes five to seven hidden years as a larva feeding on house timbers before it moves on into the hazardous open air as a short-lived winged adult. This is because the wood it eats is so poor in starch that it takes the larva that long to accumulate enough to grow and pupate. The pale-green Luna moth, among others, has such an ephemeral existence on the wing that the adult does not even eat.

Finally, winged adults are able to delay fertilization of the eggs, after mating, until the proper food plants and living conditions have been found for the young. A little sac called the spermatheca is attached to the female's reproductive system. When she mates, the male's sperm cells are stored in this sac; the eggs are not fertilized at once. Only when conditions are favorable for the offspring is the sperm released from the sac, and the eggs fertilized and deposited. After her nuptial flight, the queen bee possesses in her spermatheca approximately four million sperm cells. These last her for the rest of her life.

The insects have shared some of these six attributes for successful survival with a number of other animals since the day, some 300 million years ago, that they made their first formal appearance in the record of life. Insects have points of similarity—including external skeletons and jointed legs—with a host of creatures that are *not* insects: wood lice or pill bugs, crabs, lobsters, sand fleas, spiders, ticks, mites, scorpions, centipedes and millepedes, to name a few. This group comprises the great phylum of invertebrate animals known as the arthropods—literally, "jointed feet"—that is believed to have originated with an ancient line of marine animals that somewhat resembled today's earthworms. All arthropods, whether living on land or in water, have their bodies divided into segments, from most of which arise pairs of jointed appendages. From these appendages have developed the complicated, needlelike mouth parts, the fangs, the swimmerets, spinnerets, antennae, pincers and legs of today's arthropods.

THE insects comprise a separate class, Insecta, among the arthropods. Their bodies are typically divided into three parts: a head; a middle section, or thorax; and a rear section, or abdomen. The insect head bears the mouth parts and a pair of antennae; attached to the thorax are three pairs of legs (hence another name for the class: Hexapoda, or six legs) and, usually, wings. None of the insect's numerous relatives possess this same combination of three pairs of legs, three body divisions, a single pair of antennae and, often, wings. Spiders, for example, have four pairs of legs, no antennae and only two body divisions (the head and thorax are combined). Crustacea, such as crabs and lobsters, have many pairs of legs, two body divisions and two pairs of antennae. Other insect relatives have wormlike bodies made up of many segments. Among the millepedes, or "thousand-leggers," the legs are arranged in double pairs: no millepede actually has as many as a thousand legs; the number ranges from a dozen to over a hundred pairs. Centipedes, or "hundred-leggers," have their legs arranged in single pairs instead: sometimes these total 200, but usually the number is less than a hundred. The front pair of legs has been modified into clawlike pincers that inject venom into the centipede's prey.

There are no fossils known that show what the primitive ancestral insects looked like, but there is no doubt that they are an extremely ancient group of animals. For perhaps the past 250 million years they have been at least as numerous on the planet as they are today. A hundred and fifty million years before that, a number of different kinds of air-breathing arthropods—such as scorpions

SPEEDS OF INSECTS

The speed of flying insects can be measured by observing how long it takes them to get from one point to another in still air. The figures given in the table below for some common insects are their average normal cruising speeds; they can go considerably faster if necessary.

House fly	5	mph
Butterfly	12	mph
Wasp	12	mph
Hornet	13	mph
Honey bee	13	mph
Horse fly	25	mph
Dragonfly	25	mph
Hawkmoth	25	mph

and millepedes—were already established on land. No true insect fossils have been found in rocks of this age, but in those dating from the time of the later Carboniferous coal jungles, roughly 300 million years ago, insect fossils appear with well-developed wings and in a variety of forms. Animals of such complexity do not come into being suddenly; they must have been evolving for tens of millions of years before. Until fossils of these ancestors are discovered, however, the early history of the insects can only be inferred.

There exist today primitive, wingless insects that offer clues to what the earliest insect life may have been like; these are the bristletails and silverfish, which probably evolved from arthropods that had many body segments and a pair of stubby legs attached to each segment. As time passed, these creatures probably lost all except those appendages on the three body segments immediately behind the head, which developed into proper legs, and the rearmost ones, which became adapted into reproductive organs and organs of touch. The loss of all but these few appendages may at first seem an unimportant or even an unadvantageous development. The fact is that the three leg-bearing body segments became modified into a sort of locomotion center, specializing in transportation. These three segments relieved the rest of the body sections of the need to maintain leg muscles, so that the other segments were free to develop their own specializations.

THE next great stride in insect development came with the advent of wings. When the first amphibians abandoned the water for life on land some 350 million years ago, the insects and the other land arthropods already established on shore must have been a convenient source of food that helped these pioneers to survive in their strange new environment. The evolutionary challenge that led to wing development among the insects is not known. However, it is obvious that flying insects were better equipped to escape from the newly arrived amphibians, as well as from their older enemies, spiders and scorpions, than were their wingless relatives. Insects attained flight fully 50 million years before the first vertebrates—flying reptiles and birds—took to the air: for this long period they were the sole inhabitants of the air.

Insect wings probably developed from little flaps on top of the leg-bearing locomotion center—the thorax. Even today, all insects are wingless when they hatch out of the egg. Since an insect's external skeleton has no stretch, the growing animal must cast off its old skeleton from time to time and grow a larger one. Primitive wingless creatures like silverfish keep growing and molting throughout their lives, but for winged insects there must be one final molt into winged form, since wings cannot be molted or replaced.

In addition to the evolution of wings, many kinds of insects made a further great advance: they achieved complete metamorphosis, and their lives became divided into two active phases, each with its own specializations. The immature insect, lacking both wings and reproductive organs, abandoned the ancestral insect shape altogether—a caterpillar looks nothing like a butterfly. Many immature insects lack the usual three divisions—head, thorax and abdomen—while some dispense with legs, and still others develop additional legs to support their wormlike abdomens. They become simply efficient food-gathering mechanisms; the caterpillar of a Polyphemus moth, for example, consumes an amount of food equal to 86,000 times its birth weight in its first 24 days of life.

Such immature forms can specialize in a wide variety of foods and environments and flourish. In due course, transformation will occur. The chrysalis of a

HOW INSECTS EVOLVED

The diagrams below show how insects could have developed from a segmented worm. The first five segments gradually coalesced and specialized to form the head; the next three became the locomotive unit; and the others the abdomen.

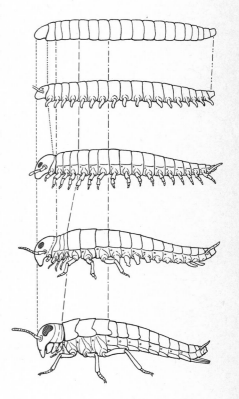

butterfly, for example, is an intermediate stage between immature and adult. This stage sets everything right again; it allows reorganization of the caterpillar's body into the ancestral insect pattern. The caterpillar's mouth, adapted for chewing, turns into the butterfly's mouth, adapted for sucking nectar; the three divisions of the body reappear, and so do the three pairs of legs and the two pairs of wings. The adult butterfly specializes in reproduction: with its wings for transportation, it can concentrate on finding a mate and seeking out egg-laying sites that are most favorable for the growth of the next generation.

Winged insects of many kinds swarmed through the coal jungles of 300 million years ago, but most of the insect species that lived in Carboniferous times became extinct. Perhaps their wings had become a liability. Spread out sometimes to spans of more than two and a half feet and lacking any means of being folded back, they prevented the bearer from hiding under leaves or in crannies. Other more adaptable insects, however, had already evolved a complicated system of joints at the base of the wings which allowed them to be folded neatly back over the body. Today, only a few insects that cannot fold their wings—notably the dragonflies—still survive.

By some 225 million years ago, all of these major advances had taken place, and nearly all of today's many insect orders had become established or at least existed in prototype. As the earth entered the age of reptiles, a wide variety of insect types still familiar today swarmed through the air—grasshoppers, crickets, mayflies, dragonflies, cockroaches, cicadas, leafhoppers, beetles and others. A few important ones were missing. Only when flowering plants arose some 130 million years ago did the insects that specialize in pollinating them—butterflies, moths, bees, wasps and the true flies—flourish. As the flowering plants expanded rapidly at the end of the age of reptiles, these new kinds of insects spread greatly and assumed a wide variety of forms.

Thus, for at least a third of a billion years, insects have consistently displayed their adaptability. After the amphibians came ashore, they took to the air. They developed a pattern of life—complete metamorphosis—that resulted in the tapping of new environments and new food sources. They took advantage of the rise of flowering trees and developed such complex social lives as those of the pollinating honey bees. They assumed a number of curious forms that protected them against enemies or made them more successful at finding prey: flowers that fly, twigs that walk and thorns that climb stems.

So adaptable have insects been in meeting the vicissitudes of life that they are the only creatures that today dispute man's dominance of the planet. It has been stated pessimistically by Dr. W. J. Holland in his classic volume, *The Moth Book*, that they will outlive man: "When the moon shall have faded out from the sky, and the sun shall shine at noonday a dull cherry-red, and the seas shall be frozen over, and the ice-cap shall have crept downward to the equator from either pole . . . when all cities shall have long been dead and crumbled into dust, and all life shall be on the very last verge of extinction on this globe; then, on a bit of lichen, growing on the bald rocks beside the eternal snows of Panama, shall be seated a tiny insect, preening its antennae in the glow of the worn-out sun, representing the sole survival of animal life on this our earth—a melancholy 'bug.'" Of course, this is always a possibility if the earth dies with a whimper of a burnt-out sun rather than with a bang. But the challenge is not one of direct combat. The insects—enormously endowed for rule within their own realm —simply do not possess the mental or physical equipment to dethrone man.

A LIVING ANCESTOR OF THE INSECTS, THE TROPICAL PERIPATUS HAS THE CLAWED FEET OF AN ARTHROPOD ATTACHED TO THE BODY OF A WORM

The Insect Explosion

Evolution has its break-throughs. A major one occurred more than 300 million years ago, when the insect body was shaped from the protoplasm of a primeval worm. In a population explosion of unmatched size and duration—it continues today—the first insects have multiplied and diversified. About 800,000 species have been found, more than three fourths of which belong to four main groups.

CARBONIFEROUS, 320 MILLION YEARS AGO   PERMIAN, 280 MILLION YEARS AGO

The Earliest Insects

More than 200 million years of insect evolution flow from left to right across the painting above. Although insects probably flourished earlier, the first readable fossil record appears in the beginning of the Upper Carboniferous, the age of the great coal forests. Most familiar of these early forms was the large roach at lower left. Flitting overhead was *Meganeura*, an immense dragonflylike creature with wings up to 30 inches across. Here also were forms unknown today, like *Stenodictya*, which had a pair of rudimentary wings in addition to two fully developed pairs.

The Permian age saw the emergence of reptiles like the sail-finned *Edaphosaurus* at center back. But while these lumbering creatures ruled the land, the insects dominated the air unchallenged by any other winged form—reptile, bird or mammal. Among these Permian species was an early grasshopper, *Oedischia*, with slender antennae and strong jumping hind legs. In the air above *Oedischia* is an ancestor of the modern stonefly and at bottom right an ancestral mayfly. Like their modern counterparts, both the creatures probably had aquatic nymphal

TRIASSIC, 230 MILLION YEARS AGO

JURASSIC, 181 MILLION YEARS AGO

forms. At right of the stonefly with wings of different sizes is *Prototelytron*, something between a roach and an earwig.

With one exception, all of the orders of insects represented in the Triassic are alive today, an example of staying power unparalleled among the higher animals. At bottom left, a small lizard gulps down what may have been a huge cricket ancestor. The wing of this species, six inches long, had a noisemaking apparatus that may have been audible for a mile. At the lower left of the feeding lizard is a primitive form of sawfly; to

its right an early species of silverfish crawls over the rocks.

In the Jurassic, dinosaurs like *Allosaurus* still dominated the landscape, and the flying reptile *Rhamphorhyncus* ruled the air. Insects thrived, and with the appearance of the first flowering plants, like the magnolia *(bottom right)*, as this period merged into the Cretaceous, they undoubtedly flourished on nectar and pollen. Few fossils have been found, mostly familiar forms: a darting dragonfly; a caddisfly on a stump; an earwig on a leaf; and on the magnolia blossom, a plant louse.

A. Petruccelli

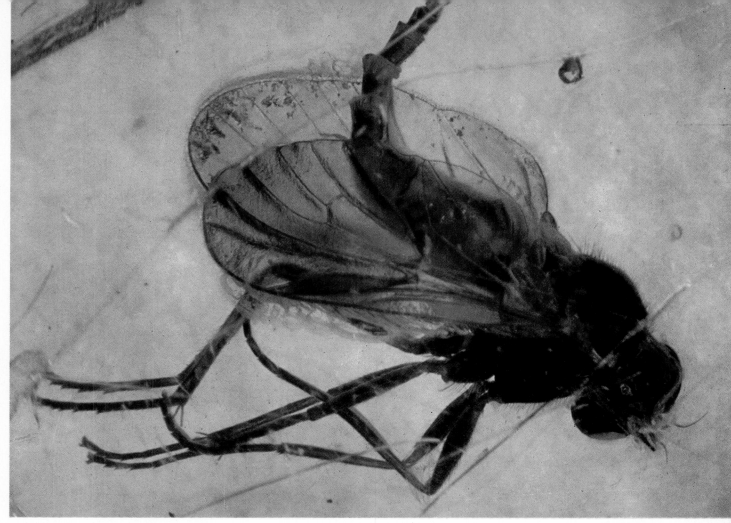

A FLY CAUGHT IN BALTIC AMBER IS COMPLETE DOWN TO ITS SMALLEST BODY HAIRS. ENTIRE SPIDER WEBS HAVE ALSO BEEN FOUND PRESERVED

Fossils in Jewels

The early insects reconstructed in the painting on the preceding two pages are known for the most part from faint impressions left in ancient rocks. Many insects from later times, and especially from a period about 45 million years ago, are found completely preserved in tiny gemlike sarcophagi, which are made of a substance known as amber. During the Upper Eocene, vast forests of trees similar to the modern white pine flourished over much of northern Europe. Resin oozed from cracks and wounds in the tree, and passing insects as well as other small animals were trapped in this sticky exudate. In time the resin hardened, was buried in the soil, then washed into the Baltic Sea. Today after a storm, bits of ancient amber can be picked up from Baltic beaches.

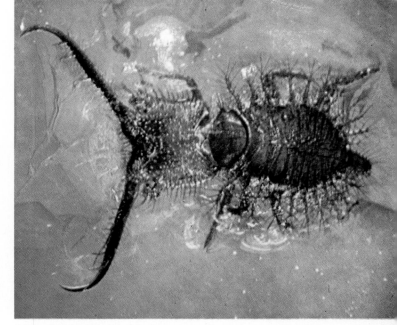

CAUGHT IN RESIN seeping from a pine, an ant and a fly take the first step toward becoming fossilized in a drop of amber. Many scenes like this took place more than 40 million years ago.

A FOSSILIZED KILLER, this sharp-jawed larva is a species related to the modern ant lion. Altogether nearly a quarter of a million fossil insect specimens have been found preserved in amber.

21

A LONG-SNOUTED PERUVIAN WEEVIL IS PARASITIZED BY A COLONY OF TINY, TAN MITES

Beetles: The Most Varied Insects

These eight insects are members of the most successful order of animals on earth, the beetles. The total number of beetle species may be as high as 280,000, an astounding number. By comparison, all the species of vertebrate animals—fish, amphibians, reptiles, birds and mammals—total fewer than 44,000. At least three characteristics contribute to this unparalleled success. First, the beetles undergo complete metamorphosis, progressing from a grub to a winged form. These stages live in different places and eat different foods. The advantages of such a double life are obvious; certainly the earth could hold many more people if human children lived and ate in the sea. Secondly, the front pair of the beetle's two sets of wings are thickened into hard covers which fold back into an effective shield, protecting the soft body beneath. This gives rise to the technical name for the beetle order, "Coleoptera," meaning "sheath-winged." Finally, the beetles have kept their primitive mouth parts, designed for chewing abundant solid foods. Many other orders have mouths fit only for sipping limited and uncertain supplies of sap and nectar.

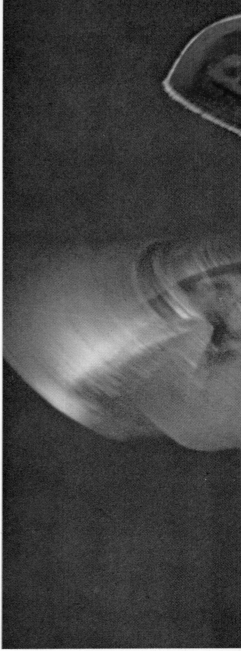

A COPPERY JUNE BEETLE COMES IN FOR LANDING.

BANDED LADYBIRD BEETLE

TORTOISE BEETLE

PERUVIAN FIREFLY

WHILE IT IS IN FLIGHT THE BEETLE'S HARD WING SHEATHS ARE HELD OPEN TO PERMIT THE FREE MOVEMENT OF ITS MEMBRANOUS FLYING WINGS

STAG BEETLE

LONG-HORNED BEETLE

SNOUT BEETLE

GREEN SILVER-LINES MOTH

FEMALE IO MOTH

The Butterflies and Moths

The bright butterflies and moths number 140,000 species, exceeded only by the beetles. "Lepidoptera," the order's scientific name, means "scalywinged," and tiny, shinglelike scales cover the wings and bodies of most adult forms. In size, butterflies and moths vary more than any other insect group. An owlet moth of South America is a foot across; the Eriocranid moth *(below, right)* has a quarterinch wingspan. Some species are even smaller.

There are no hard and fast rules for telling a butterfly from a moth. But in general, moths spin cocoons, butterflies do not. When at rest, the moth tends to fold its wings like a tent while the butterfly presses them together overhead. Usually more subtly colored and fatter bodied, the moth is most often seen as a fluttering shadow in the dusk, while the butterfly flaunts its brilliance through the day.

TASTING A DAISY, a European copper butterfly *(opposite)* can detect nectar with taste buds on its feet. Many species of this butterfly spend their pupal lives within the nests of certain ants.

HORNET MOTH

PLUME MOTH

ERIOCRANID MOTH

DUSTED WITH POLLEN, a solitary bee gathers nectar from a goldenrod blossom. The vast majority of bees are not social insects like the ordinary honey bee, but live alone or in the most rudimentary communities. The females often share a common underground burrow but each of them builds its own small egg chamber off this main tunnel, stocks it with food and seals it up.

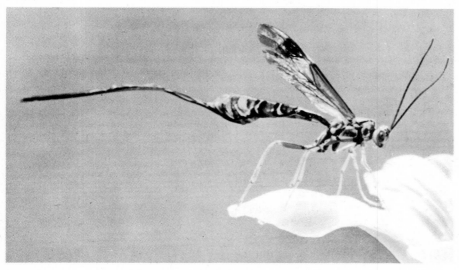

WITH PARALYZED PREY, a digger wasp staggers toward its burrow. It has immobilized a caterpillar by injecting venom into its nerve centers. After dragging the still-living creature into its nest, the wasp will lay an egg on it, then fill in the mouth of the hole with earth tamped firm with a pebble. The wasp larva will live off its caterpillar inheritance.

WITH DEADLY INTENT, an ichneumon wasp stalks a living incubator for its young. When a suitable insect is found, the wasp lays an egg deep within its flesh through a spearlike ovipositor at the rear of the abdomen. After the egg hatches, the larva starts gnawing at its host's vitals. It eats until the last organs are gone, then pupates in the empty skin.

Wasps, Bees and Ants

Third largest of the insect orders is the Hymenoptera: the wasps, bees and ants. From the arctic bumble bee of the north shore of Greenland to the Arabian harvester ant of the central Sahara, more than 115,000 species buzz and burrow. Fortunately for mankind, these are the most useful of all the insects—at least in human terms. They pollinate crops, turn over the soil more efficiently than earthworms and even furnish food directly in the form of honey. But most important, many of them, like the two wasps above, prey on other insects. This appetite is the single most important natural factor in keeping the earth's insect population in check.

Among the physical characteristics that distinguish most members of this order from the other insect groups is the familiar wasp waist, where one segment of the abdomen is pinched in. Most of them also have thin, transparent wings; the order's name is Hymenoptera (the membrane-winged).

WITH OUTSIZED STRENGTH, a giant Panamanian ponerine ant, nearly an inch long, nips away at a piece of fruit. It is also a ferocious meat eater, tearing its prey to bits to feed its larvae.

THE INSIDIOUS HOUSE FLY is a prime carrier of human disease. As many as 33 million microorganisms may flourish in its gut and a half billion more swarm over its body and legs.

THE HARMLESS HORNET FLY feeds largely on nectar. It has no stinger but its markings resemble those of the hornet, which does. This mimicry is an effective defense against predators.

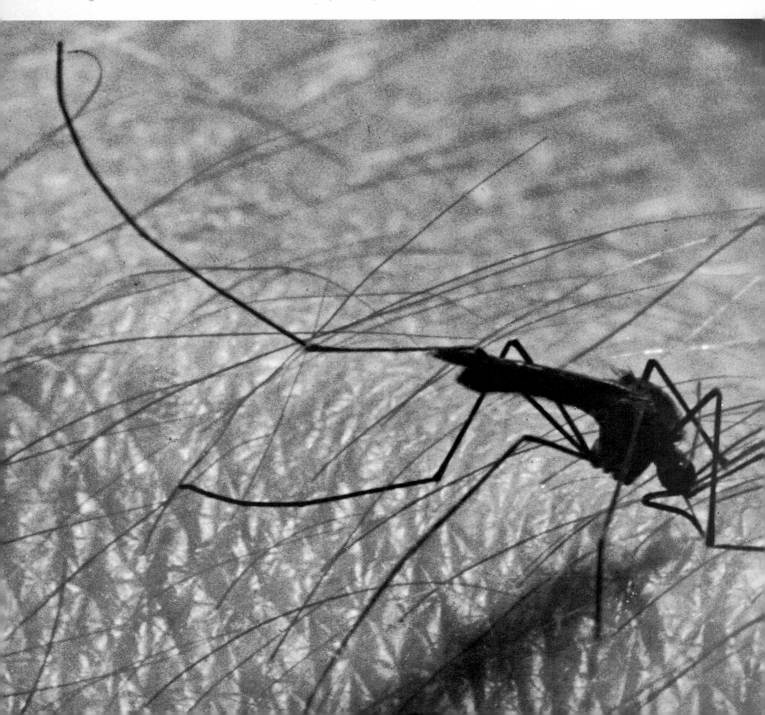

Flies, Gnats and Mosquitoes

Many of mankind's deadliest enemies hum among the 87,000 species of flies, gnats and mosquitoes in the order Diptera, fourth largest of the insect groups. Most members of the order have a single pair of wings—the source of the name "Diptera," meaning "two-winged." Most of them also possess tubular mouths which can pierce the human skin for a draught of nourishing blood. The blood loss is negligible, but as the insect is sipping, viruses and other disease-causing organisms may slip from the insect into the human host. Malaria, sleeping sickness, filariasis and yellow fever are transmitted this way.

The snubby snout of the house fly does not have to break man's skin to be dangerous. Instead, the fly, which may have just visited a cesspool, will light on a piece of human food and vomit up a drop of its own last meal. It sucks most of the material up again, but millions of bacteria, perhaps those of typhoid, tuberculosis or more than 30 other diseases, remain behind, swarming in an infectious fly speck.

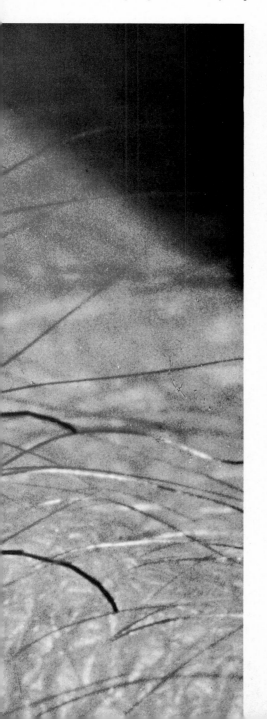

A PHANTOM CRANE FLY, denizen of swamps and wet woods, has flat places which can be spread like sails along its fragile legs. These catch air currents, aiding the insect in its flight.

A MALARIA MOSQUITO, the deadly *Anopheles quadrimaculatus*, injects an anesthetic to deaden feeling as it punctures a human arm. A saliva residue in the bite causes welts and itching.

These Are Not Insects

Anything small, creepy and crawly is an insect in the eyes of the uninformed observer. Yet many small creatures—ticks, spiders, mites, centipedes and the like—are not insects at all but are members of other, quite different, classes of animals. The spiders are perhaps the commonest victims of this misidentification. They are the best-known members of another class of arthropods—the Arachnida. Although they bear superficial similarities, on close inspection the arachnids are quite unlike insects: they have eight legs, no antennae, simple, small eyes, and their heads and thoraxes are fused together.

THE STRIPE-TAILED SCORPION is a venomous arthropod from the American Southwest. A flick of the stinger at the end of its recurved tail can inflict a painful but by no means fatal wound.

THE DADDY LONGLEGS is an arthropod whose head, thorax and abdomen are fused into a bulletlike unit. Although nonpoisonous it will give off a disagreeable odor if carelessly handled.

THE TRAP-DOOR SPIDER, a peaceful arachnid, builds burrows in the dry soil of the Southwest and western Florida. The silk-lined holes are made invisible by lids made of silk and sand.

THE HUNDRED-LEGGER, or centipede, has a pair of legs on each of its segments and is sometimes poisonous. The distantly related millepede has four legs on each division and is harmless.

THE BEACH FLEA is a 10-legged arthropod that swarms on beaches around the world. The last three pairs of legs are short and stiff, enabling it to escape enemies with enormous jumps.

THE WOOD LOUSE, or pill bug, is an inland relative of the beach flea (*opposite, bottom right*). However, it needs some water and is generally found in wet darknesses under stones and logs where it feeds on rotting wood and leaves. When danger threatens it rolls itself into a tight ball, presenting its predator with an unappetizing pill of interlocking skeletal plates.

COMPOUND EYES, like those of the horse fly at left, are made of thousands of small, complete eyes. Only the centipedes, the crustaceans and a few archaic arthropods share this complex organ of sight with insects.

2

Living
in Armor

"THE insect which astounds us, which terrifies us with its extraordinary intelligence, surprises us the next moment with its stupidity when confronted with some simple fact that happens to lie outside its ordinary practice," wrote J. Henri Fabre, the distinguished French observer of the ways of insects. The same ant that is capable of carrying out the impressive logistics of a slave raid stumbles repeatedly over an obstruction when a clear path lies a few inches to either side. A moth thumps against a lighted window, or approaches a candle in ever narrowing spirals until it flutters into the flame and is consumed.

Moths are not "attracted" to light, as many people believe; their flight into the burning candle is simply their reaction to a stimulus. Long before man's artificial lights appeared on the planet, moths and other insects developed exceedingly involved mechanisms for navigation in relation to points of light—the sun and moon. The light rays from these distant sources are practically parallel when they reach the earth; the moth can navigate a straight line by always keeping the rays falling on its eyes at the same angle. However, if the source of light is nearby, as with a candle, the rays are not parallel and the only way the moth can keep the angle roughly the same is by constantly changing its own direction toward the source of light. The result is a spiral path that eventually leads into the flame itself. The moth's reaction to light provided it with benefits for millions of years until it ran afoul of man's artificial sources. Now the insect simply appears foolish, whereas actually it has not yet had time to evolve ways to cope with the disorder that the recent arrival, man, has brought to a more ancient world of living things.

THE MOTH AND THE FLAME

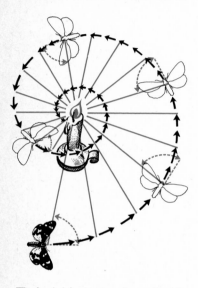

The fancied fascination of a moth with a flame has a simple scientific explanation. Ordinarily, a moth uses the light of the sun or the moon to guide it in flight. It steers a straight path by maintaining a course in which the rays of the faraway orb always strike its eye at the same angle. The moth's problem comes when it tries to use a local light source, such as a candle or electric bulb, as a beacon. In the drawing above, the moth is flying so that the light rays from the candle always strike its eye at an angle of 80°. But instead of flying in a straight line, it pursues a diminishing spiral path to doom.

Because humans regard themselves as the measure of all things, they assume that insects possess the same senses that man does and use them in much the same way. Man takes it for granted, for example, that an insect carries its senses in its head. But the insect's head is so tiny that there is simply not room enough for all the mechanisms that provide the sort of information it needs about the outside world. As a result, various insects have developed sensory apparatus that enables them to tell temperature with their feet, to hear with their legs, to detect the presence of light on their backs and even to smell an object by stepping on it.

Insects' responses to the sensory impressions that bombard them often initiate the sequences of behavior that make these animals endlessly fascinating. One stimulus leads to a reaction which, in turn, sets up the nervous system for the next stimulus. For example, the queen termite must drop its wings before it will select a mate. Then it must find a mate before searching for a home, but will not mate until it has found a home and sealed the entrance. The behavioral chain must be followed link by link; once broken, it cannot be begun again in the middle.

Man is directly in touch with his environment: when it rains, he feels the droplets spatter upon his skin. But an insect is shut off from the world, enclosed inside the insensitive surface of its external skeleton. To compensate for this, insects have abundant hairs and spines—on their antennae, scattered over their legs, mouth parts, bodies and even their wings. Each hair protrudes through the external skeleton and is connected to the skin underneath by a sort of ball-and-socket arrangement. When the hair bends in the socket, it sets up an impulse that is communicated to the brain. The hairs on the appendages at the end of the cricket's abdomen, for example, perceive earth-borne vibrations when they are touching the ground and air currents when they are held aloft. Hairs on the wings of some insects are so sensitive to air currents that they can alert their owners to the approach of solid objects. The efficiency of these hairs is clear to anyone who ever tried to swat a fly with a rolled-up paper. The fly usually darts away to safety, its hairs warning it of the air displaced by the approaching weapon.

The escape flight of the fly is automatic, as is most of any insect's behavior, and it is activated by a simple but effective nervous system which is similar to a set of beads hung on two strings running the length of the body. Each segment of the insect possesses pairs of nerve centers, called ganglia, and all of the ganglia are connected by nerve cords. The first three ganglia, fused together, form the insect brain, which initiates action and receives impressions from the sense organs. The next three pairs of ganglia, also in the head and also fused, control the workings of the animal's complex mouth parts. The ganglia within the thorax are responsible for operating the wings and legs. Other pairs of ganglia within the abdomen control this part of the body.

Thus, each of the insect's three body divisions is semiautonomous and can carry out reflex actions on its own without first having to go through the switchboard of the brain. As a result, insect behavior often consists of immediate reactions to messages received from the outside world—heat, humidity, odors, vibrations. A grasshopper has no need to think about the best place to rest; it automatically finds the sunny side of a mound and places itself so that the largest possible area of its body is exposed to the sun. A hungry insect may react by wandering about at random until it finds food. If a nest of ants is disturbed, its reaction is to carry the brood out of the light to a dark place, an automatic response that serves at the same time to protect the young. Even when an insect is decapitated it may continue to react automatically to light, temperature, humidity, chemicals and various other stimuli. A headless insect may live for as much as a year, until it starves to death. The cut-off abdomen of a moth is capable of being fertilized and laying eggs. However, this abdomen does not lay the eggs in the usual orderly rows because the ganglia that normally control this action are located in the missing thorax. Furthermore, the eggs are laid anywhere and not on the usually selected food plant, because the ganglia in the brain that regulate this action are also absent.

Two of man's most acute senses, sight and hearing, are greatly restricted or even missing in insects; indeed, most insects spend their lives in a shadowy and silent world. A specialist in human vision would find his knowledge of little use in studying insect eyes, for their structure is completely different. The insect's most prominent eyes are made up of numerous six-sided facets—28,000 in some dragonflies, 4,000 in house flies, only six in some subterranean ants. Each facet is a miniature visual system which consists of a tiny lens, a light-transmitting system and sensitive retinal cells. Each is isolated from neighboring facets and no two facets point in exactly the same direction. A single facet registers a single impression, a fragment of the total scene. All the facets together combine, like the tiles in a mosaic, to build a complete picture from many stimuli of varying intensities. No one knows, of course, what sort of picture is formed in the insect brain by the nerve impulses from a compound eye, but it is fairly certain that eyes of this type are much less efficient than the eyes of higher animals. Insect eyes have no way of focusing to achieve a sharp image; they depend on an increase in the number of individual facets for an increase in sharpness, much as a printer relies on a fine halftone screen to print the tiny dots that make up a sharp picture with a wealth of detail. A coarse screen with large dots will produce a vague, blurry picture. It is reasonable to assume that when an insect's compound eye contains only a few facets, it will produce a correspondingly coarse image.

INSECTS cannot close their eyes; they sleep with them open. Their vision is believed to be sharp only to a distance of two or three feet. Even the keen-sighted honey bee has a visual acuity equal to only an eightieth or a hundredth of man's: in a fruit fly it is about a thousandth. And these figures are for optimum conditions; they would be lower in poor light. However, compound eyes should be particularly expert at detecting movement, since an object in motion registers impressions on different facets one after the other. Detecting motion is of prime importance to the insect; a moving object means either an enemy to avoid or prey to be captured.

In addition to the pair of compound eyes, most insects have a number of small, simple eyes that lack facets. It has been something of a mystery exactly what function these simple eyes serve. If the compound, faceted eyes of bees are covered, leaving only the simple eyes, bees behave as if they are blind. But if the simple eyes, rather than the compound eyes, are blackened, the bees can still see, although they respond more slowly to changes in light intensity. Probably the simple eyes serve as boosters that somehow increase the sensitivity of the compound eyes to light.

Insects live in a world of color, but they do not perceive the same range of colors that the human does. An orange, a lemon and a green grape all look the same color to a bee, although some of the fruits are darker and others lighter in tone. However, a bee can clearly see ultraviolet, a wave length invisible to man. This color range of insects has largely determined the hues of meadow and forest, for flowers that appealed to insect pollinators had the best chance of survival through the ages of evolution. There are no bee-pollinated flowers that are solid red, for to a bee red looks the way black does to the human eye. There are, however, numerous blue and violet, yellow and yellowish-green flowers that fall within the range of the bee's color vision. In addition, there are numerous blossoms that appear muted to the human eye but that glow with an ultraviolet magnificence we are unable to detect.

Many insects rely upon the direction of the sun's rays as a sort of compass. This can easily be demonstrated by a simple experiment. Place a light-tight box over an ant carrying food back to its nest, and keep it imprisoned for a few hours. When the box is removed, the ant will not continue on its former course, but will start off rapidly in a new direction. This new route will differ from the old by exactly the angle that the sun has shifted across the sky during the time the ant was imprisoned.

The ability of insects to get their bearings from sunlight apparently depends on polarization, which is invisible to man. For the insect there is a different quality to light coming from north, east, south and west at different hours of the day. As a consequence, insects need only to see the sun in order to navigate. More remarkable, honey bees can tell where the sun is even in a cloudy sky. The explanation for this is that a certain amount of ultraviolet light penetrates the clouds and the sun's part of the sky is always about 5 per cent brighter in the ultraviolet than the rest. This difference is enough for the bees to pinpoint the sun on the cloudiest day.

Most insects inhabit a silent world. A number of them, however, can detect different kinds of vibrations. For example, the whirligig beetle, which traces winding and seemingly erratic paths on the surface of ponds, avoids obstacles by receiving wave echoes through special organs at the base of its antennae. Male mosquitoes find their mates by means of similar organs. But only crickets, grasshoppers, locusts, cicadas and the majority of moths possess hearing organs of the "eardrum"—or tympanic—sort. These are never located on the head, as in man, but rather on the legs or abdomen, and are related to the insect's breathing apparatus. Insects breathe through a system of minute air pipes that form a maze through their bodies; at a number of places, the pipes widen to form air pockets. In insects with true hearing, a pair of these air pockets has developed tympanic membranes that communicate vibrations to sensory cells.

This hearing apparatus is simple in design compared to man's, yet its range and discrimination are quite extraordinary. A number of insects can detect ultrasonic sounds more than two octaves above the highest note audible to man. They are also alert to the qualities of sound: a cricket can discriminate between the sounds made by another cricket and an experimenter's file scraped at the same pitch. The tympanic membranes of some crickets and grasshoppers are

HOW MAN AND INSECTS SEE

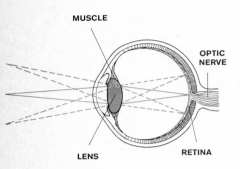

MUSCLE

OPTIC NERVE

LENS RETINA

A CUTAWAY VIEW OF THE HUMAN EYE

The human eye is one of the best in nature. It has a single lens whose shape can be changed by surrounding muscles to focus an image of either distant or nearby objects sharply on the retinal nerve cells at the rear of the eye. Each of these nerve cells transmits a tiny portion of the total image to the brain, but there are so many of them (between 15 and 20 million) that the picture they transmit seems to be a continuous whole—not broken up at all.

AS MAN SEES

situated in cavities on the front legs; by moving their forelegs in different directions, they seem able to locate a sound's source.

No insect has a true voice. Most of them stridulate (a term derived from the Latin, to creak): that is, they rub one part of the body against another. Most stridulators use sound as part of their mating behavior, either to bring males and females together or to drive off rival males. Sound may also be used to frighten away enemies: when a sand cricket is threatened, it faces the danger and produces a rasping noise. The chirp of the cricket and the snare drum of the cicada sound unmusical to us: they lack melody; their rhythms and pulsations are too rapid for man's ears to detect. But recordings of insect songs, played at slow speed, have revealed intricate inner qualities.

THE instruments used by various insect musicians differ somewhat in shape and size, thus producing different sounds and different pitches. The song of each species, moreover, has a distinctive rhythm, frequency and pattern. During the summer the air is filled with a wide variety of tunes, but each kind of insect knows only one song, the inherited song of its ancestors. Even closely related species have small differences between their songs, a fact that probably serves as a barrier against hybridization of the species in nature. For example, there are two species of short-horned grasshoppers that can be made to mate in the laboratory by dint of ingenious trickery. Male and female of different species are caged together, while a male of the same species as the female is placed in an adjacent cage. When the isolated male sings, the female is influenced sufficiently by the sound to accept the stranger that shares its cage. This mating under false pretenses is fertile and hybrid offspring are produced. Such hybrids, however, are not found under natural conditions.

Short-horned grasshoppers and locusts rub the inner side of the leg, which has a scraper with 80 to 90 fine spines, across a thickened vein on the forewing much as a violinist scrapes his bow across the strings; the wing acts as a resonator much as does a violin's body. In contrast, the long-horned grasshoppers, such as katydids and snowy tree crickets, carry their apparatus on the two forewings and rasp these together. The tree cricket produces the most musical of insect sounds: "If moonlight could be heard," wrote Nathaniel Hawthorne, "it would sound like that." The katydid is an untiring musician; during a summer it may scrape its wings together up to 50 million times. The cicada is a drummer, not a fiddler. On its abdomen is a pair of large drumheads, equipped with resonators, which it sets into vibration to produce a shrill sound, reminiscent of the creaking of an unoiled door hinge. It does not beat the drums with sticks, but instead vibrates them by muscles within its body. Only the adult males of crickets, grasshoppers and cicadas sing these loud songs; the young and the females are voiceless. This fact was recognized some 2,400 years ago by the Greek dramatist Xenarchus, who wrote, "Happy the cicadas' lives, for they have voiceless wives."

Logically enough, the ability of a species to make sounds usually accompanies an ability to hear, but there are exceptions: almost all moths are voiceless, yet many species possess acute hearing. This sort of ability to receive sound but not to produce it cannot be tied in with mating behavior. Instead, the hearing of moths is tuned to the high-pitched sounds that bats emit on their nightly forays as a sort of sonar for locating prey. When a moth detects the bat's ultrasonic squeaks, it swerves sharply in the air as an evasive maneuver, or plummets directly to the ground.

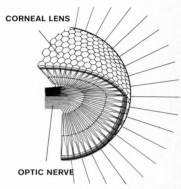

CORNEAL LENS

OPTIC NERVE

A CUTAWAY VIEW OF THE INSECT EYE

The compound insect eye consists of many tiny individual eyes, each connected to its own nerve endings. The eye as a whole does not move, nor can its lenses be focused. Each catches a small piece of the surrounding scene and the result is a rather coarse-grained picture, like a mosaic. The more facets its eye has, the more detailed a picture the insect can perceive. Insects that have fewer than 100 facets can scarcely distinguish shapes at all.

AS AN INSECT SEES

INSECT "SONGS"

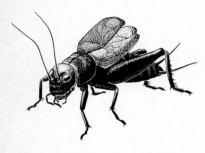

SCRAPER   FILE VEIN

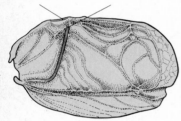

FIELD CRICKET

The "fiddling" of the field cricket is produced by the vibrations of its wings. The underside of each wing has a relatively heavy, filelike vein running across it, and the upper surface of each wing is equipped with a sharp ridge, or scraper. When the insect moves its two wings against each other from side to side, the file of one wing rubs against the scraper of the other and produces a high, soft, melodious note.

The antennae, or feelers, are the most conspicuous sense organs of most insects. Watch an ordinary ant, and the importance of the antennae as samplers of the surrounding world is quickly revealed. The feelers are constantly in motion, twisting and turning. They point in the direction of the wind, tap the surface on which the insect is moving, inspect the food before it is clasped with the mouth parts. When two ants meet on a trail, they gently tap each other's antennae; when an ant wishes the aphid it herds to produce a drop of honeydew, it taps the little insect's abdomen. The importance of the antennae is seen by the way the ant constantly cleans them with its mouth parts or its legs, which are equipped with special combs for this purpose.

Antennae are particularly large in insects that have poor eyesight, like ants, smaller in insects with good sight, like dragonflies. They come in a tremendous range of shapes and sizes. Among the long-horned grasshoppers, the antennae are longer than the entire body. Butterflies have simple, knobbed threads, male moths often have magnificent plumes. The antennae of many flies are short and swollen into knobs; in some beetles they end as a rack of flat plates. All of these strange designs serve to increase the surface area, thus making the antennae more receptive to sense impressions.

The antennae inform the insect about the feel, sound, taste, smell, temperature and humidity of the world outside its skeleton. They enable ants and bees to distinguish between dilute sugar solutions and plain water. They inform bloodsucking insects of the presence of warm-blooded prey by detecting the slight difference in temperature between the victim's body and the surrounding air. A bed bug will move toward an object that is less than 2° F. warmer than the surrounding air.

The antennae are equipped with numerous little pegs that act as odor receptors—as many as 30,000 of them are found on each antenna of the male honey bee, attesting to the importance of the sense of smell in the life of an insect. Most insects depend on smell to help them find the proper food plant or host on which to lay their eggs. Some male moths, equipped with huge, featherlike antennae, use smell almost exclusively in finding their mates. They perform what one entomologist has called "one of the most surprising feats of perception achieved by any animal." Some species of moths respond to the attracting scent of a female more than a mile away. At so great a distance, the antennae are probably stimulated by single molecules of the scent substance. Moreover, the male moths will follow the scent into a town, with its numerous competing odors, directly to the female. They do this by flying upwind, gauging the direction of the female by contrasting the number of scent molecules falling on each antenna. A male that has lost one antenna can perceive the scent of the female, but not the direction. So important is scent in the mating behavior of moths that if a female is first placed in a box and then taken out, the males will still cluster around the empty but scented box. On the other hand, males will ignore a female in an airtight glass cage.

SEASON after season, insects return to the same kinds of flowers and trees that their ancestors fed upon, unvarying in their selection. The cabbage butterfly, for example, flits through the garden seeking by odor plants of the cabbage family on which to deposit its eggs. If the caterpillars that hatch out of these eggs are moved to other plants, they refuse to eat and perish in the midst of plenty. But they can be induced to eat unfamiliar plants if the essential oils of the traditional food plant are smeared on the new ones. Throughout the garden, there is the same unerring selection of food plants by many kinds of insects, as ears of corn are bored, tomato leaves snipped, rosebuds chewed. The insects are somehow able to single out of the labyrinth of twisting stems and leaves the plants that nurtured their ancestors, often making distinctions between plants so closely related that a man could not tell them apart without a botanical handbook.

Until a few decades ago, scientists credited insects with some vague extra sense that enabled them to recognize their ancestral food plants. However, it was later learned that the finicky insects are attracted not by some instinctive knowledge of the particular plants, but by a specific chemical or combination of chemicals linked to each. For example, the cabbage butterfly will also feed on the nasturtium, which is not botanically related to the cabbage. The reason is that nasturtium leaves possess a pungent oil that smells exactly like the oil contained in the leaves of the cabbage family. The house fly is led to decaying matter by the odor of ammonia the matter gives off; the vinegar fly, which is common in wine-making cellars, is attracted there by traces of methyl acetate contained in the alcohol. Insects that lay their eggs in the bodies of other insects can even smell the difference between prey already parasitized and those that have not yet been visited.

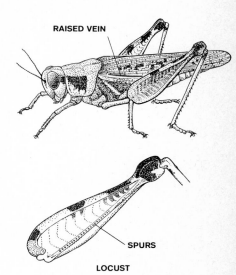

RAISED VEIN

SPURS

LOCUST

The locust, like the cricket, is also a fiddler. But its method of sound-making is somewhat different. It has a series of spurs, or pegs, on the inner surface of each hind leg (bottom) and a rough raised vein (shown in green) on the outside surface of each wing. Its rasping sound is produced when the locust rapidly raises and lowers both hind legs alternately, brushing their spurs against the tough veins on its wings.

Man has a long-range sense of smell, located in the nose, that brings distant chemical messages; his short-range chemical sense, located in the tongue, enables him to investigate his food by taste as it enters his mouth. Insects similarly have long-range and short-range chemical senses, but these play a more important part in their lives than they do in man's. With many insects, such as butterflies and flies, taste receptors are located on the front legs instead of merely around the mouth; these insects can "taste" the suitability of their food by walking on it.

The numerous taste hairs on the mouth parts of a fly are seemingly simple structures. At the base of each of these minute hairs are three receptor cells. Two of them send filaments through the hollow shaft of the hair to its tip; the third cell serves as a touch receptor and is sensitive to delicate bendings of the hair. Not much was known about the subtlety of these hairs until the development of electronic equipment sensitive enough to measure nerve impulses. A number of entomologists now have isolated individual sense hairs on the insect body and utilized elaborate amplifiers and oscilloscopes to measure their reactions to various taste stimuli.

As these studies have shown, each of the two cells leading to the hair tip has its own role in detecting chemicals. One is sensitive to salts, acids and alcohols, all unappetizing to the fly; the other is sensitive to sugars, upon which the fly feeds. Thus, one cell of the hair responds to acceptable chemicals, the other to chemicals that the fly avoids. Furthermore, the electrical impulses sent by the cell that detects sugar vary, depending upon the kind of sugar; some sugars at a low concentration stimulate even a single sensory hair, while other, less acceptable, sugars do not send an impulse unless they are in high concentration or in touch with a number of the sensory hairs. The kinds of impulses fired by the two cells not only tell the brain whether a substance is acceptable or not but indicate various shades of acceptability as well.

Further research turned up other complexities about these seemingly simple hairs. The hairs look very much the same, but some of them are excited very quickly while others are slow to send a message to the brain. The advantage of a system of this sort is that some of the receptors are always ready to fire; other-

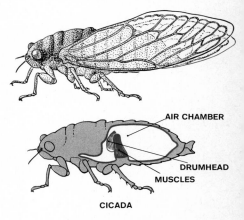

AIR CHAMBER

DRUMHEAD

MUSCLES

CICADA

The cicada's sound-making organs are internal. Most of its abdomen is hollow. Its air chambers contain a cluster of powerful muscles called the tympanal muscles. Attached to these is a kind of drumhead. When the muscles are tightened, they create considerable tension on the drumhead. When they are released, the drumhead hits the membranes lining the abdominal walls, producing the insect's shrill "song."

wise, a strong chemical would fire all of the receptors and the taste sense would be temporarily inactivated. In addition to its taste discrimination, the hairs also give the fly other information about its environment. Temperature changes of less than a degree alter the frequency of the firing of the cells; the bending of the hairs provides information about the "feel" of the substance. Thus, a sensory hair in touch with syrup signals the brain that the substance is very acceptable, that it is sticky and what its temperature is.

The sense of touch is highly developed in insects, despite their insulation from the external world. Numerous touch hairs protrude from the outer shell and are in contact with nerve endings underneath it. Insects when not flying usually try to keep their feet in contact with a surface—the ground, the ceiling, a twig or water—but when they are flying, most try to avoid touching anything with their feet; in a manner of speaking, they retract their landing gear. This is why most insects are incapable of carrying an object while in flight (though some wasps airlift their prey, and dragonflies use their legs as airborne traps). If a house fly is captured and its body gently glued to a piece of thin wire so that it can beat its wings in the normal manner of flight, it holds its legs in flight position—the front legs extended, the rear pair pointing backward, the middle pair held out at right angles. But if the legs are then put in contact with a surface, the wings cease beating and the fly moves its legs as if it were running on a solid object, even though it is still suspended. A similar response to touch explains the mystery of why an ant, dropping off a picnic table, always lands on its feet. As soon as the ant loses touch with the solid surface, it arches its body and thrusts its legs upward. Hitting the ground belly first, it at once snaps its legs downward and walks away.

MAN can sense the heat radiating from an oil burner and the cold draft from a refrigerator. It used to be believed that, being cold-blooded, insects did not possess any way to regulate their body heat—although it had long been known that throughout the winter the temperature in the center of a beehive never drops below 57°F. At that temperature, the bees switch on a behavioral heating system so efficient that during extremely cold spells the interior of the hive may be a hundred degrees warmer than the outdoor temperature. While the wasp and bumble-bee colonies are dying from the autumn chill, the honey bees save themselves by clustering into a ball around one of the combs. The size of the ball depends upon the temperature: when it is very cold, the ball is small since the bees are tightly clustered together; when it is warmer, the cluster is less dense. The bees on the inside of the cluster, being warmest, can make constant muscular movements of the wings, legs and abdomen that produce most of the heat. After a period in the center of the ball, these bees shift places with those on the outside. Even the bees on the outside of the cluster help to conserve the heat by the insulation of their fuzzy bodies.

A moth usually goes through a remarkable ritual before taking to the air. It beats its wings so rapidly that they blur like the whirling propellers of an airplane. Suddenly, after several minutes, it takes off. If a moth is captured before it has completed the ritual, and then dropped, it is unable to fly but falls to the ground instead. Obviously, the moth generates heat through the flexing of its flight muscles; if a moth is kept in a heated cage, it does not need to rev up its motor but instead can take flight immediately. For this sort of system to work, the moth should possess a mechanism for gauging temperature, but scientists do not as yet know where these heat-sensitive cells are located.

The complex senses of insects have given them ways to know their world, to sample it from afar, to touch and taste it, to be alert to its motions, to navigate by its lights. But these senses and the built-in responses to the information are of value only if the insect can benefit from them. Insects possess a variety of very efficient tools on their legs and mouth parts that match many of the tools that man has been forced to manufacture for himself.

I NSECT legs are adapted for walking, leaping, paddling, digging, cleaning and storage. The hind legs of some water beetles are lengthened and flattened and equipped with long, closely set hairs that convert them into paddles for swimming. The honey bee has pollen-collecting brushes on its front legs and pollen-carrying baskets on its hind legs. The front legs of the praying mantis and those of the completely unrelated water scorpion are modified into pincers that grasp prey. The legs of adult dragonflies are long and slender, with a row of stiff bristles on each side; when darting through the air, the dragonfly forms a sort of net with these legs and spines, into which it scoops up small flying insects. Mole crickets, which dig burrows in the earth, have unusually strong and flattened forelegs that serve as shovels, and bear a pair of shears with which they cut through rootlets that impede their excavations. The front legs of many insects bear special notches through which they can draw their antennae to keep them clean. Many butterflies—especially the brush-footed ones—have small hairy front legs that are worthless for locomotion. Instead, they are used as brushes to clean the surfaces of these butterflies' compound eyes.

The typical insect leg ends in a pair of claws with a pad between them. These two structures explain the feats of insects in climbing on sheer surfaces. If the surface is even slightly rough, the insect can gain purchase with its claws, but if the surface is mirror-smooth, the pads come into action. The underside of each pad bristles with numerous hollow hairs which are kept moist by a glandular secretion. The moist hairs owe their grip to the action of surface molecular forces.

Insect mouth parts, evolved like the legs from primitive appendages, show a variety of specializations that allow these animals to tap a variety of foods. The insect's actual mouth is merely a round hole at the front of its body. This hole has no jaws of its own but instead is surrounded by several appendages. The first mouth parts to evolve were those adapted for biting and chewing. Although these show numerous refinements in different kinds of insects, they all possess the same fundamental design. In front is a pair of jawlike appendages, known as the mandibles. These are placed at the sides of the mouth, where they swing inward like ice tongs. Behind the mandibles is another pair of appendages, known as the maxillae, that are unable to crush food but can grasp it. Behind these, in turn, is still another pair of maxillae that have become fused into the form of a large underlip. Projecting in front of the mouth parts as a kind of flap is yet another, upper "lip," which was not originally an appendage but developed as a part of the body wall.

This is the basic plan for insects that feed on solid food. But other insects—such as butterflies and moths, cicadas, aphids and some flies—dine on liquids and their mouth parts are modified for sucking. These sucking mouth parts have the same basic plan except that they have fused and extended downward, forming a hollow tube like a soda straw through which liquids are sucked up. The butterflies' and moths' tubes are often so long that, when not in use, they are carried coiled up under the head like a watch spring.

HOW INSECTS WALK

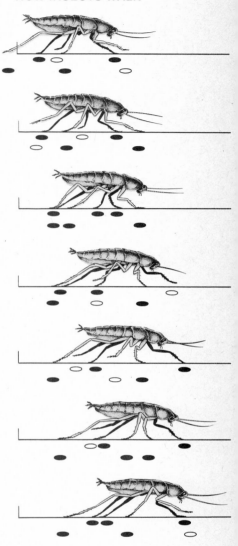

During the normal walking gait of insects, each pair of legs serves a specific function: the forelegs, for example, reach ahead, while the hind legs push and the middle legs act as a fulcrum. Since insects never lift more than one or two legs at a time, and because they support a raised leg by keeping the leg behind it on the ground, their walk appears to have a wavelike motion. These drawings of the Oriental cockroach show the complete walking cycle. The black circles represent legs which are on the ground; the white, those in the air.

41

Much to man's discomfort, among the most remarkably efficient mouth parts are those of mosquitoes and other so-called "biting" flies that plague warm-blooded animals. Actually, they should not be called biting but "piercing" flies, for these insects are unable to bite. Instead, the majority of their mouth parts are modified into needlelike stylets. Among the mosquitoes these are fully developed only in the female and in consequence only the female possesses the blood-feeding habit.

At first glance, the mosquito appears to possess a long proboscis, or "tongue," similar to that of a butterfly. This is the lower lip, which serves as a case covering the mosquito's array of delicate tools. In the six grooves of this case are fitted six lancets: four of these are a pair each of mandibles and maxillae, transformed into extremely fine needles; the other two are the upper lip, also exceedingly thin, and a sixth stylet that bears a salivary channel.

The mosquito alights on its prey so softly that it is usually not felt. It uses still another pair of appendages attached to the mouth parts, the palpi, to find a soft spot in which to make a puncture. When this place is found, the grooved lower lip acts as a positioning guide for the insertion of the six needles. The first puncture is made by the mandibles and maxillae, the upper lip and the salivary channel then follow. Saliva flows down the channel: this fluid, believed to cause the irritation and swelling that often follow a mosquito bite, serves to prevent clotting of the blood until the meal is finished. The blood itself is sucked up a groove along the underside of the upper lip and directly into the mosquito's gut.

It is the saliva of the mosquito that carries the organisms which cause malaria, yellow fever, encephalitis and some 10 other diseases of man. Even in the highland capitals of the New World tropics—such as Mexico City, La Paz in Bolivia and Quito in Ecuador—Indian builder and Spanish conquistador alike failed to escape the peril: although malaria-bearing mosquitoes are more common in the lowlands, malaria has occurred at Quito, 9,000 feet above sea level. Indeed, there is one species of malaria mosquito that deposits its eggs only in the cold, swift waters of mountain streams. The mosquito also caused most of the casualties in the Spanish-American War; it gave the Panama Canal to the Americans instead of the French, who are said to have lost one man to yellow fever for each crosstie on the Panama Railroad. As one British authority says of the mosquito's salivary channel, "Down this minute, microscopic groove has flowed the fluid which has closed the continent of Africa for countless centuries to civilisation, and which has played a dominant part in destroying the civilisations of ancient Greece and Rome."

MODERN science knows almost as much about the moon, wheeling through space a quarter of a million miles away, as it does about most of the commonplace insects of field and forest—"All those vague, unconscious, rudimentary and almost nameless little lives," as Maeterlinck describes them. Despite their abundance, insects are still largely an enigma, and ignorance has tended to clothe them in "wonders" and "marvels" that are not rightly theirs. Insects possess what appear to be many strange senses that are different from man's. These are often much cruder than man's. Although an insect only an inch long may possess as many as 50,000 eyes, these turn out to be of limited efficiency. What is more remarkable is that with such crude senses the insects have survived for 300 million years the onslaughts of fellow-arthropods—and of amphibians, reptiles, birds and mammals—to endure even in today's man-infested world.

THE VELVET ANT—REALLY THE WINGLESS FEMALE OF A DIGGER WASP—HAS A DENSE COAT OF THE SENSORY HAIRS COMMON TO MOST INSECTS

Insect Machinery

The whole huge range of insect shapes has evolved around a single basic pattern: an armored, three-part body. The head section generally has three pairs of appendages for eating; the mid-section, six legs for walking; and the rear section, guts and glands for digesting and mating. How marvelously flexible this simple plan can be is revealed by the color close-ups on the following pages.

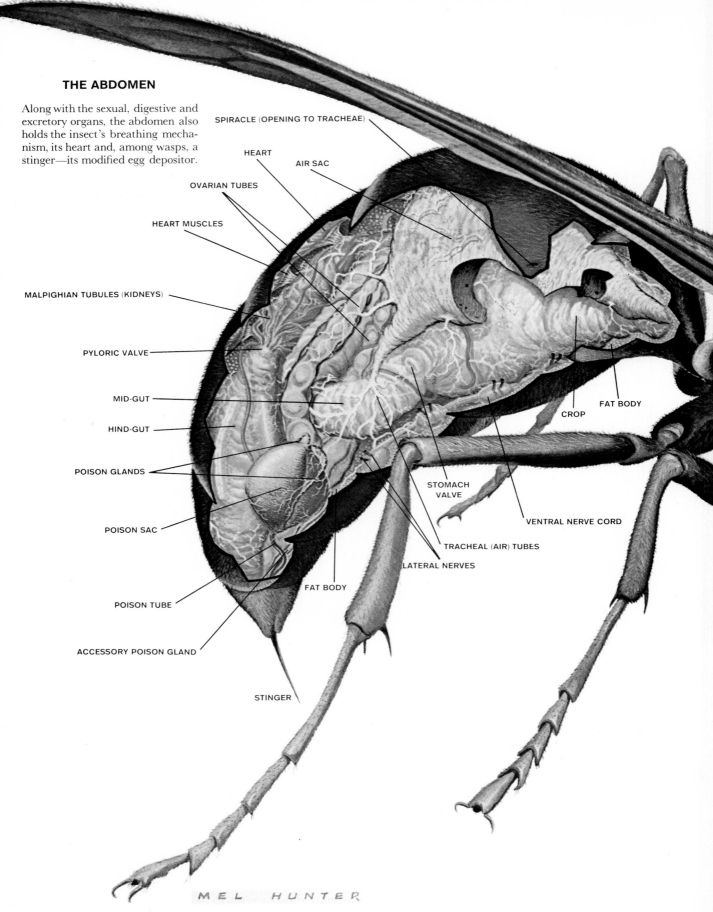

THE ABDOMEN

Along with the sexual, digestive and excretory organs, the abdomen also holds the insect's breathing mechanism, its heart and, among wasps, a stinger—its modified egg depositor.

SPIRACLE (OPENING TO TRACHEAE)

HEART

AIR SAC

OVARIAN TUBES

HEART MUSCLES

MALPIGHIAN TUBULES (KIDNEYS)

PYLORIC VALVE

MID-GUT

HIND-GUT

POISON GLANDS

POISON SAC

POISON TUBE

ACCESSORY POISON GLAND

STINGER

FAT BODY

CROP

FAT BODY

STOMACH VALVE

VENTRAL NERVE CORD

TRACHEAL (AIR) TUBES

LATERAL NERVES

MEL HUNTER

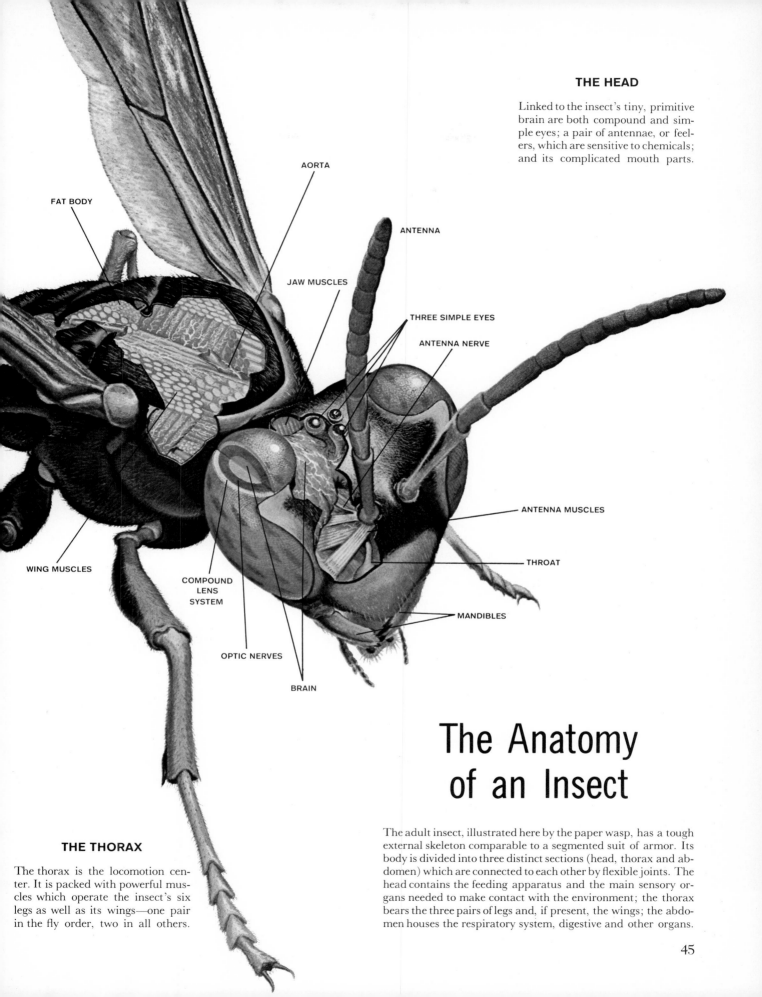

AORTA

FAT BODY

JAW MUSCLES

THE HEAD

Linked to the insect's tiny, primitive brain are both compound and simple eyes; a pair of antennae, or feelers, which are sensitive to chemicals; and its complicated mouth parts.

ANTENNA

THREE SIMPLE EYES

ANTENNA NERVE

ANTENNA MUSCLES

THROAT

WING MUSCLES

COMPOUND LENS SYSTEM

MANDIBLES

OPTIC NERVES

BRAIN

The Anatomy of an Insect

THE THORAX

The thorax is the locomotion center. It is packed with powerful muscles which operate the insect's six legs as well as its wings—one pair in the fly order, two in all others.

The adult insect, illustrated here by the paper wasp, has a tough external skeleton comparable to a segmented suit of armor. Its body is divided into three distinct sections (head, thorax and abdomen) which are connected to each other by flexible joints. The head contains the feeding apparatus and the main sensory organs needed to make contact with the environment; the thorax bears the three pairs of legs and, if present, the wings; the abdomen houses the respiratory system, digestive and other organs.

45

MANY-HUED BRILLIANCE of the female horse fly's eyes is a dazzling example of sexual differences between insects. The female's eyes are more widely separated than those of the male of the same species shown in the photograph on page 32. The stripes of color are not caused by pigmentation but, rainbow-fashion, by prismatic structures in the tissues of the lenses.

FEATHERY FEELERS of the male Luna moth, a fernlike elaboration on the basic insect antennae, are studded with sensory cells which are organs of smell. Its sole function as an adult male moth is to scent out a female and mate with it. During its life on the wing, which lasts two weeks unless its search is successful within a shorter period, it takes no food at all.

A FEROCIOUS INSECT OFFSPRING, the bristling larva of the tiger beetle, lies poised at the mouth of its burrow waiting for a meal to pass by. Its scimitar tusks can snap shut like a trap, grabbing and stabbing its prey—which is usually another small insect. The victim is then dragged down the larva's tunnel, sometimes as far as a foot underground, to be eaten at leisure.

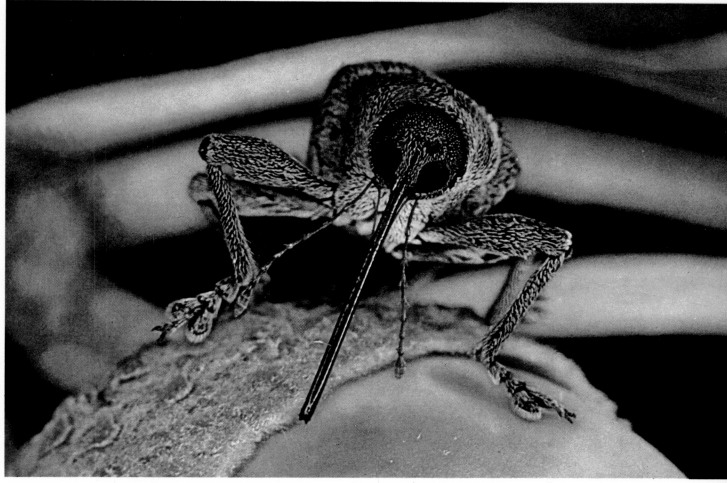

A MOTHERLY SNOUT BEETLE, or acorn weevil, prepares a home and provides for the next generation by boring a hole into the nourishing depths of an acorn. Then she will turn around and drop an egg down the hole. After the egg is hatched, the young acorn weevil larva will lead a lazy grub's life, safe within the shelter of the outer husk until it has eaten up all of the meat.

Insect Eating Utensils

The head section of an insect has three pairs of limbs which have evolved to serve as teeth, tusks, tongues, tongs, talons, tweezers, chisels, pliers, claws, jaws, saws or straws for eating. In general, the first pair of mouth parts serves to crush, like teeth; the second to grasp, like tongs; and the third to probe and taste, like a tongue. Possessing, in effect, three sets of "jaws," most insects have modified one or two sets for specialized eating techniques. In the terrible tiger beetle larva (*opposite*), the first pair has developed into tusk-shaped pincers. In the butterfly (*right*), the second pair has fused into a tube for sipping. In the acorn weevil (*above*), all three pairs have combined to form a powerful drill at the very tip of the snoutlike prolongation of its exoskeleton.

A SIPHON-TONGUED BUTTERFLY, the swallowtail, rolls up its inch-and-a-quarter-long proboscis until the scent of a suitable flower stimulates it to stiffen the tongue into a probing tube.

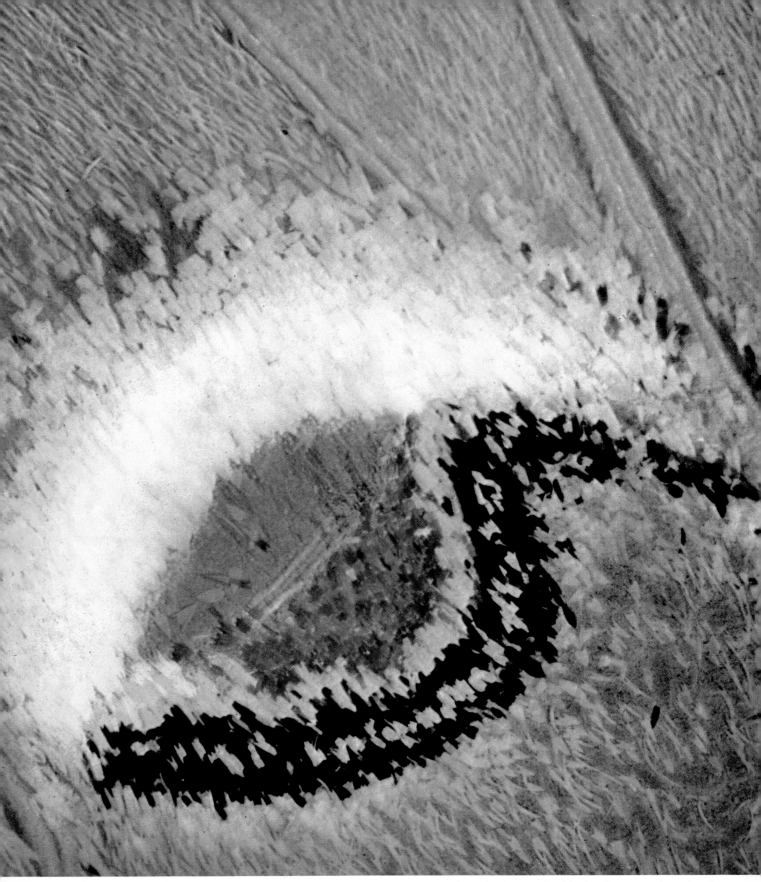

THE ETHEREAL WING of a Luna moth flaunts an exquisite, eye-shaped pattern. As in nearly all the moths and butterflies, the membrane that forms the broad surface of the wing is trans- parent; the color is contained in its dense covering of scales. Both membrane and scales are made of film-thin cuticle, the same material that makes up a beetle's armor or a lobster's shell.

A SAW-TOOTHED HALF-ZIPPER runs along the leading edge of a bumble bee's hind wing. In flight it hitches to a sturdy flap on the forewing, which has the muscles and does the work.

Insect Aviation

All the earliest known insects had wings. And although many insects now spend most of their lives grounded as larvae, they nearly all take flight as adults when it comes time to mate and spread their kind. Wings are so fundamental to insecthood that they are not mere modified limbs, like bat or bird wings, but part of the insect's back—a basic structural outgrowth of its external skeleton, delicately strutted with passages for air and blood.

Originally most winged insects had four separate wings, as do dragonflies today. But the fore and aft pairs of more recent types generally function as single flight surfaces, responding to the feel of moving air through the wonderful sail-setting of specialized flight muscles, and hitched together by overlapping (as in the butterfly), by a hook and eye (as in the moth) or by a zipperlike mechanism (as in the wasp). To gain precise flight control, the Diptera—among the most recently developed orders, including flies and mosquitoes—have given up flying with their hind wings and converted them into halteres, small stumps which act as gyroscopic stabilizers.

A MOSQUITO'S WING is a diaphanous double membrane, outlined and reinforced by veins which act as braces. The bristly hairs are sensitive to air currents, temperature and humidity.

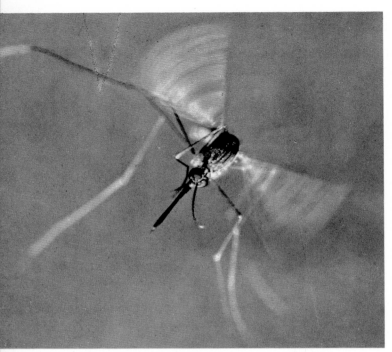

A MOSQUITO WHIRS on only two wings. By setting up harmonic vibrations in the air and in its own thorax, it gets more flaps out of its wings than its nerves or muscles could sustain alone.

A DRAGONFLY BEATS its pairs of long, slender wings independently, the front ones rising as the rear ones fall. Despite this primitive equipment, it is still the deftest of flying acrobats.

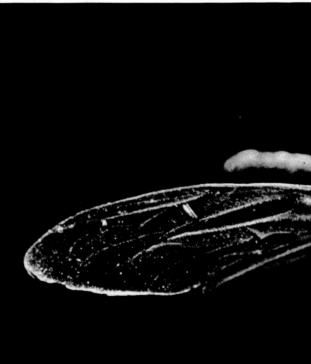

A CICADA-KILLER WASP ROWS through the air with a figure-eight motion on wings coupled together like a bee's. The wings are feathered like oars *(top center)* on the upbeat; on the downbeat *(top right)* they spank the air flat-on; in-between *(bottom)* they start to twist in anticipation of their next upward stroke.

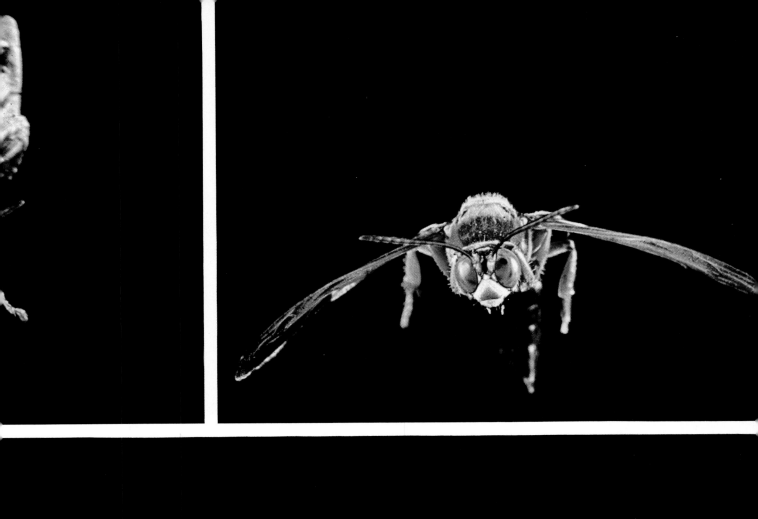

AN *APHID'S BIRTH* takes place on the stem of a goldenrod. This is a virgin birth; in the summer there are many generations of short-lived females, each of which can produce up to 100 young without fertilization. In autumn, however, aphids mate and lay eggs which survive the winter and hatch the next spring.

3

The Marvel of Metamorphosis

IN *Alice's Adventures in Wonderland*, Alice complains to the Caterpillar that she is very confused by the changes in size she has undergone. The Caterpillar finds nothing confusing about it at all. "Well, perhaps you haven't found it so yet," said Alice; "but when you have to turn into a chrysalis—you will some day, you know—and then after that into a butterfly, I should think you'll feel it a little queer, won't you?"

"Not a bit," said the Caterpillar.

"Well, perhaps your feelings may be different," said Alice: "all I know is, it would feel very queer to *me*."

"You!" said the Caterpillar contemptuously. "Who are *you*?"

The human mind has long been unable to comprehend the strange growth and development of most insects from an egg to wormlike larva, then to an inert pupa, and from that to emergence as a winged adult. More than 2,000 years ago, the Greek philosopher Aristotle explained this mystifying series of transformations very simply—although inaccurately. "The larva while it is yet in growth," he wrote, "is a soft egg." A more accurate understanding of the complex life history of insects did not develop until the past few decades: as recently

INCOMPLETE METAMORPHOSIS

EGGS

YOUNG NYMPH

LATER NYMPH

ADULT

If, when it leaves the egg, an insect resembles the adult form it will ultimately assume, and if it grows up without passing through a pupal, or resting, stage, it is said to be undergoing incomplete metamorphosis. The harlequin cabbage bug above, a stink bug, is such an insect. Although its body markings change slightly as it passes through several nymphal molts, and although it finally gets wings, it is essentially the same insect it started out to be.

as the last century, the caterpillar was still sometimes regarded as a "moving, growing and feeding egg."

The term metamorphosis has been given to this miraculous change of form in most insects—such as the transformation of the clumsy caterpillar into the bright-winged butterfly. But to emphasize this final change is to risk a complete misunderstanding of what happens during the development of the insect. The butterfly does not arise magically from the caterpillar; rather, the butterfly is the true form of the species. Instead, the magical stranger in this sequence is the caterpillar itself—a wayward form that has somehow interjected itself between egg and winged adult. Thus, two changes of form actually take place—one from the ancestral pattern contained in each egg into the peculiar caterpillar, and the other from caterpillar back at last to the ancestral form, the butterfly. It is only this ancestral form that can fertilize or deposit more eggs and thus propagate the species. There is no evidence of how such a remarkable plan of life ever came about, but the arrangement obviously has survival benefits, for about 87 per cent of all the known insect species have developed this complex metamorphosis of egg into larva, and then retromorphosis as a pupa back to the ancestral adult form.

All insects begin their lives as eggs. These eggs usually have strong outer coats and an ability to withstand unfavorable conditions. They can be frozen solid and still produce living insects; some shells are tough enough to resist the corrosive action of fairly strong acids. Insect eggs show a variety of shapes and color patterns, some of them quite elaborate. Many have knobs or sharp points on them. Their surfaces may be finely sculptured with longitudinal ribs and sometimes even with cross ribs as well. The egg-producing ability of insects varies greatly. The tsetse fly of Africa produces only one egg at a time; the larva hatches within the female and is nurtured internally until fully grown and ready to enter the resting stage. It is born alive, turns at once into a pupa and then emerges as a winged adult. At the other end of the scale stand the termites, the leading egg producers by far. A termite queen may produce 10,000 or more eggs in a single day; a single termite colony of some three million individuals can all be the progeny of one such queen.

USUALLY, eggs develop only when they have been fertilized by male sperm cells. But numerous kinds of bees, wasps, ants and other insects have been able to dispense with the male; the eggs of mature females develop without fertilization. One common black wasp is almost completely independent of the male; it has been reared in the laboratory for generations without the appearance of a single male, and only a few males have ever been captured in the wild.

The egg-laying tool of the insect is the ovipositor, inconspicuous in some species but as much as six inches long in some ichneumon wasps, which must probe deep through bark to find the live, wood-boring larvae in which they deposit their eggs. Many insects have ovipositors modified for cutting so that they can lay their eggs inside plants that serve either as a food source for the young or as a protective cover. The sawfly, whose young live inside leaves or stems, has a serrated ovipositor; the long-horned grasshopper's, shaped like a sharp blade, can be used to dig into either plant tissue or the soil. For eggs that are deposited on the outside of leaves, in bark crevices and even on rocks, many female insects secrete a fluid that acts both as a quick-drying, waterproof varnish and as a glue to cement the eggs into place. Walking sticks use this fluid to create a protective case for each individual egg. Praying mantids secrete a large amount of gummy liquid which is churned into a froth by the tip of the female's abdomen; before the frothy mass hardens, the mantis lays the eggs within it in a series of chambers that are equipped with hatches through which the young escape. The green lacewing touches the surface of the leaf with the end of its abdomen, then deposits a drop of fluid which it pulls into a delicate stalk by raising its abdomen; the egg that it lays atop this threadlike pedestal appears to be floating in air. Some mosquitoes glue several hundred eggs together, forming a raft. The eggs are long and tapered at one end, the thicker ends pointing downward. As a result, the raft has a curve something like a boat bottom. If it is overturned in the water, it immediately rights itself, for the bottoms of the eggs are easily wetted, but the tops repel water.

THE creature that eventually emerges from an insect egg may have one of three forms. Primitive insects, such as silverfish, hatch out as small-scale replicas of their parents: they grow to adult size simply by molting, by splitting their old skins when these become too tight and crawling out of them. Thus, from the time it leaves the egg until death, the insect is practically the same except for the fact that it slowly grows larger as it gets older.

The second kind of growth pattern interposes a special stage between egg and adult. What comes out of the egg is not a miniature adult but a nymph, a creature that resembles the adult in most respects but has certain important differences. Among winged insects, for example, the nymphs are wingless. Many of them hatch from eggs deposited in the water and spend their whole nymphal stage feeding beneath the surface and breathing with gills. Dragonfly and damselfly nymphs both do this. When, after several underwater molts, they are ready to emerge as adults, they crawl out of the water, crack their shells for the last time and start breathing air. Budlike growths on the thorax, inconspicuous in the nymph, are now revealed as wings and the former nymphs are adult insects at last. This sequence of egg-nymph-adult, with the emergence of wings marking the final step, is known as incomplete metamorphosis.

The third pattern is that of complete metamorphosis. In this case the larvae that emerge from the eggs are always markedly different from the adults, often live in different environments and have different habits. The larvae usually have chewing mouth parts, even though the adults may have siphoning or piercing mouth parts. They lack their parents' compound eyes. They may possess additional pairs of legs on the abdomen or they may lack legs altogether. Larvae have been given a number of different names: those of the fly group are usually called maggots; beetle larvae are known as grubs; those of butterflies and moths are called caterpillars. But before any of them can become adults they must pass through an intermediate stage as pupae.

All animals grow and show changes during the course of growth. A human child changes enormously during its embryonic stage while still inside the mother, in contrast to the changes that occur between birth and maturity. With an insect, however, the big changes occur after emergence from the egg. This is because insect growth is marked by a series of abrupt and obvious increases in size with each molt. Between molts, the insect lives through long periods when increase in size is impossible because of its all-enveloping external skeleton. These times of static size are brought to an end by a sudden surge of growth that leaves the insect wrinkled and squeezed within its armor coat. The molt follows: the insect, rid of its old shell, transforms its hitherto captive growth into an actual increase in size because its new skeleton is free to expand.

COMPLETE METAMORPHOSIS

EGG

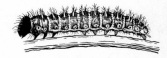

LARVA (CATERPILLAR)

CHRYSALIS (PUPA)

ADULT

If the egg yields an insect form which is entirely different from the final adult, and if this larva must pass through a pupal stage, perhaps in a cocoon, then the species is characterized by complete metamorphosis. The painted lady butterfly shown here is first a caterpillar and then a chrysalis before becoming the delicate adult creature which in no way resembles the slow-moving, segmented caterpillar, not even in its habits or food preferences.

The process of molting, then, is not so simple as buying a larger suit of clothes for a growing human child. Essentially, the insect skeleton is composed of a hard outer layer and a more flexible inner layer, both of which overlie the thin covering of living cells that might be called "skin." In molting, special glands in this skin discharge a secretion that dissolves the skeleton's inner layer, but not the outer. At the same time, an entirely new, pliable skeleton—accordion-pleated by the inner pressures of growth—is forming, still protected by the old outer layer. Finally, the insect splits this old shell down the head and thorax, and emerges in a new suit—wrinkled, soft and pliable at first—that expands and then hardens into armor.

RECENT discoveries have revealed that molting, like many other aspects of insect growth, is controlled by hormones. Ductless glands in the insect's head produce a hormone when the time for a molt approaches. The hormone is carried through the blood and acts as a messenger, causing molting glands to become active and a new skeleton to grow. This has been shown by injecting blood from an insect about to molt into another insect not approaching a molt: the insect that receives the transfusion sheds its shell prematurely.

The tremendous difference between maggot and fly, grub and beetle, caterpillar and moth must somehow be reconciled. It is the pupal stage that sees the dramatic return of all these wormlike forms to their ancestral appearance. The word "pupa," derived from the Latin for "doll," was used to describe this stage because many insect pupae resemble a doll or infant wrapped in swaddling clothes. The pupal stage is commonly called a resting stage, but this is a misnomer. Although most pupae appear lifeless and mummylike, sweeping changes are in progress beneath the still surface. During this period of fierce biological activity, the ancestral insect form is reconstructed—complete with adult mouth parts, legs and wings.

When the larva completes its growth, it stops feeding. It may spin a silken covering, such as the cocoon of a moth, inside which it is apparently immobile, or it may reorganize while protected by nothing but its naked outer skin, such as the chrysalis of a butterfly. The pupae of some insects—mosquitoes and midges, for example—are exceedingly lively, but most pupae are as still as death: the ant "eggs" sold at pet shops are actually the cocoons of pupating ants, and not eggs at all.

Lifeless as they may seem, pupae are engaged in furious rearrangement of their tissues. Among moths, the extra legs along the caterpillar's abdomen are lost. Where the stumpy legs of the thorax had been, the long, slender legs of the adult now develop. Mouth parts change from the chewing to the sucking type. The four wings develop, as do reproductive organs. Most of the muscular system is transformed. At certain stages during the breakdown of old structures and the build-up of new, the pupa's contents may be largely liquid.

The whole process of insect metamorphosis is still incompletely understood, although the fantastic nature of these transformation scenes has attracted many students. It is only within the last few decades that scientists have discovered some remarkable facts about the double life of the insect and the interplay of hormones in its life cycle. Soon after the egg is fertilized and the cells begin to divide, a strange event takes place. From a place in the egg where the future adult thorax will develop, what has been called a "wave of determinism" spreads out over the embryo. Like a stage director, this wave arrays certain cells for the specific roles they will play in the life of the larva. Shortly thereafter, a second wave assigns still other cells to the roles they will play in the insect's pupal and adult stages: the clusters of adult cells that result are known as imaginal buds. Thus, a forming caterpillar has within it two separate growth patterns: the one that it uses to continue its growth into a caterpillar, and another which is held in storage and which will come into play when the time comes for it to turn into a moth.

This isolation of larval and adult cells from one another occurs at a very early age; among house flies and fruit flies it can be detected only seven hours after the egg begins development. Although the embryo at this stage appears to be only a ball of cells, the plan of two future organisms—the larva and the pupa-adult—is already laid out. This early segregation of cells with two individual potentials helps explain how insect larvae have been able to develop such strange adaptations and to follow courses of evolution that are sharply different from those of the adult forms. This independent evolution has resulted in the remarkable specializations of insects and thus has vastly increased their adaptability. The adult insect can follow one steady evolutionary path, while the larva can change course markedly without in any way affecting the adult.

The cells that are committed to the formation of the larva quickly go through their development. The tiny larva that emerges from the egg is a wingless mechanism with a single purpose: consuming food. It grows and molts a number of times. It increases in size *not* by increasing the number of its cells but by enlarging the size of the cells with which it was born: a mature larva usually has no more larval cells than were present when it emerged from the egg, although it may be many thousand times larger. All the time that the larva is feeding hungrily, molting and escaping from enemies, it carries within it the clusters of adult imaginal buds, but these cell clusters take no part in the larva's activities. They do not mature and are held constantly in check.

When caterpillar, grub or maggot enters its pupal stage, however, its larval cells begin to die. Now the clusters of adult cells put on a burst of growth. Unlike the cells of the larva, these adult cells grow *not* by enlargement but by division. They develop into specialized organs, utilizing the dead larval cells for nourishment. First, larval tissues are replaced by pupal tissues; then the pupal organs are transformed into those of the adult.

Obviously there must be some control center that directs this complex dissolution of the larva and the assembly of the pupa-adult, nourished by these raw materials, into what amounts to a new organism. Investigations have revealed that, as with molting, head hormones play the key role. One such hormone triggers the secretion of a second hormone in the larva's thorax. This second hormone acts upon the waiting clusters of pupal-adult cells and provokes them into transformation. It also acts as a regulator of the head hormone: feeding back to the brain, it shuts off that flow. These growth-and-development hormones thus direct much of the insect's life: they tell it when to molt, when to end the larval stage, when to pass from a pupa to an adult.

But what keeps these hormones in check? What prevents them from acting upon a tiny caterpillar long before its appointed time, causing it to turn into a midget adult? Just behind the insect brain, investigators have found a pair of glands known as the corpora allata. Dissection has revealed these glands in every fully metamorphosing insect thus far examined. By delicate surgery, scientists have been able to remove them from living larvae. Wherever this was done, the caterpillars ended their larval life immediately. No matter what their stage of development, at their next molt they spun midget-sized cocoons and emerged as dwarf adults. Thus, the removal of the corpora allata cuts short the youth of an insect and thrusts it prematurely into the adult world. Since it maintains insect immaturity, the secretion of these glands has been named the "juvenile" hormone.

Just as removal of the corpora allata causes a larva to become a pupa prematurely, the artificial implanting of these glands in a mature larva, on the brink of pupation, rejuvenates it. The larva postpones metamorphosis and continues to grow, until finally it turns into a giant adult. It is believed that this sort of thing happened naturally during the time some 300 million years ago when insects with two-and-a-half-foot wingspreads existed. The corpora allata of these giants must have continued to pour out the juvenile hormone for a long period, resulting in a longer larval stage and consequently a larger adult.

As a normal larva matures, the corpora allata halt their production of the juvenile hormone and the insect's array of pupal-adult cells is liberated. These immediately respond by growing and differentiating into pupal organs. At the same time, the larval cells receive their own hormone from the thorax, signaling that it is time for them to reach biological death and transfiguration into the raw material of the adult.

When the great changes within the pupa are complete and the time has come for the transformed adult to emerge, it undergoes its last molt by shedding the pupal skin. For some insects, this presents a problem. Some fly species have a special bladder in the head which is inflated until the pupal skin breaks and the fly is free. This is the only use to which the bladder is put; after the fly's emergence, it is deflated and withdrawn into the head. Some moths, which pupate inside a cocoon, secrete a liquid that softens one end of the silken chamber. Among certain silkworm moths the habit is not to glue the threads together at one end of the cocoon. Instead, these threads are woven into a cone. This is the reverse of the sort of trap that lets an animal in but not out again. The cocoon's strands are so arranged that the adult can easily leave, but enemies are not able to enter.

The adult that emerges from the pupa is not fully formed at once. It is soft and helpless. In a moth or butterfly the wings look like small, folded parachutes. The adult climbs up a stem, wings drooping. In a few minutes, blood pressure and muscular contraction help them unfurl like a leaf bursting its bud. After some 20 minutes a moth's wings have reached full size, but they are still moist and soft; it may take two hours for them to become firm and assume their full color. Among some insects the height of color is not reached for days or weeks. Meanwhile, final perfections are taking place in the legs, antennae and other external parts of the body. At last the adult insect assumes its familiar shape, beats its untried wings a few times and flies off. It has now reached the end of its long path of development and will no longer grow or molt. Small flies do not grow into larger flies, as many people believe; they belong to different species, even though they may look very much the same.

W INGS are the emblems of the adult insect; flight, for the brief hours or many months that the adult may survive, is a way of life. Of all insect flights, the most impressive is that of the locust, whose swarms have plagued mankind around the world, particularly in South America, Africa and the Near East. They were one of the 10 plagues that Jehovah visited upon Pharaoh. The inexorable advance of the black cloud of these insect destroyers upon the land is

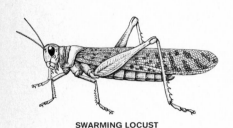

SWARMING LOCUST

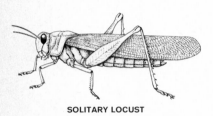

SOLITARY LOCUST

Gregarious, or swarming, locusts differ from solitary locusts in having darker bodies and darker, spotted wings. According to one theory, not yet substantiated, the reason for this is that swarming nymphs eat faster, burn up more material than they can normally excrete and transform this waste into dark body pigment.

described in the Book of Joel in the Bible: "A day of darkness and of gloominess, a day of clouds and of thick darkness, as the morning spread upon the mountains. . . . A fire devoureth before them, and behind them a flame burneth: the land *is* as the Garden of Eden before them, and behind them a desolate wilderness; yea, and nothing shall escape them."

"Locust" is the common name for several species of short-horned grasshoppers that often increase suddenly in numbers and undertake mass migrations. There are seven or so species that can bring desolation and famine in their wake. One such locust swarm in East Africa was over a hundred feet deep on a mile-wide front: it took nine hours to pass at a speed of about six miles an hour. When assisted by tail winds, desert locusts have appeared in England after a journey of at least 2,000 miles, probably begun in southern Algeria.

The sudden appearance of swarms of locusts long remained a mystery. Under normal conditions, locusts live as solitary individuals, differing in both color and shape from swarming locusts and causing no more serious damage to crops than do ordinary grasshoppers. Not until 1921 did scientists discover that the swarming locust and the solitary shorthorn locust, despite appearances were, in fact, one and the same insect.

WHAT causes the transformation from a scattered population to a swarm that may number in the billions, with each individual eating its own weight in vegetation every day? One of the first clues to the mystery was the discovery that solitary locusts could be transformed into gregarious ones in the laboratory simply by rearing them under crowded conditions. Once again, the influence of hormones provides the answer. The development of eggs in many insects, the locusts among them, is controlled by the same glands—the corpora allata—that produce the juvenile hormone. It was found that the presence of mature male locusts, such as would be the case in crowded circumstances, makes female locusts mature rapidly. A chemical that the male secretes over its entire body stimulates the female's head glands, which release a hormone that speeds the maturation process. If female locusts are reared in the absence of males, many of their eggs fail to develop at all; those eggs that do require about 28 days to mature. But when the females are reared together with mature males, their eggs grow to full size within 14 days or so.

This interaction between crowding and physical change in the female lies at the root of the mystery. All that is required to produce a swarm is a favorable season followed by an unfavorable one. In a favorable season, with abundant food, the population of solitary locusts will naturally increase. If the next season is a poor one, this increased population will be forced to crowd together in the few suitable areas that remain. The crowding exposes the females to male stimulus on a massive scale, females and their eggs mature at a headlong pace and a population explosion brings the locust horde into being.

Many people believe that insects are all short-lived, but that is not always so. Some insect species do have brief spans of life: one kind of aphid, for example, can become adult in as little as six days, spend the next four or five days in reproduction and then die. The males of some insects live only brief hours as adults, although their developmental stages last a number of months. At the other end of the scale, there are some insects that are enormously long-lived: queen termites may survive for more than 50 years.

In the Temperate Zones most insects produce only one generation a year, although some have two, three and even more. In the tropics many insects breed continuously and the generations overlap. But many insects at some stage of their lives can enter a state of arrested growth called diapause.

This arrested state is often immensely more complicated than the simple dormancy of an insect during the cold of winter. For many insects, diapause has great survival benefits. An example is the yearly cycle of the silkworm moth: these insects pass the winter as eggs and then hatch in the spring, with the larvae quickly changing into pupae and then to adults. These adult moths then lay eggs that hatch immediately, in early summer. The moths that result from this second set of eggs, in turn, lay their eggs in the fall. It is this final set of eggs that overwinters and does not hatch until the following spring.

Why do eggs laid during the summer hatch almost immediately, while those laid during the fall go into diapause for the winter? This is obviously a satisfactory arrangement for the silkworms, since eggs can endure the cold winter but adults cannot. One wonders, though, what has informed the silkworm moth that it is time to lay special, overwintering eggs. It has been shown that the explanation lies not in some mystic silkworm foreknowledge but in the varying degrees of sunlight and darkness in each day as the summer passes. The key to this is the fact that the moths that deposit these special eggs grew to maturity at a time of year when the days were longer than the nights. Females raised to maturity when periods of light exceed periods of darkness are able to pass on a subtle influence, which delays hatching, to the eggs they eventually produce. This influence, investigators have proved, is still another hormone produced in the head of the female. It seems to have no effect on larva or adult; its influence is only on the eggs and on their time of hatching.

THE life and growth of insects are thus seen to consist of the intermeshing of many delicate mechanisms. Swept along on tides of hormones, triggered by such stimuli as temperature and light, influenced by the presence of other species, insects at every stage of their lives must follow exacting rituals that have evolved over millions of years. Turning the complexities of the insect's life cycle against itself may be man's best hope of eventual control over insect pests. Much research is currently under way in this field.

The juvenile hormone, for example, has great potential: it could prevent larvae from turning into adults and reproducing themselves. If some method could be developed to manufacture this hormone in large quantities and spray it on immature insects, they might die before metamorphosis. Similarly, if the swarming hormone could be counteracted, the build-up of locust hordes might be prevented. The screw-worm fly has already been eradicated as a pest in the southeastern United States and elsewhere by interfering with its reproductive habits. Because the female fly mates only once in its lifetime, this pest's life cycle was easily disrupted. When males, sterilized in the laboratory by radiation, were released in immense numbers, they competed with fertile males for the available females. Where irradiated males were successful, only sterile eggs resulted and the next generation was greatly reduced in numbers. The same technique was then used with this smaller generation and with the even smaller one that followed until, finally, no more females were born.

There is an additional advantage in turning the insect's own mechanisms against it. Insects could scarcely become resistant to their own life processes as they so frequently do to insecticides. Perhaps it will be in these exquisite intricacies of insect lives that their ultimate vulnerability—and the means for future control—can be discovered.

THE TRANSLUCENT PUPA OF A MONARCH BUTTERFLY HANGS DORMANT ON A TWIG. IN 12 DAYS ITS CELLS REORGANIZE INTO A WINGED ADULT

Forms in Flux

All but a few insects undergo the remarkable transformation of their bodies known as metamorphosis. The fat, creeping caterpillar —a veritable eating machine—turns into a graceful, winged moth which is able to fly far outward from its cocoon shelter in search of a mate or a promising spot to lay its eggs. Recent delicate experiments have disclosed how some of the changes are brought about.

Mystery in the Making of a Moth

The metamorphosis of caterpillar to moth is one of the most familiar of all biological phenomena, yet until a few years ago it was one of the least understood. An egg, laid by a moth, hatches into a tiny caterpillar which feeds voraciously for six to eight weeks until it reaches maturity as a fat, four-inch worm. The sated larva then spins a cocoon and within it the mummylike pupa forms. During a period of dormancy the pupa is somehow rearranged to form the body of the mature moth which will find a mate and repeat the cycle. But what brings about this incredible change of body form and function? What mechanism controls its timing so the frail moth leaves its cocoon only in the warmth of spring? Within the last two decades, some elegant experiments (*next pages*) have explained these mysteries.

FROM EGG TO PUPA in the life cycle of a cecropia moth is shown above. An egg hatches after 10 days (1). The caterpillar, turned green to match its background, grows enormously, splitting out of four skins in the process (2). A cocoon is spun of liquid silk extruded from glands near the caterpillar's mouth (3). Pictures 4, 5 and 6 show the developing pupa with the cocoon removed.

A MOTH ESCAPES from the dry skin of the pupa. The skin begins to split at the head end and the moth pokes its head out. Then, using its legs, the moth pulls its body free and exposes velvety, tightly folded wings. Blood expands the wings, enabling the moth to fly. The mature moth is a reproductive machine; it is unable to eat and lives only long enough to find a mate.

Clues Hidden in the Pupa

In 1942 a young Harvard biologist, Dr. Carroll Williams, began a brilliant piece of scientific sleuthing which went far toward solving the mystery of metamorphosis. Working with the cecropia moth, Dr. Williams soon learned that whatever directed metamorphosis was located in the front section of the animal. If a pupa was cut in two, the front half went on to develop into half a moth while the back part remained a pupa. Continuing one step further,

Williams sought to find out what in the head section was triggering the change. His experiments, some of which are shown on these pages, pinpointed two interdependent hormone centers, one in the brain and the other in the thorax, just behind the head. Further experiments showed that a warming of the temperature—in nature the first warm days of spring—triggers the flow of the brain hormone to start the transformation of the dormant moth.

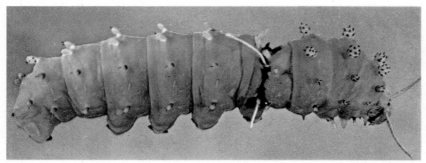

WITHOUT HORMONES, a caterpillar cannot develop. To prove this point, Williams first tied off the head from the thorax, and then the head and thorax from the tail. Thus divided, the caterpillar continued to live but did not begin metamorphosis.

WITH ONE HORMONE, development begins. This insect was tied off after the brain hormone began to flow but before the thoracic hormone was produced. The thorax developed, but the tail, which received no stimulus from the thoracic center, did not.

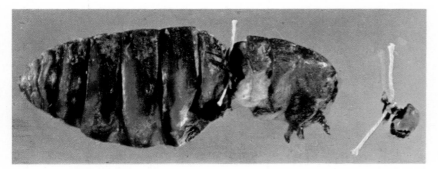

WITH BOTH HORMONES, full metamorphosis occurs. Head and thorax sections were tied off after both hormones had been produced. Experiments proved that the brain hormone stimulates the thoracic hormone, which in turn initiates metamorphosis.

A HEADLESS MOTHER grows to maturity and lays eggs (three-picture sequence at right and below). When brain and thoracic hormone centers are inserted with tweezers (*right*) into a pupal abdomen whose severed end is sealed with a plastic cover, it develops into the fully functional rear section of an adult moth (*far right*). This fragment of a female not only attracted a normal male moth but it also was fertilized and deposited eggs (*below*).

HALVED PUPAE test the effects of injury on metamorphosis. For purposes of comparison, Dr. Williams used four moth pupae of exactly the same age. The pupae are from left: a whole pupa; a halved pupa whose two raw ends are covered with a plastic coating; a halved pupa whose two ends are connected with a tiny plastic tube; and finally a halved pupa with the sections connected by a plastic tube but with a movable ball bearing in the tube to stop any tissues from extending between the segments.

A MONTH LATER the experiment is complete (left). Pupa Number 1 developed normally. In Number 2, the front end metamorphosed but the tail did not. In Number 3, the wounds healed and a tissue thread grew through the tube, providing a bridge across which hormones could flow. Both ends developed. In 4, where the motion of the ball bearing prevented tissue growth, no development took place. Dr. Williams concluded from these experiments that injuries must heal before the insect metamorphoses.

A FATAL FLIGHT climaxes the experiment. Pupa 3, now a moth, expands its wings and flies away. Though both sections of the body developed, the weak bridge of tissue in the tube broke and the insect fell to the ground and died.

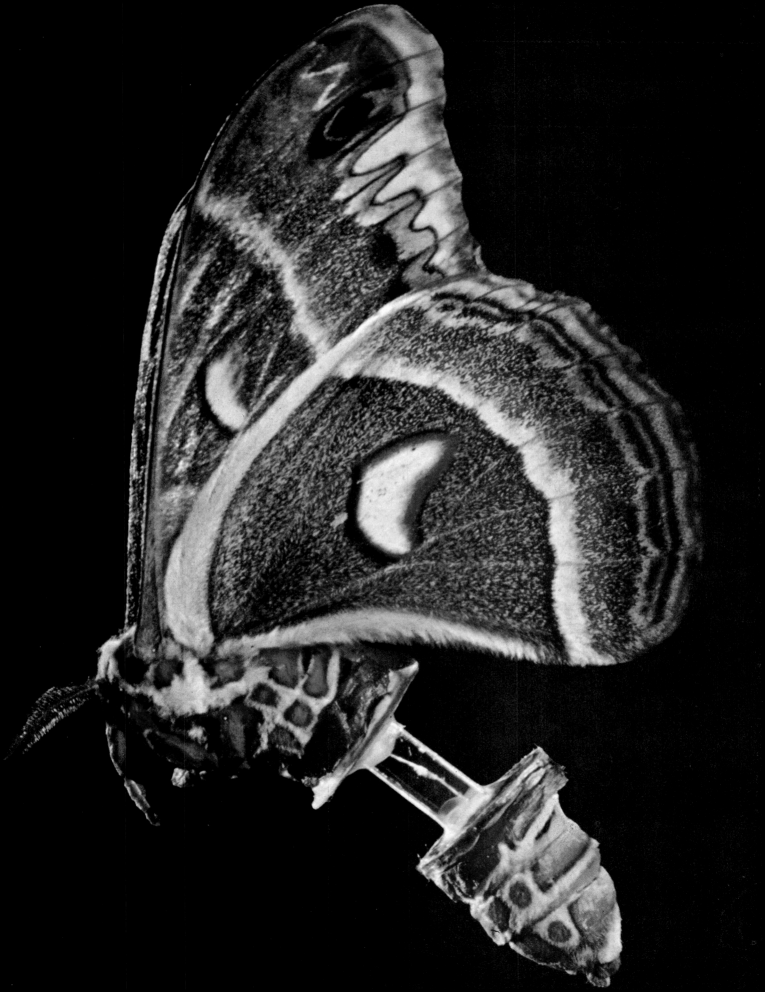

KENTISH GLORY MOTH

HANDMAID MOTH

COPPER BUTTERFLY

IO MOTH

STINK BUG

HARLEQUIN BUG

PAINTED LADY BUTTERFLY

FALL CANKERWORM MOTH

LADYBIRD BEETLE

The Profusion of Eggs

If a biologist from another planet were to take a census of the earth without the aid of a microscope, he could only report that the principal form of land life in this world—in terms of absolute numbers—is the insect egg. The fertility of insects is staggering. The average female will lay 100 to 200 eggs in its brief lifetime, but a house fly will produce a thousand and the long-lived queen termite 500 million. Yet most people have never seen an insect egg; they are inconspicuously deposited in protected places where the larvae will be close to food, and they are tiny—the largest is only a quarter inch long. Despite their small size, many kinds of eggs are distinctively colored and sculptured, as seen in the highly magnified photographs opposite.

A COCKROACH BABY squeezes from its egg. Roaches clump 30 to 40 eggs in a casing like the one above. The mother carries the capsule on its abdomen until it finds a place to hide it.

LACEWING EGGS ARE ELEVATED ON GOSSAMER PEDESTALS, POSSIBLY TO KEEP THE FIRST HATCHED LARVA FROM CANNIBALIZING OTHER EGGS

A PALE BEETLE GRUB dug out of a rotting log has little resemblance to the adult form *(opposite)*. The larva lives exclusively on a diet of decaying wood, on which it slowly fattens.

A GHOSTLY BEETLE PUPA, here removed from a protective case formed of wood fragments by the larva, shows many of the characteristics of the adult which is slowly taking form in its interior.

Metamorphosis of an Insect Behemoth

Like some antique war machine, the grotesque stag beetle *(opposite)* rattles through the dead leaves of a European forest searching for a mate. It holds its enormous jaws cocked, ready to fight a ponderous, butting love duel with any rival male. If it is victorious the beetle will transfer its sperm to the female's body, then lurch onward, perhaps to find itself still another mate, but certainly soon to die by violence or of insect old age.

In its essential steps, the life cycle of the stag beetle follows that of the most delicate butterfly. It began some four years earlier as an egg laid in the decaying heartwood of an old tree. The egg hatched and the larva slowly grew into a plump grub and then into a pupa. Within the pupa, most of the tissues of the larva distintegrate into a kind of cellular soup. Only a few body structures, such as the breathing apparatus and circulatory system, stay on to serve the adult. New adult tissue begins to form slowly out of the soup, taking shape from tiny clusters of cells called imaginal buds which have been passed along from the larva. After perhaps a month of this biological alchemy, the soft white worm is totally converted into a hard-coated black beetle.

A MANDIBLED MONSTER, the two-and-a-quarter-inch-long adult form of the European stag beetle is so named because its branching, outsized jaws resemble the antlers of a stag. Despite their formidable size, the pincers of this male beetle are quite weak. The female, with stubbier jaws, has a more powerful pinch and has been known to draw blood from a man's finger.

Seventeen Years in Darkness

The patient seventeen-year locust, more properly known as the periodical cicada, is one of the relatively small group of insects that makes an incomplete metamorphosis. Its immature form looks much like a miniature version of the adult cicada and is called a nymph. Millions of cicada nymphs live underground, sucking juices from tree roots until the spring of their 17th year, when they push their way to the surface all at the same time, crawl up bushes or trees and molt into an immense horde of winged insects. The damage these adults do is not by defoliation, as with the true locusts, but by slitting tender twigs to lay eggs. The newly hatched nymphs fall to the ground and dig in for another 17 years.

HONEYCOMBED SOIL is left by surfacing cicada nymphs. The insects here are dead remnants of the swarm. Unlike adults, nymphs are wingless and have strong front legs for burrowing.

IN A FINAL MOLT, A MATURE CICADA PULLS ITSELF THROUGH A SLIT IN THE NYMPHAL SKIN. LIFE ABOVEGROUND LASTS ONLY A FEW WEEKS

A JUNK YARD OF SKINS shed by swarming cicadas clutters an Indiana orchard following a large emergence in 1953. The progeny of this horde, now underground, will appear in 1970. There are at least 20 different broods of cicadas in the United States, each developing on its own timetable. This explains why there may be several different cicada swarms in one 17-year period.

HONEYCOMB CELLS are the basic
storage units of the beehive. The
dark cells contain honey, and are
waiting to be capped with wax like
the full ones at top left. The open
cells at lower right contain pollen
and the closed ones pupating larvae.

4

Insect
Architecture

HONEY bees have long been lauded for their selection of a six-sided shape—
the hexagon—as the structural unit that composes their honeycombs. Not
only does a hexagonal cell hold more honey than a triangular or a square one,
but it is also strengthened by its contact with all the neighboring cells. Darwin
regarded this example of the bee's architecture as "the most wonderful of known
instincts" and "absolutely perfect in economising labour and wax." The bee,
of course, has no knowledge of geometry nor any way of comparing the storage
capacities of variously shaped containers. Then how did bees ever stumble upon
the neat, hexagonal rows that make up their combs?

It is probable that the bees could not construct a cell of any other shape.
Visualize a neat pile of cylindrical plastic tubes, stacked so that five tubes are
on the bottom row, four on the next, then five again and so on. If these tubes
are subjected to equal pressure on all sides, as they would be if additional tubes
were placed tightly around them, they become compressed—into a series of
hexagons. The tubes assume a hexagonal shape because each is in contact with
all surrounding tubes at six points; under compression, these six points are
converted into the hexagon's six walls. It was once believed that something of

this sort took place in the construction of a honeycomb, the pliable beeswax cylinder assuming a hexagonal shape in which it hardened. But studies of combs at all stages of construction show that the bees both start and finish their cells as hexagons.

Thus a simple explanation cannot be found for the honey bees' adept architecture, and it is no easier to find explanations for many of the other structures that insects make. In all probability, insect architecture evolved over immense stretches of time and the structures that survive today do so because they confer some benefit upon their builders. The insect world is notable for the constructions made by its inhabitants. Their only basic raw materials are earth, wood and other plant materials, and their own silk, wax and saliva. Their tools are the ones they are born with, on their mouth parts and legs. With these they are able to make homes and nurseries that take such various forms as paper cartons, adobe huts, wooden labyrinths and silken pavilions.

ALTHOUGH the honey bee is probably the best builder among the bees, it is by no means the only one. There are over 3,000 species of bees in North America. All but 100 or so are solitary rather than communal, although several hundred solitary species do live in what might be called villages. Each female bee in such a village constructs and provisions its own nest in the ground without help from its neighbors. Nests only an inch apart may crowd a patch of soil, and a larger bee town may cover several acres of tightly packed burrows.

Among the solitary bees, some make their nests in abandoned snail shells, in the burrows of other bees and even in cavities of soft rock. Carpenter bees chisel their own tunnels in wood or utilize the borings already made by beetles. But most solitary bees build in the soil. Their burrows usually take the form of a main corridor with smaller branches that contain the brood cells. The burrows are often only a few inches deep, but some bees drive shafts downward into the ground for two or three feet. Some construct their brood cells in bunches, like a cluster of grapes, while others hollow all of them out at one end of the tunnel, like petals on a flower spike. Each kind of bee usually follows its ancestral building design, never improving but instead constructing a replica of the burrow in which it was born. The solitary bee fills each brood cell with a mass of honey-moistened pollen, known as honey loaf or beebread, lays its egg directly upon this store of food and then seals the nest.

As a rule, the female solitary bee has nothing further to do with its offspring after laying the egg, but some species show faint glimmers of the organization that reaches its height in the honey-bee hive. A common type of solitary bee known as *Halictus* occurs almost everywhere in North America and Europe. It is mostly black or greenish-black and less than half the size of a honey bee. The fertilized female *Halictus* usually passes the winter in a hibernating burrow; in the spring it emerges and constructs underground brood cells which are provisioned with honey loaves. Because the female has been fertilized, its offspring are also all females. They make their nests in side burrows of the parental nest or else dig new ones of their own nearby. Their offspring, in turn, develop from unfertilized eggs and are all males. But the first female is still present and it now lays more eggs on the honey loaves of its daughters. These eggs produce females, which mate with the males, and these fertilized females dig hibernation burrows for the winter and repeat the cycle.

Higher on the social scale are the bumble bees. The female that survives the winter is a large individual known as a queen. Emerging in the spring, it does not make a burrow of its own but rather seeks out a deserted rodent nest. A large quantity of wax starts to exude from the segments of the queen's abdomen. With this wax the bee constructs a honeypot and fills it with as much as a thimbleful of nectar for use during the night or during bad weather. Then the queen makes a cell and places a pollen ball in it, on which the eggs are deposited. The queen sits on the eggs, and later on the larvae, like a brooding hen, protecting them from the cold to which they are very susceptible. Brooding, like the queen's other behavior, stems from unreasoning instinct. When stimulated to brood, the bumble bee broods. If an experimenter removes the eggs, the queen will utilize any nearby object, even a pebble, as a substitute.

The first bumble-bee brood develops into a handful of diminutive worker bees, which the queen assists in cutting their way out of their cocoons. Once on the scene, these workers free the queen from all duties except egg-laying. As the workers take over building and maintenance, the nest's brood cells increase in number and soon form a comb. These cells are not used for brooding a second time: instead, the workers rim them with wax, converting them into storage tanks for nectar and pollen. Bumble-bee towns never become as populous as honey-bee cities: a thriving bumble-bee colony may number 1,000 or 2,000 individuals by summer's end, but most contain only a few hundred.

Another remarkable engineer is the leaf-cutting bee, whose handiwork in the garden can be seen in the neat ovals cut out of the leaves of roses and other plants. The insect makes a solitary nest of a series of cells in the ground or in hollow wood, each cell containing layers of leaf or flower petals, all cut to approximately the same size, as if the bee were following a pattern. In point of fact, the bee is, and the key to the pattern is its own body. In cutting each dime-sized oval, the female anchors itself by the hind legs to the edge of a leaf and then, as if its body were a compass, describes a circle, cutting through the leaf with its mandibles as it turns. The bits of leaf are always about the same size because the bee's body size does not alter. The pieces of leaf are then laid one atop the other and trodden into the shape of a thimble, which is stocked with pollen and nectar. After laying an egg in the first cell, the bee begins to build another one directly above it in exactly the same way. One leaf-cutter bee was observed constructing 30 cells in nine rows under a porch, using at least a thousand ovals of leaf.

THE greatest diversity in building operations is found among the wasps. These insects have perfected methods of constructing dwellings and nurseries both of paper and of mud. The manufacture of paper is a simple operation—for a wasp. It collects fibers of rotten wood, the stems of plants, or even man-made paper and cardboard, all of which are thoroughly chewed. Mixed with a salivary secretion, the result is a pulpy mass, a sort of papier-mâché that usually turns into a firm gray paper when dry. Yellow-jacket wasps construct paper nests underground, but the large paper balls suspended from the branches of trees and the eaves of roofs are built by the kind of wasp known as a hornet. A hornet nest consists of horizontal combs, with the cells facing down and the combs enclosed together in paper wrappers. Each time a new comb is added—below and parallel to the original one—the hornets cover the entire nest with a fresh outer layer of paper.

The hornet's building site is located with no apparent care given to suitability: the nests are often in places exposed to the hazards of wind and rain, open to predators, or built in cramped quarters where there is no room for enlarge-

THE MUD-DAUBER WASP

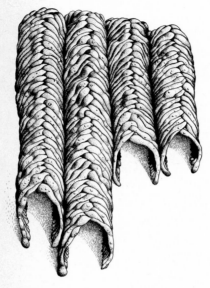

The mud-dauber wasp is a solitary rather than a social insect. It builds a pipe-organ nest for its young and provides them with food without the help of workers. Its nest is a long tubular structure of hardened mud subdivided into separate cells (above). The wasp stocks the cells with an abundant supply of paralyzed spiders and deposits an egg in each. Unlike most other solitary wasps, the female mud dauber gets some help from the male, who guards the nest while she is hunting.

ment. Ghost towns of abandoned nests are commonly seen, showing that some catastrophe has occurred. Nevertheless, hornets that have been displaced usually attempt to rebuild in exactly the same location. This is why merely knocking down a nest at night does no good: in the morning, the hornets start to build again. Even after one nest was moved a mile from its original location, the adults abandoned the elaborate structure, with their larvae still inside, to return to the old site and begin anew.

PAPER nests are also made by *Polistes* wasps. This common, slender wasp, with a narrow waist and usually black or yellow and black in color, is so abundant around man's structures that it is semidomesticated. It is among the most gentle of wasps, stinging only when disturbed. The small *Polistes* paper nests hang from the eaves of houses and garages, and the queen shelters for the winter inside the nests of man. In the spring, it leaves the human household by a door or window. It usually does not go farther than a nearby eave, where it lays a foundation by regurgitating a sticky material and smearing it on the place where the nest will be attached. Here the queen constructs a paper rope that dangles for perhaps half an inch. The end is again smeared with the same material that was used in laying the foundation. The first group of vertical cells, forming a horizontal comb, is then hitched to the rope, the eggs are glued into place, one to a cell, and the developing larvae hang downward.

Further cells are added to the sides of those already formed; as the comb grows, the hanging support is strengthened until it may be more than an inch in diameter. Even though papier-mâché is the only building material used, these nests are extremely strong. One was found to be able to sustain a pull of seven pounds, although the entire comb, even when filled with larvae, could not have weighed more than four ounces. Each bit of building material arrives at the nest, piece by piece, in the queen's jaws. When the larvae hatch, the wasp captures insects which it tears apart and feeds to its young. As the larvae grow, their cell walls are lengthened by the addition of more paper.

Like many of the solitary bee queens, the *Polistes* wasp is on its own at first. It performs all the duties of nest construction, maintenance and feeding until the first larvae develop into mature workers. The nest thrives as these workers carry back plunder to feed the next generation. The population may reach a hundred, although it is usually less than that. Suddenly, after midsummer, males and young queens appear and mate. Soon the old queen, the workers and then the males die; the last brood of larvae fails to develop.

The dissolution of this summer empire does not seem to be correlated with a drop in temperature: it usually occurs before the onset of cold weather. The weakness in the *Polistes* body politic is that this social organization is held together not by emotion and ethics, as human societies are, but by chemistry. As summer advances, secretions from the worker wasps' glands are exhausted; these secretions had presumably been mixed with the food fed the midsummer larvae when it was pre-chewed by the workers. The late larvae, deprived of this substance, fail to develop.

Unlike hornet nests, which are protected by an outer wrapper of paper, the *Polistes* nests are usually exposed—heated by the sun during the day, cooled at night. When the sun's rays fall directly upon the nest and threaten to overheat it, the wasps have two effective methods of cooling it. They fan vigorously with their wings and they also bring in droplets of water that probably serve to air-condition the cells. The natural cooling of the nest at night, in turn, seems to play a part in determining whether an immature wasp will develop into a worker or a young queen. Experiments show that if mature wasps are kept warm, the larvae develop into queens. Strangely, it does not matter at what temperature these young themselves are kept. Instead, variations in temperature seem in some way to alter the bodily workings of the mature workers who pass the effect on, again probably because of some change in the secretions they mix with the larvae's food.

The mud-dauber wasps, as their name indicates, use mud as their architectural raw material. Some of these wasps build a number of long tubes, side by side, so that the nest resembles the pipes of an organ. Each tube is divided into a number of compartments: the wasp provisions each one with paralyzed spiders and deposits an egg. But not all mud-builders produce pipes. The twigs of trees and the stems of flowers often bear little earthen jugs, some only half an inch in diameter and as delicately fashioned as if they had been turned on a wheel. These are the work of the potter wasp, easily recognized by its almost pear-shaped abdomen and bulge in its petiole (the normally thin stalk that connects abdomen to thorax).

A potter wasp usually visits only a single mud pit to get the materials for its jug, although two-toned jugs, the result of the use of two different kinds of mud, are found occasionally. Despite the numerous trips needed to haul the required supply, a jug can be built in the space of three or four hours. Each is nearly a perfect globe, except for a thin neck with a tiny lip that sometimes makes the whole resemble a tilted pitcher. The outside is usually left roughened, but hidden from view is a carefully smoothed interior surface. Each jug is provisioned with paralyzed caterpillars, and then a single egg is laid and suspended inside by a silken thread. After this the jug is sealed.

A COMMON wasp often found digging burrows in dry, bare soil is *Ammophila*, the "sand lover." *Ammophila* is easily recognized by its long, slender body, usually black with an attractive blotch of red or orange-red at the end of its extremely thin abdomen. The sand lover is an accomplished digger and uses two sets of tools: strong, pointed mandibles, with which it bites into the soil to loosen it; and its front legs, which bear a sort of broom of stiff bristles which it uses to rake the loosened grains away. It never leaves evidence of its excavating operations around the nest. Instead, the grains of soil are seized between head and thorax—the wasp tucking them under its chin, so to speak—and are carried a few inches away from the shaft in a brief flight. When the wasp has dug the shaft downward to a depth about equal to the length of its own body, it widens out a chamber at the bottom, large enough to hold a few caterpillars and its own offspring. Despite the considerable amount of soil that must be removed by digging and the repeated flights that are needed to carry this away a few grains at a time, an *Ammophila's* excavation takes only about 45 minutes.

The female then sets out in search of prey but, before leaving, it closes the nest and camouflages the burrow mouth with lumps of earth, pebbles or bits of wood. When it captures a caterpillar, sometimes larger than itself, the prey must be dragged all the way home, except for short, gliding flights. Out of the multitude of nests surrounding its own, the female goes directly to the correct one, opens it and drags the prey into the chamber. A single egg is deposited on the body of the caterpillar and the nest is then sealed. This time the wasp not only blocks the burrow, but also works sand among the pebbles and rakes the surface so that the entrance is completely hidden.

THE POTTER WASP

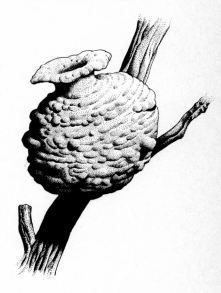

The potter wasp is also a solitary insect, getting its name from the vaselike shape of the mud or clay nest it skillfully constructs. The nest is attached to twigs and paralyzed caterpillars are heaped on its floor by the busy female. She then suspends her egg from the top of the nest by a delicate thread, so that it hangs over the pile of caterpillars until it hatches. Although the adult wasp lives mostly on nectar and sap, the larvae can only survive on the fresh meat they are supplied with.

Ammophila had early attracted naturalists by its industry and skill, but it was not until two Dutch entomologists studied these wasps closely that an incredible story emerged. After sealing one nest, they noted, the female might start digging a new nest—or it might open up a nest built previously. This in itself was rather unusual, for most solitary wasps do not return to burrows they have sealed. The Dutch investigators also saw that the female might sometimes make an inspection call—and nothing more—at a previous nest while, at other times, it returned to the inspected nest with prey. It was soon learned that the wasp was provisioning such a nest with a fresh supply of food for a larva that had already consumed its first caterpillar. After the nest was restocked, it would be sealed and left for a few days. Meantime the wasp would continue work on a third nest, make an inspection of the second nest and return to the first nest once again, bringing in several more caterpillars and then sealing it with finality.

Not only does *Ammophila* place pebbles in the first nest's entrance to block it, but it also uses its head forcibly as a hammer, pounding the pebbles into place. In some cases it even clasps a pebble in its mandibles and uses it to tamp the soil down: this is one of the two known uses of a "tool" by any insect. The nest is now bolted closed and the female is finished with the first of its young, which has been provisioned with enough food for it to complete its larval life and pupate in the safety of the chamber. This done, *Ammophila* restocks the second nest, completes provisioning of the third, and perhaps even starts work on a fourth.

Thus, this little wasp was found to maintain at least three nests at the same time, each at a different stage of development. The female was able to locate each nest quickly, although all were disguised and surrounded by a multitude of similar nests. It apparently knew which nest to visit, and when. After each visit the wasp seemed to remember exactly what had to be done: whether to lay an egg, to complete the excavation of an unfinished burrow, or to bring a second or third supply of caterpillars to a growing larva. Moreover, it knew whether to carry back a single caterpillar, many caterpillars or none at all. The stimulus it received from each nest was kept separate from the stimuli it received from the others. The female usually called at the nest most in need of fresh supplies of food; there it was evidently stimulated to search for caterpillars. When it called at another nest immediately afterward, it may have received an entirely different stimulus. But even while receiving this second stimulus, the female neither forgot where its other nests were located nor what their needs were.

Most insects are content to go their own way, buzzing across the landscape as individuals, recognizing no ties or responsibilities, encountering other insects only as predators or prey, or as temporary mates. But a few, such as hornets and some other wasps, honey bees and bumble bees, and ants, are social. In addition to these, there is one less well-known group of social insects, the termites, or "white ants." Despite this name, they are not ants—they belong to a very primitive group of insects related to the roaches—nor are they always white or even very pale in color. There are about 2,000 known species of termites around the world. They lead hidden lives and exist in fantastic numbers.

Cut into any stump or log in the woods and it will probably be tunneled through by numerous galleries; some small wingless insects may be seen scurrying back to darkness and safety. These are among the hidden monarchs of the earth, but few insects are so ill-equipped for their rule. Termites lack the sting of the bee or the hard skeleton of the ant. Their thin cuticle gives them scant protection against cold or heat; if taken from the shelter of their dark tunnels, they die in a few hours. They can live only in warmth, yet they perish in sunlight. They require constant moisture, yet they often live in places where more than half the year is parched. Most are blind, small, soft-bodied and almost completely defenseless. Yet the termites have won a place among the planet's most indestructible residents. They have accomplished this by means of a social life more complex than that of bees and wasps, by the formation of a strange partnership with certain microbes and by the creation of flourishing cities engineered for climate control.

IF a termite nest is broken open, it is seen that not all of the members of the colony are alike. The great majority of them are small, soft-bodied and wingless, with rounded heads and inconspicuous jaws; these are the mature workers or the young nymphs. But others, the soldiers, are much larger and have enormous jaws. The soldiers have dedicated their jaws to the defense of the colony: indeed, they are not even able to feed themselves and must have their food placed in their mouths by the workers. Termite soldiers congregate at places where the nest has been invaded or is in danger, and they remain until the breach is sealed again. Another function they may serve is to spread alarm in the colony; when disturbed, they often knock their heads against the wood, making loud sounds. Among the termites, both workers and soldiers exist as males and females, not just as females, as among the hornets, bees and ants.

If one continues to search in the termite nest at the right time of the year, darker forms, with gauzy wings much longer than their bodies, will be found. These are the reproductive males and females; they will soon issue from the nest in a huge swarm, mate and set off to found new termite colonies. Finally, if one searches through the entire nest, he will find one unusually large termite bearing stubs from which the wings have broken off: this is the queen. An old queen in the tropics may grow as thick as a frankfurter and four inches long, its abdomen so swollen with eggs that it is completely immobile. The queen is surrounded by attendants who constantly groom it and carry off the eggs that issue in a steady flow from its body. In some species, the termite queen lives with its tiny mate, the king, in a royal chamber. There, amid a confusion of attendants, the queen sprawls "like a whale surrounded by minnows," as Maurice Maeterlinck described the scene.

These various forms of termites within a single nest are known as castes. The king and queen once were winged reproductives whose wings broke off along a pre-existing line of weakness after their nuptial flight. They found a dark cavity in wood or soil and launched a new colony. They are adapted to the single task of reproduction—the endless spawning of a torrent of nymphs. Some of the nymphs in the colony can develop into reproductive forms if the king or queen dies, but the two castes—worker and soldier—are usually sterile. These castes were once thought to be hereditary—that a termite was born to be either worker, soldier or monarch—but what determines caste has been found to be much more complex than that.

Any nymph may develop into a queen, a king, a soldier or a reproductive—but somehow it never does so until members of this particular caste are needed. When the sole soldier in a new termite colony is removed, a replacement quickly develops from a nymph that normally would not have developed into a soldier at all. If this replacement soldier is also removed from the colony, another new soldier develops from another nymph. In the same way, removal of

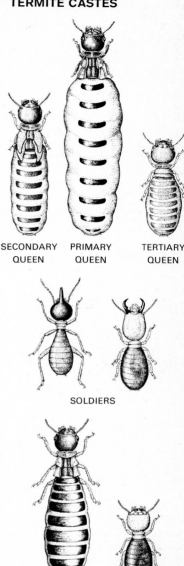

TERMITE CASTES

SECONDARY QUEEN   PRIMARY QUEEN   TERTIARY QUEEN

SOLDIERS

PRIMARY KING   WORKER

To carry on their complex social life, termites long ago evolved a rigid caste system in which each type of insect performs specialized jobs. The workers are responsible for all the labor necessary to build the nest and keep it in operation. They also act as nursemaids to soldiers and the royal pair, who are incapable of feeding themselves. Soldiers, whether scimitar-jawed or equipped with snouts for spraying an ant-entangling sticky fluid, defend the nest. The pampered king and queen—with smaller secondary and tertiary monarchs ready to step in as replacements in case they should die—are mated for life and serve but a single function: to produce the eggs which keep the species going.

A SYMBIOTIC ODDITY

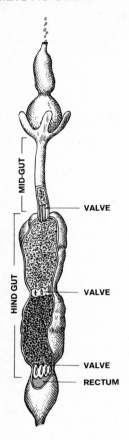

Two curious partners are the Cryptocercus cockroach and the microscopic protozoans living in its large intestine. Without them the roach cannot digest the wood it eats. As the wood (shown in green) enters the digestive tract, it is ground into tiny bits by valves until it reaches the greatly enlarged hind-gut. There millions of protozoans (shown in black) consume the bits and turn them into sugar and other nutrients. This liquid is released by the protozoans and filters back to the mid-gut, to be absorbed into the insect's blood stream. Below is an enlarged view of a single protozoan with bits of wood floating in it.

the king or queen causes a nymph to develop into a replacement reproductive. However, if the king and queen are not removed, no competing reproductives develop, nor are any new soldiers added until the colony increases in size.

Obviously, the nymphs possess the potential to change their social position, but in an undisturbed colony they do not. It seems that the very presence of soldiers and reproductives in the colony somehow inhibits the development of replacements. After numerous experiments, some scientists have come to believe that just such an inhibitor—a "social hormone"—exists in the termite colony. There is a certain critical period in the development of the nymph during which it has the capacity to change into one of the adult castes. Whether or not it does depends upon the make-up of the colony at that particular moment. If soldiers and the reproductive pair are present, the nymph develops into a sterile worker. If any of these key members is missing, however, the nymph can develop into a reproductive adult or soldier within a week or two. The balance among the castes thus seems to be maintained by means of the inhibiting hormone, produced by the adults and restricting the development of the nymphs into anything except workers.

An entire termite colony, sometimes numbering more than three million individuals, may feed exclusively on wood. This is astonishing, for wood consists largely of cellulose, a substance that most animals find indigestible. The fact is that when one looks at a termite, he sees only half of a remarkable partnership. The other half is hidden inside the termite's gut and consists of a population of microscopic, one-celled protozoa that digest the wood into a form that can be used by the termite as food.

A termite is not born with these protozoa; it receives its dowry of them in the food given to it by the older workers. Probably the protozoa harbored by termites today are direct descendants of those that inhabited termites millions of years ago. Generally, all the termites of a particular species, wherever they exist on the planet, harbor the same species of protozoa. That the protozoa are essential to certain kinds of termites has been demonstrated by subjecting the insects to high temperatures or to oxygen under pressure—processes that kill the protozoa but do not harm the termites. The treated termites, deprived of their intestinal partners, starve to death.

For termites, survival also depends upon use of their social organization to maintain correct temperature and humidity in the nest. An entire colony of termites might perish in half a day if exposed to dry air; individuals die in as little as five hours. There is no place on the globe, not even the tropical rain forest, where termites can find favorable temperature and humidity hour after hour, month after month. They have survived by creating their own climates. Except for the brief mating flight of the winged colonizers, the termites' entire existence is passed in walled-up darkness. Even when they venture outside their homes, many kinds of termites carry their eternal night and their special climate with them by building tubes that reach back to the nest.

THE termites of the Temperate Zones are usually inconspicuous, except for the damage they cause, but various tropical species erect huge structures that are among the most arresting features of the landscape. Some of these mounds are so plentiful and so high that from a distance they give the impression of being the huts of a human village. There are termite mounds in Africa that closely resemble gigantic mushrooms with a stalk and cap, or pagodas with a series of overhanging eaves. Nests with protective caps of this sort are usually found in the damper forests and obviously are an aid in keeping the interior of the nest dry.

Not only have their mounds been found to be marvels of engineering, allowing termites to survive in places that would normally be uninhabitable, but these insects seem to vary their structures depending upon the conditions they meet. For example, one termite species in a wooded part of Trinidad usually builds a cartonlike nest on a tree trunk; in the open grassy areas of the same island it builds its nest in the soil. Some of the termites of Africa, which feed on fungus they cultivate inside the hothouses of their mounds, have numerous architectural styles. In one place they may construct a sort of castle with turrets, but in another, with a different kind of soil, their mound may be like a steeple, 20 feet high.

The fungus grown inside the nests of many mound-building termites serves not only as a source of food, but also as an air-conditioning unit as well. The fungus generates heat as it grows, and absorbs surplus moisture which it gives back to the air when the humidity falls. One of the most extraordinary structures built by an insect is the compass mound of certain Australian termites. As much as 10 feet long and about 12 feet high, it is less than 4 feet thick and nearly always built so that it points north-south, the flat sides facing east and west. This peculiar orientation of the nest has yet to be explained. However, one possibility is that it offers some protection against the fierce rays of the midday sun, which would strike only the wedge-shaped summit and thus not overheat the mound.

T HESE are enduring structures, so tough that when land is cleared for cultivation they often must be dynamited out of the ground. Their surfaces will make sparks fly from a hatchet; a pickax is needed to break into them. Repairs are made swiftly: in areas where the mounds have been leveled off to clear airfield runways, new structures—large enough to make take-off and landing a hazard—may be erected in a day or two.

Inside the mound, dependent on the species of termite that built it, a particular architectural plan is followed. Typically the center is occupied by the royal chamber in which the king and queen, with their attendants, spend their entire lives. Surrounding this throne room are galleries with connecting passageways. The thick outer walls of the nest are often perforated with tiny holes, too small for the termites to pass through: these probably serve for ventilation. Most mounds have some sort of a rainshed which, like the pitched roof of a house, allows quick runoff of water, and overhanging eaves from which the rain can drip without splashing on the nest itself. Some termites, particularly those in South and Central America that construct carton nests the size of a barrel in trees, build projecting ridges along the tree trunk to deflect rain runoff that might otherwise threaten the nest. Whatever their size or shape, all of these structures are undertaken with a limited variety of simple building materials. Some termite species use only bits of soil fitted into place with a mortar of saliva, while others bind the soil with an intestinal fluid. Still others combine fresh or partly digested wood with the soil particles.

A variety of behavioral mechanisms and engineering works marks the termites' control of nest ventilation, humidity and temperature. Some desert dwellers construct vertical tunnels as much as 130 feet deep into the sandy soil in order to reach water, which they carry up to the nest. The evaporation of this water keeps the humidity inside the nest close to the saturation point, although

TERMITE AIR CONDITIONING

This cutaway of the mud nest of a type of South African termite shows how the species has engineered its hard, thick-walled mound for proper ventilation. Air in the labyrinthine living quarters of the colony is heated by the bodies of the millions of termites and ascends to the dome-shaped space at the top of the nest. From here it enters large ducts which branch into smaller tubes honeycombing the ridges on the sides of the nest. As the stale air passes through these ridges, close to the outside air, it gives off suffocating carbon dioxide, picks up new oxygen supplies, then passes back into the nest to be recirculated.

the air outside may be almost completely dry. Some termites construct their mounds only in the deep shade of tropical forests where the temperature is fairly uniform. Some species build mounds with unusually thick walls: within these, the temperature stays more constant than in the open air. So successful are some South African termites in adjusting temperature that on a summer afternoon the outside wall of a mound may be too hot even to touch while the temperature in the center of the nest is only about 85° F.

A termite mound must also have a ventilation system to take away carbon dioxide and replenish the nest's atmosphere with oxygen, since even a medium-sized colony, numbering some two million individuals, requires about 1,100 quarts of air a day. It has been calculated that if there were no exchange of air whatever, the oxygen inside the nest would last the termites only about 12 hours. The only way to get oxygen is by an exchange of the air inside the nest for air from the outside. This presents a problem: the thick walls that provide such good temperature and humidity control make such gas exchange difficult. One of the mound-building termites of Africa has solved this engineering problem remarkably well. Its nest is constructed in the shape of a miniature mountain that may be as much as 16 feet high and 16 feet broad at the base. Inside the mound, the nest proper stands on pillars that rise above the floor, forming a sort of cellar. Above the nest is another hollow space that serves as an attic. The outside surface of the mound bears a number of hollow ridges running from top to bottom. Since the nest proper is kept warm by the metabolism—or body heat—of the termites themselves, together with the heat from their fungus gardens, there is a constant current of warm air rising in the nest. This current passes into the attic and then enters the tubular ridges jutting out from the mound, which connect the attic with the cellar. The air current travels down these tubes into the cellar and circulates through the nest again.

These ridges not only protrude, but also have thin walls. This gives them considerable surface area for the diffusion of gases, and in fact, as the air passes down through them, there is a loss of carbon dioxide to the outer atmosphere and a balancing gain of oxygen. It is believed that these channels also have something to do with the remarkably constant temperature inside the nest. The termites are ceaselessly at work within the channels, possibly opening and closing them in some way and thereby regulating the flow of air as one might open or close the vents in a heating unit.

TERMITES developed their wood-eating way of life long before man appeared on the earth, and they possess no sensory equipment to tell them the difference between a fallen tree and the timbers of a human's house. In undisturbed areas, particularly in the tropics, they fulfill a vital function in breaking down the endless rain of forest debris into the raw materials that nourish new trees. Thus termites are largely responsible for keeping the forest cycle of birth, death and rebirth working efficiently. If man can momentarily forget the potential threat that termites pose to his own wooden architecture, he may come to appreciate something of their usefulness and their fascination. "Their civilization, which is the earliest of any, is the most curious, most complex, the most intelligent and, in a sense, the most logical and best fitted to the difficulties of existence which has ever appeared before our own on the globe," wrote Maurice Maeterlinck in *The Life of the White Ant*. "From several points of view, this civilization, although fierce, sinister and often repulsive, is superior to that of the bee, of the ant, and even of man himself."

A PAPER-WASP NEST BUILT INSIDE AN ABANDONED CAR SHOWS VARIOUS HUES, INDICATING MATERIALS GATHERED FROM DIFFERENT PLACES

The Homes of Insects

Master designers and engineers, insects have been constructing elaborate shelters for themselves for hundreds of millions of years. Long before man appeared, termites were building skyscrapers, wasps were making paper and mortar, caterpillars were weaving in silk and ants were creating mounded metropolises. But impressive as these activities are, they are done entirely by instinct.

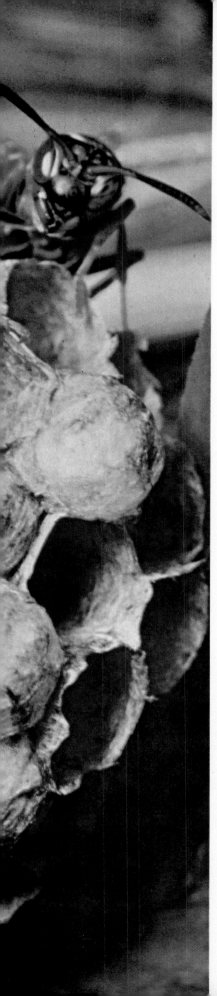

A TOOL-USING WASP, *Ammophila* holds a pebble in its jaws to tamp down the earth over the entrance to its burrow. This solitary hunting wasp has previously stocked its underground nursery with a paralyzed caterpillar, upon which it laid a single egg.

Papermakers and Masons

Closely related to bees and ants, wasps are equally noted both for the ingenious shelters they build for their offspring and for the ways in which they provide them with food. By far the best known are the paper wasps, which make their nests of weathered wood chewed to a pulp and mixed with saliva to form a durable papier-mâché. Colonies are started in the spring by a fertilized queen who has hibernated through the winter in a sheltered spot. Building the first cells itself, it quickly rears helpers who assist in enlarging the nest and feeding the young. *Polistes (left)* constructs horizontal open combs which are typically suspended from a sheltering eave or overhang by a single stem which is slender, yet surprisingly strong. Hornets build huge covered nests hung from branches, while yellow jackets make their spherical paper houses in underground hollows.

The hunting wasps excavate their own underground nurseries, or build mud shelters which they stock with food for their larvae. Some construct their adobe compartments in wood crevices or in the hollow stems of plants. One mud dauber builds its exposed cells in parallel columns, like the pipes of an organ. The potter wasp fashions a beautiful little clay jug, complete with narrow neck, flaring mouth and perfectly fitting clay lid. Whatever the method of sheltering and feeding, all of the wasps provide handsomely for their offspring.

PAPER WASPS clamber across the cells of their nest. Many of these wood-pulp cells form hexagons. Eggs are visible in the center cells, while larvae fill adjacent units. The cells closed with silk contain the pupae. Adults feed caterpillars to their offspring, which reciprocate by secreting a sugary saliva which adults eat.

A WINGLESS CRICKET, the Carolina leaf roller, makes a new house each day. Hunting aphids by night, this remarkable insect starts building its daily shelter before the dawn each morning. After having cut incisions in a leaf, the cricket rolls it around itself like a blanket and then "sews" up the edges with silk thread formed in its thorax and spun from its lower lip. Next it weaves shut the open end, curls its long antennae over its back and retires for the day.

THE PRICKLY SHELTER of a caddisfly larva is made of tiny twigs and stems bound with silk. Many species of caddis worms may be identified by the distinctive cases which they build.

Netmakers and Tower Builders

Among insect architects, the termite is the champion skyscraper builder. The African landscape is dotted with sun-baked, rock-hard towers like the one shown opposite, some of them 15 or 20 feet high. Far less conspicuous are the silken nets of the underwater larvae of a caddisfly *(below)*. The traps function as efficiently as man-made nets, are usually less than an inch long and remarkably durable. The silk of which they are made is the same as that produced by spiders and caterpillars. It is also used to glue together twigs or grains of sand to make the small underwater houses inhabited by caddisflies.

A SILK NET is the creation of *Hydropsyche*, a predatory caddisfly larva that usually lives in swift water and seines its food. Anchored to stones at either side, the net captures insects and other prey swept downstream by the current. Hidden at the side in a loosely constructed shelter of silk and sand, the larva comes out periodically to dine on its catch and repair the net.

A TERMITE TOWER in northern Kenya may house a colony of close to a million inhabitants. Constructed of earth and vegetation mixed with termite saliva and excreta, the thick walls become as hard as rock and efficiently control internal temperature and humidity. In some mounds, a network of channels near the surface provides air conditioning for inner chambers.

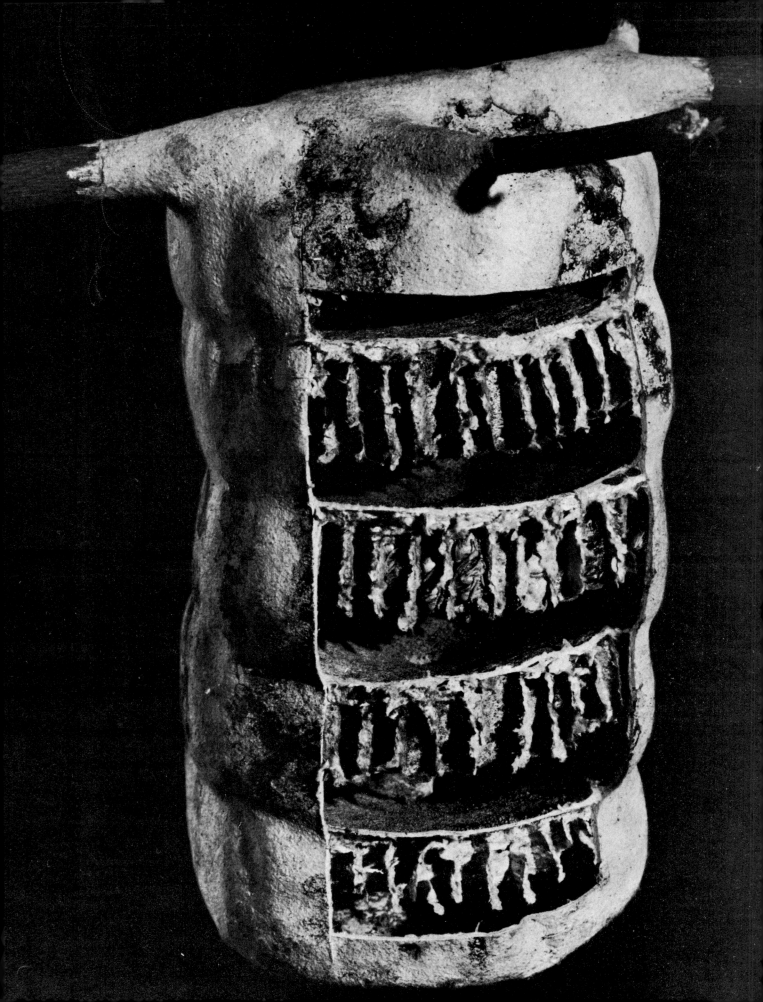

A CYLINDRICAL CARTON houses the multistoried combs of a tropical papermaking wasp. More combs, all firmly attached to the outside walls, are added from beneath as the colony grows.

A HORNET'S NEST shows successive rows of combs all encased in an envelope of tough paper. This outside wall can be as effective an insulator against heat and cold as a 16-inch brick wall.

Workers in Wood

In the trunks of trees, in dead limbs, in weathered fence posts, and in the wooden structures that man builds, myriad insects dig, bore and tunnel, carving out nests and nurseries for their young. Ambrosia beetles cultivate fungus gardens deep in the sapwood of trees, growing their crops on beds of wood shavings and excrement. The grubs eat the wood-nurtured fungus. One ambrosia beetle

STRIATED SECTION of a twig has been carved by engraver beetles. After boring through the bark, adult beetles drilled out the egg chamber in center. The grubs bored out the many tributary channels, widening them as they grew.

COLONNADED GALLERIES show the work of the black carpenter ant. Armed with saberlike jaws, this destructive insect chisels out spacious nest

is known as "Tippling Tommy" because it does its digging in the staves of wine or rum casks.

Furniture beetles carve up antiques. They work only in old wood, 20 years old for softwoods, 60 years old for hardwoods. The death watch beetle can actually be heard as it bores away in the dark. It sometimes stops to tap its head loudly against the walls of its tunnel.

cavities in softwood, often causing extensive damage to buildings. Growing to a half inch or more in length, it is one of the biggest of U.S. ants.

BARK, OR ENGRAVER, BEETLES usually construct galleries between the bark of a tree and the vital sapwood, frequently destroying much timber. The form and arrangement of the channels often exhibit features unique for each species.

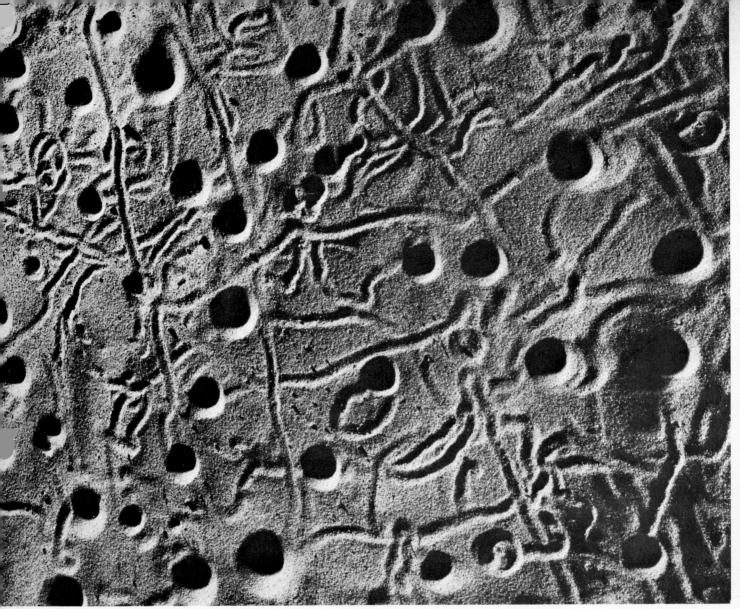

PITS AND TRAILS ARE THE WORK OF ANT LIONS. THESE LARVAE LIE AT THE BOTTOMS OF THE PITS, READY TO SEIZE ANY INSECTS THAT FALL IN

Excavators and Tunnelmakers

A host of beetles, termites, wasps and other insects is constantly at work all over the world, excavating underground nest chambers and tunneling elaborate mazes of subterranean passages and highways. Of all the movers of earth, ants are by far the most remarkable. They excavate huge and intricately organized underground cities which often extend hundreds of feet under the forest floor and house a half million or more inhabitants. Traveling to and from their diggings, countless individual ants sometimes clear well-worn trails that crisscross through the underbrush like a maze of superhighways. The earth excavated for these ant metropolises is sometimes heaped up in huge mounds containing several hun-

dred cubic yards of soil. Entomologists estimate that Brazilian ants turn over in this way an average of 16 tons of earth per acre per year. The champion digger of them all, however, may be a North African species which was observed moving more than a ton of earth in one 15-square-yard area in a hundred days.

Ants have an enemy that is also a formidable digger. This is the ant lion, which scoops out a funnel-shaped pit in sandy soil for trapping insect prey. Scuffling backward in a spiral movement, this predatory larva plows up the soil with its bristly posterior and flicks out the loosened grains with its spadelike head. When the hole is done, the ant lion digs in at the bottom and waits for a meal to fall into its jaws.

MOUND-BUILDING ANTS often construct great cities like this one in Pennsylvania, which is 3 feet high and 10 feet in diameter. The colony inhabits the upper chambers during the summer, retires to deep galleries in cold weather. To take this photograph, a section of the mound was sliced away and the surface covered with a glass pane until the insects rebuilt the tunnels.

5

The Hunters
and the Hunted

ONE of the most hostile of all environments is the sand dune. Intensely hot and nearly bone-dry, the dunes support few kinds of animals other than insects, which are able to burrow into the ground or to take wing to escape the burning sands. Even in this world of scant vegetation, the insects make up a varied and often bizarre population. Predators for the most part, they subsist largely by preying upon each other and upon the few plant-feeding species that have become adapted to dune life. Here the complex intermeshing strands that link the prey and the predator, the parasite and the parasitized can be observed with textbook clarity.

The inhospitable dunes provide living space for ants that gather the nectar from flowering plants adapted to a dune existence, and for termites that manage to survive by feeding on the wood of trees and shrubs buried by the shifting sands. A number of kinds of solitary bee construct underground cells and honeypots. The cuckoo bee capitalizes upon their industry; it follows a bee back to its burrow and lays eggs in the honeypot, thus appropriating it for its own young. Typical of the dune hunters is *Bembex*, the sand wasp. Even during the warmest part of the day in the hottest season of the year, the dunes seem to teem with these short, chunky bembecids, brightly banded with yellow and black or green-ish-gray and black.

The sand wasp hunts by sight; it must provision and dig its nest during the hot daylight hours. It possesses no physical modifications, such as insulating hairs, to protect it against the sun's fierce rays. In fact, if kept at the surface it quickly succumbs to heat prostration. But the sand wasp avoids overheating by its behavior. Above the hot surface, the temperature decreases rapidly; it is at least 10° F. cooler a foot above the sand. The wasp hovers in this cooler zone, then suddenly descends to its burrow and digs hurriedly with its front legs. As it begins to overheat, it rises briefly into the cooler air; then, refreshed, it drops again to the site and continues its excavations. The wasp alternates between the hot sands and the cool higher air until the burrow has been dug deep enough to reach the cooler sands beneath the surface; it can then remain in the burrow without interruption, digging the tunnel in comfort to a depth of two or three feet.

Like the tool-using *Ammophila*, *Bembex* is a socially advanced wasp: it keeps its nest provisioned with captured flies—as many as 20 a day—as its larva grows. Both these flies and the succulent *Bembex* larva attract numerous other predators and parasites. Velvet ants—actually a species of wasp in which the female is wingless—travel over the blazing dunes, searching for a sand-wasp burrow. They lay their own eggs in the nest and their own larvae, when hatched, feed upon the immature bembecid. The velvet ants themselves are often parasitized by bee flies; the bee flies, in turn, are prey for robber flies. These robber flies pounce on their victims in flight with the swiftness of a falcon; they girdle the quarry with their long, spiny legs and pierce them with strong beaks. In the intermeshing of predator and prey that makes up the dune community, robber flies in turn fall victim to the predaceous sand wasps.

Hunters and hunted alike must not only track down prey and escape from enemies but also wage continual battle against the heat. Hunting wasps and flies cruise the cooler air above the dunes. The flightless velvet ants are protected by a dense growth of hairs that cover their bodies. Other insects have their own methods of survival. Some beetles migrate up and down the stems of plants in response to the changing temperatures. Grasshoppers simply extend their long legs, lifting their bodies above the hot surface; if it becomes intensely hot, they fly a few feet into the cooler air above.

Other hunters escape the problem by living in burrows beneath the blazing sands. One of the most voracious is the larva of the tiger beetle, an insect that is equally voracious as an adult. The larva constructs a vertical burrow that may be a foot or two deep; the diameter of the shaft is only a little greater than the larva itself, about the thickness of a lead pencil. When hungry, it stays at the top of the shaft, waiting for an unwary insect to pass within grasping distance. The beetle larva has an enormous head, bent at a right angle to its body, that makes a living plug for the burrow opening. Its powerful crescent jaws can quickly seize any insect walking over the trap. It cannot be pulled out of its shaft by the struggles of a large victim: it has a special anchor on its abdomen, a hump with two large hooks which it digs into the burrow walls. When it is not hungry, the larva retreats to the coolness of the shaft bottom.

Another predaceous larva that lives beneath the surface of the hot sands is the ant lion; it digs a funnel-shaped pit, and buries itself at the bottom except for its head and massive scimitar-shaped jaws. When an ant or other prey steps close

A DEADLY AMBUSH

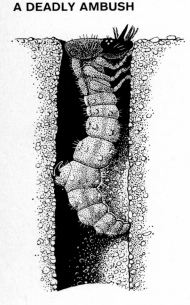

The tiger beetle's attack resembles the action of a jack-in-the-box. Keeping its lid-like head flush with the top of its burrow, it waits until a victim passes, then springs out in a partial back somersault, snatching it with its jaws. The tiger beetle's humped back is equipped with two barbed spines which hook into the burrow wall and prevent the creature from being dragged out by strongly resisting victims. When danger threatens, the beetle can relax the hump and plummet safely down to the bottom.

to the rim of the pit, the sand collapses and it tumbles downward to the waiting jaws. Occasionally, a scrambling insect gains a foothold on the rim, but the ant lion loosens the victim's grasp by flinging a shower of granules upward with a snap of its head. The ant lion continues to hurl sand until the victim slips to the bottom of the funnel, where it is grasped in the jaws and pulled under the sand. The ant lion's jaws are grooved and through them flows a glandular secretion that paralyzes the prey within several minutes and liquefies its body tissues so that they can be sucked up. When the ant lion has thus drained its prey, it flicks the dry carcass out of the pit. Pit-making ant lions are restricted to soil that is loose and dry: if wet and packed, the rim of the funnel would not collapse in an avalanche and bring the victim tumbling down within reach. They are therefore abundant in desert areas and dunes, but any other place where they can find dry, loose soil—under a cliff edge, a projecting porch or even a leaning tree— will serve to house these ingenious trappers.

The ant lion larva is squat and fat, with disproportionately large jaws. After pupating, it undergoes a striking change: it emerges as a graceful insect with gauzy wings and slender abdomen that somewhat resembles a damselfly. It floats away on feeble wings and lives only long enough to mate and deposit its eggs.

WALKING through the woods or meadows, one is usually not aware of the constant warfare among the swirling insects. Dragonflies, darting in the sun, scoop up prey in flight with their basketlike legs. The larvae of the delicate lacewing—stout, flattened and extremely voracious insects—patrol plant stems and leaves, sucking aphids and scale insects dry. Ladybird beetles, both adults and grubs, consume immense numbers of aphids. Praying mantids wait motionless, and then suddenly grasp prey in their long forelegs which fold over the victim like closing jackknives. In addition to these comparatively obvious predators, swooping down on or grappling with their prey in the jungle of foliage, parasites are busy laying their eggs in the living bodies of other insects. They use their victims not as food for themselves but as living larders for their young.

Assassin bugs are among the most expert of insect predators: the roughly 2,500 species throughout the world display various hunting methods. Some kinds run down their prey and pounce upon it. Even a large, fast-moving quarry is held firm by the adhesive pads on the assassin bug's legs; each pad may consist of as many as 75,000 hairs, covered by a thin film of oil that adheres to the victim. Other assassin species wait for their quarry in some likely location. There are intricate and subtle variations of this method. Some species plunge their legs into the resin of coniferous trees and hold these sticky limbs aloft as traps. Other assassins, specialists in capturing bees, have strong bristles on their legs with which they entangle this hairy prey. One assassin that lives in the West Indies secretes flavorsome fluid from its underside: ants are attracted to the nectar, become intoxicated and thus easily fall victim.

Once the assassin makes its capture, it uses other specialized organs to kill the prey quickly. Glands in the assassin's thorax produce a powerful venom, which is forced by a small pump in the head through elaborate mouth parts into the victim's body. The assassin's venom glands are complex. Two lobes secrete a toxic fluid that the bug seems able to store almost indefinitely; another lobe produces a nontoxic fluid that appears to act as a diluting agent—and possibly also as a sort of mouthwash that flushes the bug's hollow mouth parts after the venom has been pumped through. In any case, the fluids' action not only renders the victim helpless but also reduces its tissues to a thick soup. In addition to its

A GAME OF CATCH

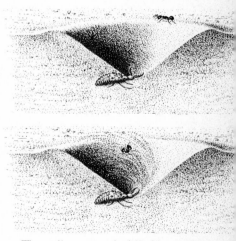

The ant lion ensures the fall of its victim from the rim of its funnel-shaped pit into its outstretched mouth with a powerful salvo of sand granules. But the fierce predator rarely succeeds in clasping its prey firmly on the first try. Often, the ant lion must repeatedly toss its quarry against the walls of the pit, or release it and recapture it with a new barrage of sand, until the tips of its jaws are in a position to inject a paralyzing poison into the body. It is then dragged beneath the sand and sucked dry.

INSECT MOUTH PARTS

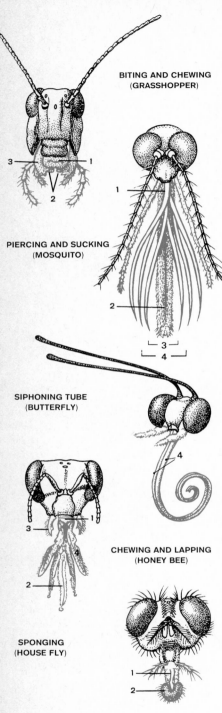

BITING AND CHEWING
(GRASSHOPPER)

PIERCING AND SUCKING
(MOSQUITO)

SIPHONING TUBE
(BUTTERFLY)

CHEWING AND LAPPING
(HONEY BEE)

SPONGING
(HOUSE FLY)

Although the mouth parts of insects are superficially dissimilar, they have all developed and been modified from the same original plan—still retained by insects like the grasshopper. Essentially, these mouth parts consist of a labrum, or upper lip (1); a labium, or lower lip (2); and two pairs of horizontally working jaws: the mandibles (3) and the maxillae (4).

force pump, the assassin's head houses a suction pump that draws the liquefied tissue of the prey into the predator's digestive system.

All insects face instant death—from other insects, from long-tongued lizards, snakes, frogs and toads, from sharp-beaked birds, from insectivorous mammals. They have survived by evolving an extensive repertoire of protections and deceptions. Some insects simply wait out danger by feigning death. Usually the insect falls to the ground like a pebble, folds its legs tightly under its body and remains motionless. But there are numerous variations on this sort of playing possum: the caterpillar of the sphinx moth raises the front of its body and curls its head down, thus resembling somewhat an Egyptian sphinx. At a sign of danger, some of the inchworm caterpillars suddenly become rigid at awkward angles. Most insects remain motionless only a few minutes, but experimenters have been able to keep a giant water bug in a death feint for eight straight hours by a repetition of the danger. An insect is thought to achieve its motionless pose through a block against responses to touch. It does not react to any touch stimuli and the entire sensory system becomes inhibited.

A NUMBER of insects—such as crickets, grasshoppers and fleas—rely upon leaping as a method of escaping from enemies. The click beetle combines a jumping organ with sound and death-feigning. When picked up, it gives a startling click that might cause a bird to drop it in alarm. It then tucks up its legs and drops to the ground, where it usually lands on its back. It lies motionless for a few moments, then snaps its body, producing the same clicking sound and jerking itself into the air. If it lands on its back again, as often happens, it repeats the jerking movement and continues doing so until it lands right side up and can scurry away.

The jump of a common grasshopper is a most remarkable accomplishment. It can leap horizontally about 20 times its body length, equivalent to a human covering the length of a football field in just three broad jumps, or its trajectory might be straight up, a distance in human terms equal to jumping over a five-story building. The hind legs of a grasshopper differ from the rest of its legs, and from the legs of most other insects. They are extremely long and large, and the angle formed between the thigh and shin portions is very small; it is when this angle is suddenly increased that the grasshopper is launched. Thus, the hind legs push instead of pull, as in most other insects. Furthermore, both hind legs are synchronized to work together rather than alternately, as most insect legs do in walking. Evolution has endowed the grasshopper with delicately controlled muscles in the hind legs, both of which are capable of generating a take-off thrust nearly eight times the total weight of the insect. To deliver this kick, the tiny muscles must exert an astonishing amount of thrust, about 20,000 times their own weight.

Sometimes grasshoppers jump for no apparent reason, and they sometimes fail to jump when their lives are obviously in danger. The jump is probably not an automatic reflex action, but rather the result of a complicated series of controls. If these controls did not exist, the grasshopper would constantly be jumping at false alarms and expending vast amounts of energy. Grasshoppers always jump if there is some stimulation of the cerci, the two tail-like appendages on the end of the abdomen. These sense organs respond to the slight changes in air pressure that sound waves or the approach of an enemy might produce. When such a stimulus takes place, impulses travel to the nerves that cock the jumping muscles. The first impulse halts the nerve fibers that control normal walking and puts them temporarily out of action. Then it excites the muscles that cock the leg itself and warns them to be on the lookout for the order to fire. The grasshopper is thus primed to leap instantly should a second burst of impulses come. The enthusiasm of the jump depends upon how many impulses are received in the second message; a few impulses stimulate only a short hop, a rapid burst makes the insect give a prodigious leap. For this sequence of events to take place, some 3,500 muscle fibers in each hind leg must be activated; nevertheless, the entire sequence can take place in a mere thirtieth of a second.

A number of insects possess chemical armaments which they use to discourage aggressors. Some insects are simply endowed with an evil smell or a vile taste; after sampling one, a predator often learns to leave that species alone. Many plant bugs and lacewings give off foul-smelling secretions when handled. There are some ants that do not sting, yet their poison glands produce large amounts of formic acid; these ants can squirt the acid as far as a foot from the hind end of their bodies. The soldiers of several kinds of termites have their whole heads—and sometimes also the greater part of the thorax and abdomen—modified into a sort of atomizer that sprays a fluid highly repellent to ants, their hereditary enemies. The Spanish fly—actually not a fly nor especially Spanish, but a widespread beetle instead—gives off a secretion that can raise blisters.

One of the most elaborate pieces of armament in the insect world is possessed by the bombardier beetle. This creature's realistic artillery consists of a turret which forms the rear of its abdomen. When the beetle "fires," there is an audible "pfft" and a spurt of mist as its defensive fluid comes in contact with the air. Located in the beetle's last abdominal segments, which can telescope and bend in any direction, the "cannon" is able to "fire" to the front, rear or sides. When an ant or other predator attacks, the beetle instantly aims its turret and discharges the fluid. Hit by the spray, the ant retreats quickly, and is subject to periodic seizures.

An upside-down click beetle rights itself with a self-cocking mechanism like that of a pistol. When the insect is on its back, it bends up its thorax until it succeeds in hooking a sharp spine into a notch on the abdomen. When this is let go, the beetle is hurled into the air under the sudden release of muscular tension, usually landing right side up. When seized by a bird or lizard, it may also click in the hope of startling the predator into dropping it.

This is effective artillery: not only can the spray be aimed but the beetle can discharge repeatedly and in rapid succession. Some bombardiers, that had not fired in several days, have fired as many as 29 times in less than four minutes. One series of experiments pitted bombardiers against large ants in 200 separate encounters; in none of these did the beetles ever receive a noticeable injury. In addition to dealing with ants and beetles, bombardiers are able to repel such fierce predators as praying mantids and spiders.

At first it was thought that the bombardier's spray was simply a liquid that turned into a vapor when it left the beetle's body and came in contact with the air. However, it has been shown recently that the beetle actually creates an internal explosion. Situated at the end of the beetle's abdomen are paired compartments that serve as reservoir and reaction chamber. Three chemicals are secreted by glands and stored in the reservoir, which is normally kept closed by a valve. To fire, the beetle opens the valve and allows the secretions to flow into the second, strong-walled compartment where, catalyzed by an enzyme, the mixture reacts explosively and is forcibly expelled.

MANY insects use color, pattern and shape as means of pretending to be something they are not. Some butterflies have tattered wings that resemble dead leaves or oddly patterned wings that look like lichen-covered bark. Other butterflies have gone the limit in masking themselves: their wings are devoid of scales and thus transparent, allowing the foliage on which they settle to show through. The caterpillar of one moth hatches from the egg in late summer and feeds on birch leaves; at that time its color is reddish-brown with some green markings, thus harmonizing well with the early fall foliage. This caterpillar hibernates during the winter: when it awakens in spring, its color has changed—concealing green has replaced most of the brown.

Some caterpillars and grasshoppers are countershaded—the upper parts of their bodies show a dark tint that gradually grades to light on the sides and bottom. Sunlight from above strikes the dark upper part, but does not reach the insect's underside: the countershading has the effect of making the whole body appear to be evenly illuminated. A caterpillar that is countershaded in this way creates an illusion of flatness despite its cylindrical shape: this illusion is of great benefit to caterpillars that live among flat leaves. In one experiment, caterpillars were mounted on twigs, half of them dark side up—thus receiving the benefit of their countershading—and the other half, light side up. These twigs were then distributed around an aviary occupied by jays. The birds located and ate many more of the inverted caterpillars than they did those that were protected by their countershaded camouflage.

Not all protective coloration is concealing, as many people believe. On the contrary, some color patterns make the insect clearly visible—but disguised as a twig, bark, leaf or thorn, which predators regard as inedible. A bird sees such a protectively colored moth not as a moth but as the dead leaf it resembles; since the bird does not feed on leaves, it ignores the insect in plain view. Some of the most fantastically camouflaged insects are those that resemble twigs; they are strikingly similar to the plant they feed on not only in color but in structural details as well. One kind of twig caterpillar has a smooth, slender body, like the twigs of birches on which it feeds. Another, which feeds on oaks, is stouter and rougher; it even shows what appear to be the scars where the previous season's leaves were joined to the twig. The bodies of these caterpillars may display the wrinkled texture characteristic of many twigs. Their legs often fit so smoothly around the real twig that the place where the two join cannot be seen and no shadow is cast.

Some skeptics of protective coloration have argued that many insects are successful despite the fact that they wear garish colors which actually advertise their presence rather than hide it. Experiments have revealed that these insects survive not in spite of their gaudy colors, but because of them. Many such brightly colored and patterned insects possess unpleasant taste, odor or stings that make them unpalatable to predators. A foul taste or odor is of no benefit to the insect when it is dead, but if unpleasant features are combined with a warning, then most such brightly colored insects are not attacked. The garish warning gives to the predator a sign that it can recognize and remember. In general, warningly colored insects tend to congregate, thus displaying their signals en masse and increasing the chances that a predator will learn his lesson rapidly. The few insects that the predator does sample are sacrificed, but the population as a whole benefits.

One unusual kind of coloration—seen on some mantids, bugs, beetles, butterflies and moths—consists of bright patterns that closely resemble the eyes of vertebrate animals. These "eye spots" are often located on portions of the insect's body normally kept concealed—such as on wings that are closed or covered when the insect is resting—but are displayed suddenly when the insect is attacked. Experiments have been carried out in which birds were closely watched for their reaction to butterflies that flash their eye spots. As the birds approached, the butterflies suddenly spread their wings and revealed the spots. The birds jumped back as if they had been stung. These experiments were repeated after the scales that formed the eye-spot pattern were rubbed off: the birds then attacked the butterflies.

There is definite survival value for insects that possess such prominent eye spots. One possible explanation is that insectivorous birds recognize their own predators—such as cats and owls—partly by their eyes. The insects thus seem to receive protection by playing upon the birds' fear of their own predators. Eye spots may also give benefits in drawing the attention of predators away from the vital parts of the body to the edge of the wings, which can be damaged without serious effects. The lizard that snaps at the spot receives only a dusty mouthful of scales and not an insect. Finally, the spots may afford protection during the crucial hours when newly emerged adults—their wings still hardening—are relatively helpless.

Patterns of black and yellow are remarkably predominant among bees and wasps as well as among some unpalatable caterpillars. Birds, like people, usually ignore insects with these colors, for the birds have found that insects garishly colored in this manner are usually endowed with an unappetizing odor or a sting. A bird that once samples them has learned a lesson it does not quickly forget. A bird's memory for this sort of surprise is long-lasting; one refused a wasp eight months after it had last tried one. Birds have no built-in instinct that leads them to avoid these colors: each generation of young birds learns by unhappy experience.

As a bird learns to avoid repugnant insects by their colors, it also learns to reject other, palatable insects that display similar colors. These insect mimics have adopted the colors and patterns of inedible insects with remarkable precision. It is not enough merely to look like another insect; for effective resemblance, the mimic should also act like the model. There are some moths, for example, that go to great ends to mimic hornets. They possess long stinglike appendages on their abdomens, and some even mimic their model's stinging behavior, twisting and bending as if searching for a place to insert the stiletto. The wings of these moths, instead of being covered with scales, are transparent, as are the hornet's; their bodies are usually colored black and yellow. They imitate the hornet's style of flight and they even fly by day instead of at night. Inexperienced birds eat these mimics with relish until they have their first experience with a hornet; thereafter they refuse the hornets and their mimics as well. Tests have revealed that the mimic need not show an exact reproduction of the pattern of the avoided insect; even a superficial resemblance is enough to offer some protection.

THE exquisitely precise patterns of defense are no more accidental than the huge pincers or curved jaws of the predator. So utterly fantastic are the ways in which insects use color and pattern to deceive their hunters that the whole subject of insect camouflage becomes unbelievable. How does the insect "know" what it should look like? How did it manage to achieve such a perfect likeness? The insect, of course, knows nothing about it: it cannot achieve the likeness by some conscious act of will. Instead, these resemblances come from the amazing potentialities of the evolutionary process—variation and natural selection.

The natural selectors in such cases are the predatory animals: they destroy the insects whose disguises they can see through more rapidly than they do those that have achieved a more perfect sham. A major flaw in the armament of masquerade may mean instant death; those insects that survive are those that have developed at random the most artful disguises. It is probably that the protective pattern first evolves as a mutation from some insect that has no special defenses. If this mutant has markings on its wings that frighten a bird about to snatch it, for example, it survives to reproduce. Out of the many hundreds or thousands of its young, more of those that possess this favorable characteristic, however slight, are more likely to survive and reproduce in their turn. Natural selection continues to favor the descendants that have additional, bird-frightening patterns on their wings. Those that lack such markings are more subject to attacks; their numbers dwindle, and the nonmutants may even become extinct.

Over the years a number of scientists have questioned the theory of camouflage and protective coloration, but the preponderance of research confirms the advantages for the species possessing it. For example, the fact that warning coloration protects insects against birds was demonstrated by a three-year experiment that consisted of observing the food brought by parent starlings to their nestlings in the wild. Neck collars were placed on the nestlings, thus preventing them from swallowing the food. During the three years, 16,484 insects were carried back to the nest. Of these 4,490 were beetles—but only two were the common gaudily colored ladybird beetles which have a repugnant taste. Only a single wasp was brought to the nest, and not one bee.

Another series of experiments was carried out with dead twig caterpillars and jays. The caterpillars were mounted together with the twigs they resembled and placed in a large aviary, after which the jays were admitted. Although the jays had not been fed previous to the experiment, it took them a very long time to locate the caterpillars. The jays hopped over and pecked near the caterpillars for as much as 40 minutes but, since the dead specimens were motionless, they were not discovered. Only when the jays stepped on the caterpillars—and presumably recognized the yielding corpses as edible—did the birds realize that food was available. Then most of the jays started pecking at twigs and caterpillars indiscriminately. But after seizing a few real twigs, the birds became discouraged and stopped pecking.

This study clearly demonstrates that twig caterpillars receive a high degree of immunity from predation through their immobility and their resemblance to the plants on which they feed. Because twig caterpillars do not live in groups but rather far apart, even the bird that accidentally finds one will probably peck enough real twigs thereafter to become discouraged before it finds a second.

THE greatest single factor in preventing insects from overwhelming the rest of the world is the internecine warfare which they carry out among themselves," concludes one entomologist. It is certain that insects, if somehow released from the controls that limit their populations, would increase in numbers fantastically. If all the offspring of a single pair of flies were to survive and breed, and their offspring did the same, and so forth, for a single year, the resulting mass of flies—tightly packed—would form a sphere some 96 million miles in diameter, more than the distance from the earth to the sun. On the other hand, were there not the balancing controls of camouflage and warning in nature, the grim efficiency of predators might sharply reduce or even eliminate some insect species. Man boasts of his chemical onslaught against the insect realm—but among the most efficient insecticides are other insects, while the most efficient repellent of predators is a suitable disguise.

CONCEALED IN PLAIN SIGHT, A GEOMETRID MOTH LARVA APES A TWIG OF THE TREE IT EATS, TO DECEIVE BIRDS BY WHICH IT MIGHT BE EATEN

The Fine Art of Survival

The swiftness of insect reproduction has let evolution perfect an
endless variety of predatory and protective devices: frozen faking
like the caterpillar's above, marksmanship with smoke and stench,
trade-marks advertising undesirability, masks for murderers, silks
for ensnarers and inflating pumps for swaggerers. A variety of
insect cloak-and-dagger acts is played out on the following pages.

SHAPED LIKE A DRIED LEAF, AN INSECT HIDES ON A FOREST BRANCH

How to Vanish

Being plated, cocooned, tusked, clawed and jawed, winged, armed with hypodermics or simply expendably proliferous, most insects have many ways of protecting themselves against other insect species.

But against sharp-eyed, brainy predators of bigger animal kinds such as birds, reptiles and mammals, the first insect line of defense has to be concealment and camouflage. Camouflage takes many forms: disappearance into the background, mimicry of twigs or leaves which are not worth eating, or mimicry of other insect species which taste bad or have poisonous stings. Some forest grasshoppers go so far as to resemble fresh-cut green leaves being carried by irritable echelons of ants.

Since even insects have to rest, many of them use their most general camouflage to disappear while resting. Nocturnal moths like the five shown opposite will often rest through the dangerous, shifting lights of daytime, hanging flat against the bark of suitably colored trees. Beetles and bugs often snooze in the brown litter on the forest floor. Caterpillars normally take their siesta as leaves, twigs or bird droppings up in the trees. But the most specific patterns on insect backs are used when an insect is up and about and eating its favorite food. Then its splotches and gradations of color—even the most gaudy ones—become precisely attuned to the moving shadows in its own part of the forest, and it can munch and move in comparative privacy and safety.

THE CUCUMBER STRIPES of light and dark green running up a pine sphinx larva's back enable the caterpillar to look like bitter needles as it eats its way up a pine tree.

A BLACK AND WHITE NOCTUID MOTH FINDS COVER ON BIRCH BARK

A "PROMINENT" MOTH BECOMES LESS DEFINED ON A PINE TRUNK

THE ROUGH, MOTTLED STINK BUG SEEMS LIKE A SHARD OF BARK

SPECKLING OF AN OWLET MOTH MATCHES MANY FOREST DECORS

A GEOMETRID MOTH BLURS ITS SHAPE WITH BOLD SHADED BANDS

A WHITE SPOTTED MOTH CLINGS CLOSE TO A LICHEN-COVERED LIMB

A PUSS MOTH CATERPILLAR, AS IT CRAWLS UNDISTURBED ON A TWIG, BLENDS ITS BRIGHT COLORS AMAZINGLY WELL WITH ITS BACKGROUND

LOOKING DANGEROUS AND LOOKING INEDIBLE

If an insect cannot vanish, its best hope is to appear dangerous or distasteful. The gaudy species at right have all developed orange colors to warn birds that they are milkweed eaters and hence taste very bitter. The puss moth larva above them has a pale-rimmed contrasting saddle that breaks up its succulent outline. It is also shaded—from light on top to dark below—so that when it feeds on the underside of a twig, its sunlit belly will look as dark as its shaded back. Even so, if it is touched it inflates a terrifying scarlet face and erects its harmless tails as if they were stingers, to discourage enemies.

MILKWEED LEAF BEETLE

MILKWEED BUG

WHEN IT IS TOUCHED, THE CATERPILLAR ABANDONS ITS CAMOUFLAGE, REARS ITS TAIL AND HEAD AND LOOKS AS FRIGHTENING AS POSSIBLE

FOUR-EYED MILKWEED BEETLE

MILKWEED TUSSOCK MOTH CATERPILLAR

A TOMATO SPHINX MOTH CATERPILLAR STILL CRAWLS, STUDDED WITH COCOONS OF PARASITES THAT HAVE DEVOURED ITS INTERNAL ORGANS

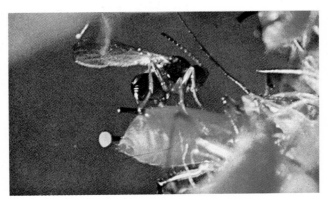

A HELPLESS APHID, although oozing drops of offensive fluid, fails to repel a black wasp that lays an egg in its abdomen.

Caterpillar against Parasite

Camouflage or startling shapes are all very well in protecting insects against some of the larger predators, but the fact remains that their worst enemies are frequently other insects. Nearly half of the insect species known to scientists get their living from each other, with many of them acting as parasites. The two caterpillars above are completely helpless to combat the tiny larvae inflicted on them, and which, in the end, will literally eat them alive. But

A HUGE RAIN FOREST MOTH LARVA IS GAUDILY COLORED TO WARN BIRD PREDATORS, AND POISONOUSLY SPINED AGAINST INSECT PARASITES

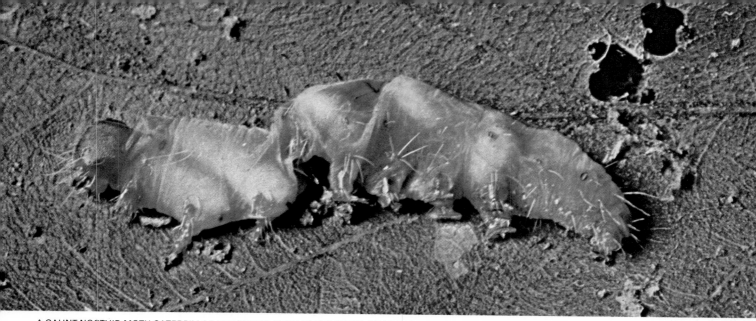

A GAUNT NOCTUID MOTH CATERPILLAR IS NOTHING BUT A LIVING SHELL COVERING THE TACHINID FLY LARVAE WHICH ARE SLOWLY EATING IT UP

there are ingenious defenses against even these formidable threats. The caterpillars shown below are protected by poisonous or sticky hairs that keep egg-laying enemies at a safe distance from their juicy bodies.

The crudest insect parasites ultimately kill the prey they feed on. More highly developed types generally maintain a hostile balance of power. But some of the most successful species have evolved a symbiotically agreeable relationship with their hosts called mutualism. Some of the world's most complex symbiotic relationships exist among insects. Many aphids are given cradle-to-coffin security by ants because they excrete a sweet "honeydew." Some small beetles live only in ant nests and earn their keep merely by their exciting aroma. Thus it is hard for biologists to know whether to classify them as symbiotic parasites or simply pets.

A PLUME MOTH CATERPILLAR EXUDES DROPS OF GLUE FROM ITS HAIRS, TRAPPING TWO WASPS THAT TRIED TO PARASITIZE IT WITH THEIR EGGS

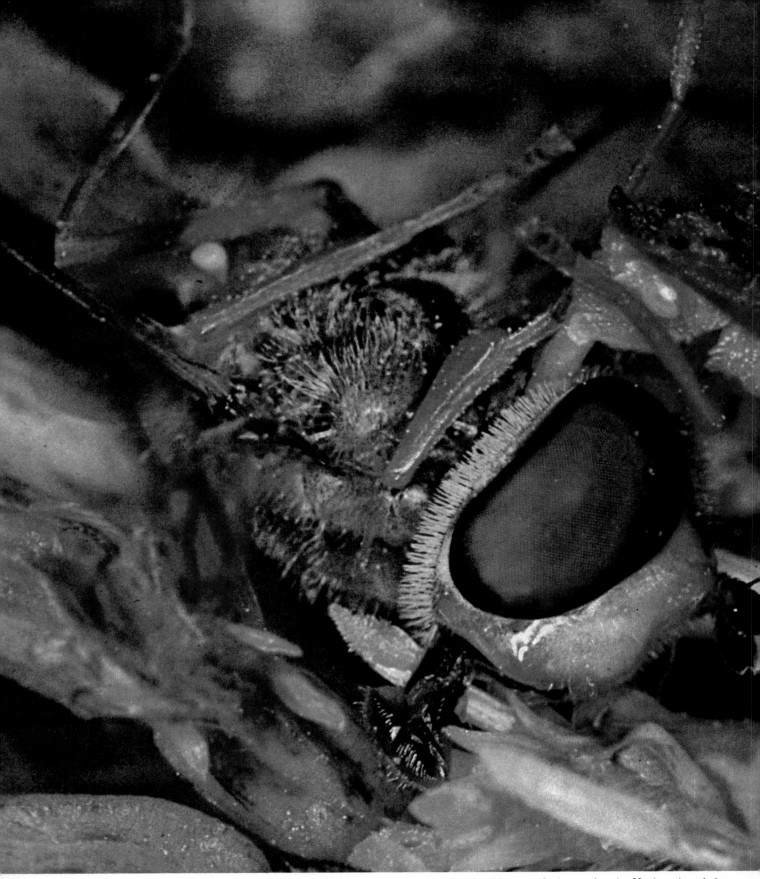

AN ORANGE-BROWN AMBUSH BUG, which lurks inconspicuously in the orange throats of goldenrod flowers, falls upon an unwary hover fly, seizing it with clawed front legs and quickly poniarding it with a paralyzing proboscis. Having sipped the fly's juices, the bug will throw away the corpse and retreat into its deceptively lovely lair to await a new victim. Under other

circumstances the fly itself would gain protection from its own appearance, which generally mimics the bee's and hornet's. But this means nothing to the half-inch ambush bug, which tackles large wasps as a matter of course. Like the hover fly, the ambush bug is a common insect throughout North America and stages its swift savageries wherever concealing blossoms bloom.

A STARRY UNIVERSE underground is created on the ceiling above a subterranean river in the Waimoto Caves of New Zealand by the glow of thousands of luminous larvae which trail silken threads down like fishing lines. Insects attracted by the light of the larvae stick on the threads and are then reeled in. The larvae grow into true fire flies, *Arachnocampa luminosa*.

WHEN BACK-LIGHTED, WAITOMO'S LUMINOUS CAVE WORMS ARE SEEN TO HANG OUT THIN STALACTITES OF SILK FOR ENSNARING THEIR PREY

Live Sparks in the Dark

The unique cavern opposite is inhabited by a luminous gnat of the family Bolitophilidae. Like the common lightning bug of North America, these tiny creatures light up the night by a difficult act of organic chemistry which they perform in specialized organs located in their abdomens. They synthesize an enzyme, luciferase, and with it oxidize a fat, luciferin, to give off light. The light is without parallel for its coolness, radiating only $1/80{,}000$ as much heat as a candle flame of equal brightness. Presumably its gemlike radiance originated as an evolutionary accident, but today it is clearly advantageous, attracting prey and enabling mating fire flies to signal in heliographic codes which differ from one species to another. The steady burners that are found glowing in the cave are the plump larval forms of the fly. The staccato flashers are species of air-borne adults.

ADULT WAITOMO FLY, shown in the first photograph ever taken of it, resembles a gnat but has eyes that are much reduced in size, owing to the fact that the fly lives in perpetual darkness.

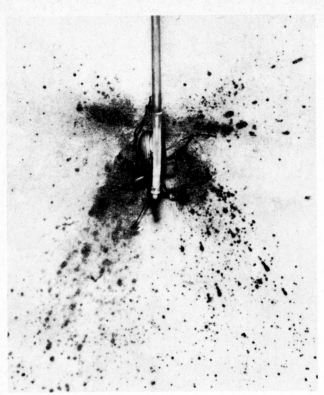

FOUR-POINTED SHOT PATTERN laid down by a bombardier beetle when it was nudged from four different quarters shows that it can aim its noxious spray accurately in all directions.

A SELF-ASSURED BOMBARDIER BEETLE AWAITS THE ONSLAUGHT OF A

GAGGING ON AN EXPLOSIVE BURST OF IRRITATING GAS SPRAYED DOWN

Insect Chemical Warfare

As anyone knows who has ever disturbed an ant nest or wasp hive, insects can do much more in their own defense than merely play dead or look threatening. Some bite, some sting and some simply stink. The common Spanish fly contains a blistering potion. Certain lacewings exude foul smells. One kind of termite soldier has its entire head specialized as an anti-ant atomizer. In some cases the irritation and damage are caused by complicated toxic substances, difficult to analyze in the laboratory.

The bombardier beetle on these pages secretes three chemicals—two hydroquinone compounds and hydrogen peroxide: an explosive mixture in the presence of a catalyst. They are stored mysteriously together in the beetle's weapon glands and secreted when needed into a hard-walled reaction chamber where the mixture is ignited, probably by an enzyme. The blast of unpleasant mist from their interaction is aimed from a flexible abdominal duct which the insect can point in any direction, sending ants into seizures and even deterring frogs.

FROG. AS THE FROG IS ABOUT TO SNAP ITS UGLY TRAP, THE CANNON IN THE BOMBARDIER'S REAR SWIVELS INTO POSITION AND BLASTS THE FROG

ITS GULLET BY THE BOMBARDIER'S WELL-AIMED GUN, THE FROG BACKS OFF AS THE BEETLE CONTINUES ON ITS WAY, HURRYING ONLY SLIGHTLY

6

Flowers, Pollen and Bees

A TREE standing in a forest is besieged by myriads of insects—no part of it escapes unscathed. From root tip to leaf canopy, the insects chew and suck on the green abundance. Aphids and leafhoppers pierce leaf tissue with their beaks and draw out the juices; caterpillars browse at random; leaf miners have found a domain in the narrow layer between a leaf's upper and lower surfaces, and there eat out serpentine galleries. Fruits are riddled, nectar and pollen stolen. Wood-boring beetles seek weak places in the bark to lay their eggs in; later their grubs spread through the wood. Carpenter ants gouge out nesting hollows deep in the trunks. Hordes of other insects feed on the maze of roots hidden in the soil. Still others lay their eggs within the tree's ripening seeds.

About half of all known insect species feed upon living plant tissue, leaving no known variety of higher plant immune from their attacks. Even when not feeding upon plants, insects use them in a multitude of ingenious ways for protection, rest and pupation. So complex is the relationship between plants and insects that some species in their larval stage, such as butterflies and moths, are such voracious plant feeders that they can ravage a midsummer forest, although the adults of the same species are the pollinators that ensure the flowers, fruits and seedlings of a new generation of the same plants. Under this endless insect assault, some plants have evolved defenses against insect attack—such as hairiness, toughness of leaves or repelling toxic substances—but most plants are assured of survival only by their profusion.

THAT insects should feed upon plants seems inevitable: the reverse of this process—plants that feed on insects—is also known. Despite the myth of a "man-eating tree of Madagascar," there are no carnivorous plants sufficiently large to endanger man or the larger mammals, but many kinds efficiently prey upon insects and other small creatures. Some 450 species of carnivorous plants have developed a wide variety of insect traps—with slippery surfaces, glue, spines and closable leaves. Some are like pitchers, in which the insects are drowned; others work like steel traps to imprison their victims or like flypaper to mire them. The insect is often attracted by lures: the odor of violets, honey or nectar, attractive colors or brilliant points of light. These traps are no accident. They confer a real advantage for, by digesting insect tissue, the plants obtain nitrogen and perhaps other substances such as mineral salts that are absent from the marshy soil in which they usually grow.

One of the most elaborate traps is the bladderwort's underwater one. Each of this plant's small bladders is kept closed by a valve surrounded with long, sensitive hairs. When an aquatic insect or other small prey touches one of these triggers, the valve snaps open and the bladder expands suddenly, sucking in water and victim as well. Then the valve closes on the prey, which is digested. Afterward the insect's remains are expelled and the trap resets itself in preparation for the next victim.

In contrast to the mechanical complexity of the bladderwort is the simple efficiency of the pitcher plant. Its leaf is a hollow container that is a combination of lure, trap and stomach. Nectar, which attracts insects and leads them to the rim, is secreted from glands near the mouth of the pitcher. The insects learn too late that they have been deceived. They tumble down the walls of the pitcher, which is lined with slippery, downward-pointing hairs that form a sort of toboggan slide into a pool of liquid at the bottom. Winged species try to escape by flying, but they knock against the sides of the pitcher or against the top of the leaf, which overhangs like a lid to prevent rain water from entering. An insect that attempts to crawl out finds its escape blocked by the tangle of downward-pointing hairs. Its struggles only work it lower and finally it falls exhausted into the liquid, where it is digested by enzymes. The food material is absorbed by the plant through the walls of the leaf.

Most insects do not survive their encounters with pitcher plants, but a few live out their lives in a constant seeming flirtation with a watery death. These species use the pitchers as their homes, and are found living nowhere else; they feed on the walls of the pitcher or hijack the mass of insects captured by the plant. A small mosquito and a tiny gnat breed only in the fluid at the bottom of the pitcher, where their larvae grow to maturity. It is believed that these insects are protected against the digestive action of the enzymes in the plant's fluid by possessing antienzymes of their own.

Three small moths lay their eggs in the mouth of the pitcher plant. The caterpillars that hatch out make a snug retreat for themselves either by sealing the mouth of the plant with silk or by eating away the tissue below the mouth, causing the top part of the pitcher to die and collapse, clogging the entrance. Thus protected from above against weather and predators, the caterpillars feed

THE LEAF MINERS

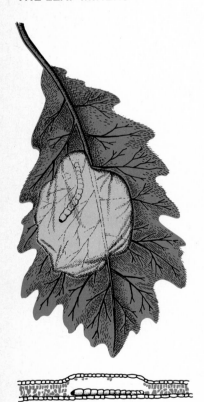

Leaf miners spend their larval lives between the upper and lower skins of leaves, eating the tissue between. Some species create a series of distinctive winding galleries as they burrow through the leaf, while others, like the white oak leaf miner (above), cause a blotchlike patch to appear on top of the leaf.

Although they are most numerous in the tropics, leaf miners (the adult forms of which are flies, wasp relatives, butterflies and moths) cause much damage to crops in northern latitudes, since they attack nearly all families of plants and trees.

and hibernate in their closed chambers. One caterpillar cuts an exit hole above its point of pupation so that, when it turns into an adult, it can escape: it guards against rain entering and flooding the chamber by cutting another hole for drainage in the bottom of the pitcher.

A plant that grows in Ceylon is an example of a less predaceous trap. Its flowers attract flies by their odor and color and, once the insects enter the blossom, a set of recurved hairs on the petals keeps them captive. The imprisoned flies pollinate the flower in their efforts to find a way to freedom and, in due course, the bloom relaxes and the flies escape.

In a world where some plants eat insects and many insects eat plants, there are a few alliances that are beneficial to both sides. The pulp-filled thorns of an acacia tree in the New World tropics are nearly always tenanted by stinging ants. The ants eat away the interior pulp and then use the resulting hollow as a nest, encouraged to stay by secretions of a sugary fluid from the tree as well as by tiny false fruit borne on its leaves. The trees, in return, are thought to receive the pugnacious ants' protection from defoliating insects, and even from mammals that attempt to browse the leaves. Ants are also congeners with certain tropical aerial plants that live perched on tree branches and cut off from the soil. The bases of many of these plants are often riddled by chambers and passages; the ants live in these spongelike structures and fill them with soil and organic matter useful to the plants. It was once thought that ant and air plant were essential to each other, but it is now known that the so-called ant plants can grow without the insects being present, although certain kinds of ants nest nowhere else. Thus the ants seem to enjoy the major benefits of this rather one-sided partnership.

BUT the prime association of mutual benefit between insects and plants is the act of pollination. The landscape is full of flowers that must be pollinated by insects in order to produce fruit and seeds. The pollen must be transported from plant to plant so that each kind of flower receives its own kind of pollen. It must be placed precisely on the female parts of the flower, and this must be done swiftly, for many blossoms remain open for only a short time. A huge army of insects accomplishes this immense undertaking with remarkable efficiency. Ants and beetles crawl over the flowers, butterflies and moths dip their long, sucking mouth parts into blossoms, flies and wasps buzz and whir through the sea of petals, the efficient and purposeful bees tirelessly make their rounds.

Pollination is simple in theory. Plants have developed attractions for insects in the form of color, nectar and pollen. The insect brushes against the pollen-bearing organs of the flower, becoming dusted with pollen which it carries to another flower of the same species. Over millions of years there have developed numerous delicate refinements among plants that attract insects and among insects that steal pollen. Worker honey bees, for example, possess dense body hairs that catch pollen, which is removed by comblike structures on the legs and transferred to pollen baskets on the hind legs. Many insects have greatly elongated, siphonlike mouth parts that can reach the nectar deep inside bell- and trumpet-shaped flowers. One moth from Madagascar has such a proboscis, which measures more than nine inches long.

The parts of a mountain laurel flower are so arranged that a visit from a bee virtually ensures cross-pollination. The laurel blossom is shaped like a bowl, with the female organ—the stigma—rising prominently in the center. Surrounding the stigma in a ring are 10 pollen-bearing stalks. These if they stood

THE BIRCH LEAF ROLLER

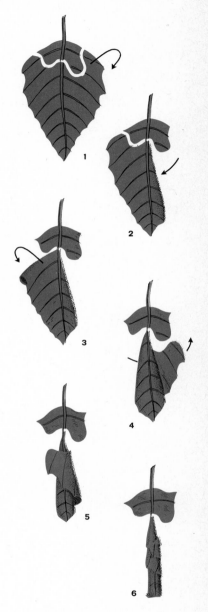

The European weevil, or birch leaf roller, is uniquely adapted to transforming leaves into snug nests which provide both food and protection for its emerging larva.

After making two S-shaped cuts (1) in a leaf, the female uses its legs to roll one half of the leaf into a cone (2). Then it rolls the other half around the cone in the opposite direction (3) through (5). Finally, it enters the cone, cuts a few slits on the surface of the inner leaf and inserts an egg into each opening. Only an hour after it began, the leaf roller tucks over a fold at the tip of the leaf (6) in order to seal the eggs inside against predators.

upright might come into contact with the stigma and fertilize the plant with its own pollen. Instead, they are bent outward and downward like tiny springs with their tips caught in little notches in the petals. When a bee visits the laurel blossom it first collides with the upright stigma. Pollen caught in its body hairs during a visit to another laurel brushes off on the stigma and fertilizes it. Then, as the bee descends to the bottom of the bowl for nectar, it brushes against the pollen stalks. These are dislodged from their notches and spring up like catapults, showering the bee with a new cargo of pollen which it will carry to the next laurel flower it visits.

Flowers display numerous other mechanisms for getting the full benefit out of insects' search for nectar and pollen. Some blossoms open and close only at certain times of the day, to accommodate honey bees that have internal clocks to help them keep track of time and visit the right flowers at the right hours. The lady's-slipper orchid has a nectar-filled trap that imprisons the visiting insect: to escape, the visitor must take a path which not only pollinates that flower but dusts the insect with pollen for the next flower as well. The milkweeds have their pollen bunched in the form of little clips: when an insect alights on the edge of the flower to sip its nectar, the pollen mass becomes clipped to its legs for transport to the next flower. Some tropical orchids have evolved blossoms that look like female bees. The orchid puts out its flowers as the male bees are emerging but before the females have left their pupal cases. A male, flying in search of females, will eventually arrive at an orchid flower. So realistic is the orchid's mimicry of the female bee that even the male is deceived. In its attempts to mate with the pollen-bearing parts of the flower, it becomes dusted with pollen which it carries to the next orchid that seduces it.

So closely are the lives of the small *Pronuba* moth and the yucca, or Spanish bayonet, of the Southwest intertwined that without the yucca the moth could not produce young, and without the moth the plant could not produce seeds. When a female *Pronuba* visits a yucca, it forces its ovipositor through the flower's ovary wall and there deposits its eggs. Then it gathers a ball of sticky pollen grains and fastens them to the plant's stigma. This step is absolutely necessary, for unless the moth pollinates the yucca, no seeds will develop and the caterpillars will starve, since it is the seeds that they eat when they hatch. The yucca, however, produces many more seeds than the caterpillars can eat, thus providing for its own survival as well as that of the moths. In the autumn, the caterpillars cut holes through the ovary walls and fall to the ground where they dig burrows and pupate; the adults that emerge in the spring seek out new yucca blooms and repeat the endless cycle.

M ANY kinds of bees visit flowers, but none of them, not even the acclaimed bumble bee, possesses the remarkable efficiency of the honey bee at pollination. Honey bees are foremost among all insect pollinators because their whole economy is based solely upon the collection of nectar and pollen. Nevertheless, the importance of the honey bee as a pollinator has been somewhat exaggerated. It has been claimed that were it not for honey bees no flowers would bloom, no fruit would be produced and numerous familiar plants would disappear. This is not true at all. When European settlers first arrived in North America, they found an abundance of flowers, fruits and vegetables—but no honey bees. Furthermore, the pioneers were able to grow their familiar European crops for more than 50 years before honey bees were introduced to the New World in the 17th Century. This was because an abundance of native insects was able to handle the pollinating task. However, many of these native pollinators have become greatly reduced in numbers as forests have been logged and meadows plowed. In their stead, the honey bee does a remarkably efficient job. These bees collect nectar and pollen from a wide variety of plants and yet the bees of one hive will concentrate their efforts on one plant species in a small area, thus ensuring cross-pollination. Furthermore, honey bees are semidomesticated and their hives can be moved easily from field to field.

Each hive seethes with unbelievable activity as bees buzz in and out of the entranceway, swarm over the combs, store honey and pollen and care for the brood. Yet, in all this apparent disorder is a strict division of labor. It is sometimes supposed that each worker bee is a specialist—a comb builder, a nurse or a forager—but this is not so. Each bee passes through an entire roster of professions, altering its activities as it grows older. Since new broods of bees constantly arise, there are some bees engaged in all of the tasks of running the hive at the same time.

U PON its debut from the pupal case into the life of the hive and for a period of about two weeks thereafter, the bee's principal occupation is that of nurse. It brings honey and pollen from the storage cells to feed the queen, the drones (or males) and the larvae. This is a demanding job, since a single larva averages some 1,300 meals a day. As it gets older, the bee becomes able to produce wax from glands on the underside of its abdomen and begins working on the combs. The wax exudes from between the abdominal segments, is scraped off by the hind legs and passed to the front legs; then it is thoroughly chewed before being molded into the cells of the honeycomb. In addition to constructing new combs, these middle-aged workers also take care of house cleaning in the hive and stand guard at the entrance. It is they, not just any bee, that do the stinging when an intruder comes too close to the hive.

Unlike the smooth stiletto of a wasp, the sting of a honey bee has small barbs like a porcupine quill that prevent its being withdrawn. After the bee stings and tries to fly away, the hind part of its abdomen is torn off and the bee dies of this injury. Rather than being inefficient, this kind of weapon actually benefits the hive by making the sting more effective. In the torn-off part of the abdomen are the poison gland and the nerves controlling it. This apparatus continues to pump poison into the wound even after the dying bee has flown away. Efforts to pull out the sting succeed only in squeezing more venom from the gland into the puncture. Thus, even though stinging is fatal to the individual bee, the added protection that such attacks afford the hive against a honey-hungry bear or other predator is well worth the loss of a few barren females out of the entire hive population. When the sting is used against other insects, the bee does not lose its life; the barbs can be extracted from the skeleton of another insect.

About three weeks after its emergence from the pupal stage, the bee enters the last period of its life—old age. During the active summer months, a worker bee may live as long as four or five weeks, but often less than that. When the worker goes foraging, it is already past its prime. It is logical that only after the bees have carried out their other duties do they undertake this strenuous and hazardous work, for many dangers threaten when a bee ventures beyond the protection of the hive. In the course of a year, however, not all workers become elderly foragers. Those that emerge during late summer and autumn live through the winter season, when no new brood is reared, and survive to care

Mutualism is a relationship between living forms that is beneficial, occasionally vital, to both. The tiny yucca moth (above) cannot get along without the yucca bloom that it lives on. And without the moth, the desert-blooming yucca would die out.

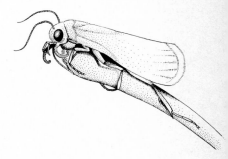

The moth plays its part in the relationship by gathering pollen from the yucca's anther (above) with its special curved proboscis and carrying it in a ball to another blossom, which it fertilizes by forcing the pollen down the stigmatic tube of the flower.

The plant cooperates with the moth by providing seeds as food for the insect's larvae. After the insect deposits its eggs at the base of the ovary (above), they hatch and the larvae consume the seeds, leaving a surplus to ensure the plant's survival.

A WORKSHOP OF LEGS

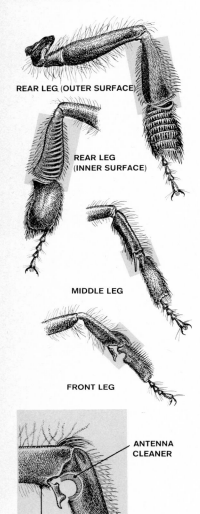

REAR LEG (OUTER SURFACE)

REAR LEG
(INNER SURFACE)

MIDDLE LEG

FRONT LEG

ANTENNA
CLEANER

EYE COMB

Each pair of a bee's legs performs a special function. The rear legs scrape pollen from each other and deposit it on pollen baskets (shaded in green at top). The stiff hairs of the middle legs brush pollen from the thorax and front legs. The sharp little spur (in green, center) removes wax from wax glands on the abdomen. Each front leg has branched, feathery hairs for collecting pollen. It also has a special joint (enlargement, bottom) with a comb for cleaning the eyes, and a hairlined notch through which antennae are drawn for cleaning.

for the first spring brood. The queen herself may live for four or five years.

The old bees search abroad not only for nectar and pollen, but also for water, for propolis and possibly for balm. Propolis is derived from the resin of trees; the bees use it to block holes in the hive and also to seal up the corpses of such small intruders as mice that they may have stung to death. Balm is a substance like propolis but more liquid: it is used to varnish the inside of honeycomb cells before the eggs are laid. It is not certain whether balm is collected or, instead, secreted by the bees. Finally, very large amounts of water are needed in order to cool the hive by evaporation, to keep the humidity high and to dilute honey that has become too concentrated.

Most foraging, however, is for pollen and nectar. A laden forager may return to the hive with pollen balls nearly a quarter of an inch in diameter in its leg baskets. Nectar is gathered from a wide variety of flowers, but each bee usually keeps to a particular kind of flower until the supply diminishes. Nectar is sucked up by the proboscis and is stored in an organ called the honey sac. In order to fill its honey sac, a worker bee has to visit between 1,000 and 1,500 individual florets of clover. About 60 full loads of nectar are necessary to produce only a thimbleful of honey. Nevertheless, during a favorable season a single hive might store two pounds of honey a day—representing about five million individual bee journeys.

The contents of the bee's stomach are not its own: rather, most of it belongs to the hive. To feed itself while out foraging, the bee opens a valve that empties some of the nectar from its honey sac into its own stomach. When the bee returns to the hive, it empties the sac by disgorging nectar onto the mouth parts of the younger bees. By alternately sucking and blowing, these bees move the nectar back and forth over the surfaces of their tongues; this evaporates some of the water and concentrates the nectar. Glandular secretions further transform it. Finally, more water evaporates in the storage cell and the nectar gradually thickens into honey.

THE tasks performed by the worker bee seem to depend on the stage of bodily development it has reached. Sometime between the sixth and the 14th days of its adult life, a worker bee secretes from glands in its mouth a substance called royal jelly, which is essential for feeding the larvae and the queen. These glands later dwindle, the worker's wax glands reach full development and it switches to comb-building. At least that is what happens in an active hive with many bees of all ages. However, hives pass through crises, particularly during bad winters, and experiments have been performed in an effort to find out just how rigidly the activities of bees are controlled by their glandular secretions. In one such experiment all the old foraging bees were removed, leaving only the young workers. Since there were no bees to bring in food, the supplies in the combs were quickly used up. Some bees lay motionless, starving to death, while others dragged the larvae from their cells and sucked them dry. Then suddenly some of the young bees, although their feeding glands were still active, flew out to forage. This experiment showed that it was the state of the colony, and not the state of the glands, that directed the bees' behavior. In fact, the feeding glands of the bees that went out to forage soon conformed to the bees' new behavior and became reduced in size. Such a severe disturbance in the routine of a healthy hive would be unlikely to occur under natural conditions. But occasionally the requirements of the hive do change, as when there is an abundant nectar source or an unusually large brood. The bees can then meet the demands of the hive by developing the appropriate glands earlier or later; they are ruled not by calendar but by need.

But what bee informs the others of the need for foragers? Studies of colonies in glass-walled observation hives have revealed that each bee gathers on its own the necessary information about the needs of the hive. It does this by apparently aimless wandering. On such a tour of inspection, it looks into empty cells to see if they have been cleaned and examines larvae to see if they need feeding. At other times, the bee simply loafs, an idea that may seem incompatible with man's concept of the industry of bees. However, idle workers are needed in the hive, just as an army requires reserve troops. These bee reserves may be called up at any time to defend the nest or to air-condition it by beating their wings.

THE way in which bees undertake tasks that require cooperation is more complex. When a hive begins to grow warm in summer, numerous bees set about cooling it. At first they fan their wings but as the outside temperature rises mere fanning is not enough. Water must be brought into the hive and evaporated for cooling purposes. The bees accomplish this much as they thicken nectar—by spreading droplet after droplet on their tongues until these evaporate. Such water-cooling often achieves a remarkable stability in temperature. One hive which was exposed to full sunlight at about 160° F. remained a constant 95° F. inside.

It might be imagined that as soon as a bee detects a need for cooling, it flies off in search of water. This is not so; the need may be detected by a young worker that has not yet been foraging and does not know the terrain. Only old workers are water collectors; the young workers act as water sprinklers, distributing the droplets brought back by the foragers. The collector learns whether or not to continue carrying water during the brief moment when it returns to the hive and delivers its droplet. As long as overheating of the hive continues, the young sprinklers rush up and take the water with great enthusiasm. Their apparent greed shows the worker that water is still needed and it makes another collecting trip. If the hive has cooled by the time it returns, the sprinkler bees are no longer as enthusiastic and the collector does not go out for another load.

Females do all of the work in the hive, including the very occasional laying of unfertilized eggs, all of which develop into drones, or males. But the principal egg layer is the queen. There is only one queen in a hive and it does nothing but reproduce. The question of what determines which larva will be a queen and which will become a worker is a fascinating one. Apparently, all of the female larvae are exactly alike upon hatching. Their destiny is determined by the kind and amount of food they receive. During the first three days of their lives, all larvae are fed on the royal jelly exuded by the glands of the young workers. If a larva is thereafter switched to beebread—a small quantity of honey mixed with pollen—it develops into a worker. If it continues to be fed royal jelly, however, it develops into a queen.

The eggs destined to produce queens are not different from those that produce workers, but they are placed in special large cells, which may serve as a memory aid to the nurse bees when they are distributing food. If an old queen dies, the colony can usually produce another queen simply by transferring one of the dead queen's latest eggs to a queen cell and feeding royal jelly to the larva that hatches. But what causes the workers to build a queen cell? The answer seems to revolve

THE LANGUAGE OF BEES

To "tell" each other where nectar may be found, worker bees have developed two distinct kinds of dances, a round dance for nearby nectar and a tail-wagging dance for distant nectar. Each of these dances is performed on the vertical face of the honeycomb.

The round dance is the simpler. When a forager returns to the hive it disgorges a drop of nectar to announce a source of honey within 100 yards of the hive. It then whirls around in one spot while the surrounding bees use their feelers to pick up the flower scent clinging to its body. They then leave the hive to look for a nearby flower of that kind.

The tail-wagging dance is for distances beyond 100 yards and tells bees in what direction to go for nectar. In this dance a bee makes a flat figure 8 with a straight line between the loops. This line acts as a pointer. It cannot, of course, point right at a flower, but it does tell other bees how far to the right or left of the sun to fly when they leave. The dancing bee does this by laying out its "8" on the comb in such a way as to locate the sun at the top—regardless of where it really is in the sky. Then it makes its run at an angle from this imaginary sun: to the right if the real flower lies to the right of the real sun, and so on. The other bees comprehend this angle, and apply it when they look for nectar.

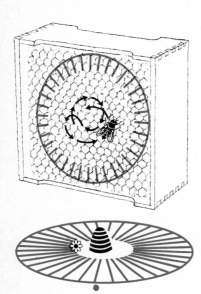

The round dance, performed when the nectar source is close at hand, stimulates other bees only to search in the general area of the hive. Because this dance does not use the sun as a compass, it cannot tell them in what direction they must look.

around a tiny gland in the mouth parts of the queen bee. This gland is the source of a substance that the queen spreads over its own body when grooming itself. Worker bees serve as courtiers. Constantly licking and grooming the queen, they receive a supply of this queen substance. Their supply passes by mouth from bee to bee throughout the hive and with it the information that the queen still exists. The queen substance inhibits the workers from constructing a queen cell.

However, if the queen dies, the substance is no longer available and the colony's inhibition comes to an end. The workers quickly prepare the outsized queen cells and stock them with the dead queen's most recent eggs. Within two weeks a number of new queens will reach maturity; they duel until only one emerges the victor. The conqueror assumes power and produces a supply of the inhibiting queen substance; thereafter, no additional queen cells are prepared.

The queen substance seems to dominate much of the life of the hive. In a flourishing hive with a great many bees, for example, the queen substance becomes so diluted in being shared by a large population that its chemical message is no longer felt everywhere in the hive. As a result, some of the workers start queen-raising activities; the colony divides, roughly half of the bees going with the old queen to found a new hive.

IF a large bouquet of flowers is left on a table, it will eventually be found by a foraging honey bee that will fill its crop greedily with the nectar and then fly back to the hive. If this scout is identified with a dab of paint, it will be seen that the same bee returns—accompanied by dozens of other workers. Somehow, the scout bee has announced its discovery to its hivemates, informed them of the location of the nectar source and worked up sufficient enthusiasm to make them fly there. It is amazing to think that a lowly insect could convey so complex a message, and yet it does. Numerous experiments have gone far toward unraveling the language of the bees.

If the nectar source is located within a few hundred feet of the hive, the following sequence of events takes place. The returning scout enters the hive and runs upon the combs, where it is immediately surrounded by other bees. It disgorges a drop of nectar from its honey sac and then begins to "dance." Its dance is in the form of a circle, going clockwise and counterclockwise. Disregarding the hubbub in the hive, the scout continues its whirling. The dance soon infects other bees nearby and they troop behind, taking part in each of the turns. Then it stops, goes to another part of the hive, disgorges another drop of nectar and again dances. Even while the scout is still going through these motions, some of the bees take off and arrive at the nectar source. When the scout has disgorged all the nectar in its crop, it returns to the source for another load.

This is the so-called round dance; it is used by bees only when the nectar source is less than 100 yards from the hive. Stimulated by the dance, other bees go out in search of nectar. The reason they do not have to wait for the scout to lead them is that they have already received a valuable clue. Even before setting off, they know what kind of flower their target is: its scent adheres to the dancing bee. They also have a scent clue awaiting them outside the hive, for the scout bee has left its mark on the flower. Every worker bee has a so-called scent bottle at the end of its abdomen. Upon discovery of a nectar source, this organ is extruded and a trace of scent, the bee's own "trade-mark," deposited on the flower. Other bees can detect this clue at a considerable distance, pinpoint the source and return to the hive with full nectar loads of their own. Then they, too, dance. This stimulates more foragers and soon all the nectar is drained from the blossoms.

If the nectar source is 100 yards or farther from the hive, the scout bee must give more detailed instructions. Not only must the scout tell how far away the source is, but it must also indicate the direction. Now, instead of a circle, the scout traces the outline of a squat figure eight in its dance. The speed with which the bee dances around the figure eight and the rate at which it wags its abdomen on the straight track between the two loops tell the other bees exactly how far away the source is. When investigators placed nectar 400 feet from a hive, for example, the scout ran 11 figure eights in 15 seconds; but when the source was placed more than a mile away, it ran only four figure eights in the same length of time. At the same time the scout wagged its abdomen much more rapidly when the source was near than when it was distant.

Thus, the other bees learn from the speed of the dance and the rate of abdomen-wagging almost exactly how far away the nectar source is. They also know the scent of the flowers that make up the source. But how do they know in which direction to fly? The dance gives this information as well. Direction of flight depends on the direction the bee is facing when it makes its straight run between the loops of the figure eight. If this run is made straight up the face of the comb, it means that the source is exactly in the direction of the sun; a run straight down indicates a direction away from the sun. An angle to the left or right of vertical indicates the angle of the course to the left or right of the sun that must be followed to reach the source. This is an extraordinary feat in communication: the scout bee has taken an angular measurement and transposed it into a linear display on the comb. Thus it is that the other bees are able to make a "beeline" directly from the hive to a newly discovered nectar source that may be a mile or more distant.

The language of the bees seems unbelievable, yet it has been confirmed by countless experiments. There is no doubt that the bees understand the language, for they fly directly to the indicated flowers. They ignore others closer or farther away, and waste no time searching among flowers that have no nectar to offer. However, as in human communication, there are always a few bees who misunderstand the dance. Despite the precise instructions they are given, these few bees do not go directly to the source. Instead, they search far afield. But these nonconformists are also of benefit to the hive society. While the major strength of the bee forces is being committed to exploiting a known supply, the wanderers may well discover another field in flower elsewhere. In this way, new sources are brought to the attention of the hive.

A worker, no matter what hive it comes from, instinctively communicates and understands the dance, so long as it is introduced into a hive of the same kind of bee. However, there are a number of distinct species and geographical races of honey bees: instead of communicating in exactly the same hive language, each kind possesses its own "dialect." If bees that belong to different races are placed together in a hive, they attempt to cooperate but the result is confusion. Although aroused to set off from the hive in response to the dance, they misunderstand directions and go to the wrong places. The Italian race, for example, uses the round dance for distances only up to 30 feet; between 30 and 120 feet, it dances in a sort of sickle pattern, with the opening of the sickle facing in the direction of the food. At distances beyond 120 feet, it switches to the tail-wagging dance, but it uses a different scale of speeds to indicate distance.

In the last few years it has been discovered that bees not only dance to give information about food sources, but also to tell of potential new homes. When

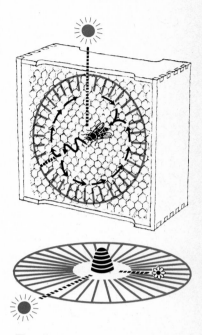

The tail-wagging dance, for distant nectar sources, tells other bees where to fly in relation to the position of the sun. In this example the flower lies about 120° to the left of the sun, and the bee has traced its "8" accordingly on the comb.

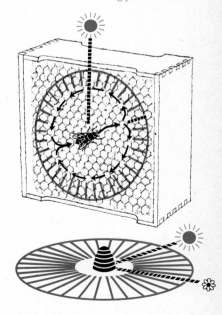

With the flower about 70° to the right of the sun, the "8" is laid out to match. In this case the flower is very far away, and the bee signals this by wagging its abdomen slowly across the "8." At top the flower is nearer and the bee wags faster.

the numbers in a hive increase to the bursting point, the old queen moves out with about half the population, leaving the combs and food supplies to be taken over by new queens. The old queen and the followers must now find new quarters. The swarming bees assemble in a tight cluster in the neighborhood of the old hive, and scouts soon fly out in all directions. After a short time, some return with information about new sites. They indicate the locations by means of the tail-wagging dance. Each dancer enlists adherents who fly to the potential site to inspect it.

Reports start coming in to the cluster from all directions—a hollow in a tree here, a crack in a barn wall there. One such swarm was observed to receive reports on 21 possible sites from its scouts. By the fourth day, there seemed to be increasing interest in a nesting place some 400 yards to the southeast of the swarm. Other sites were still advertised, but their adherents' dances grew fewer and fewer. Finally, on the fifth day, none of the competing sites was being advertised; only then did the whole swarm fly off to take possession of the site to the southeast.

Not only does the wagging dance give precise directions for finding the site, but it also assesses its value as well. The worth of the site is declared by the enthusiasm or the sluggishness of the dance. A lively dance, soliciting the acceptance of a prime building site, may last for several hours and attract more followers than a short sluggish dance. The more dancers, the more bees that fly off to inspect the site. If their reaction is favorable, they do a lively step on their return and attract even more followers. Who makes the final decision? It is not the queen: experiments have shown that the swarm can reach agreement on a new location even with its queen isolated in a cage so that there can be no contact between royalty and the dancers. Somehow, the swarm—consisting of as many as 30,000 bees—comes to a unanimous decision, with each worker apparently having an equal vote.

Thus, the choice of the bee home seems to rest solidly on what might be called advertising. Is this bee ballyhoo any more reliable than the kind that humans indulge in? When a bee performs a lively dance, is the site it sponsors actually superior? To find out, investigators have placed swarms on a level wasteland, lacking trees or any other natural sites for hives. There they offered the bee scouts a number of artificial hives that varied in quality. The bees returning from the best of these hives gave lively dances, while those that inspected inferior hives were fainthearted in their praise. Soon the bees that had visited inferior sites went off to visit the one that had attracted the lively dancing. They were convinced; they returned to the swarm and switched their vote. Their wagging dance indicated their favor: in agreement, the swarm flew off to take possession of this better hive.

THE hive of the bees has been pictured as a totalitarian government, a matriarchy in which the workers are mere automatons, senselessly carrying out the ruthless laws of the hive. Now that the language of the bees has been learned, this is found to be untrue. What a remarkable society this is, where nonconformists are not only tolerated but are of value to the state. What a strange dictatorship, where the ruler is voteless but the ruled have equal votes and the right to change them. The honey bees have, in fact, evolved a well-nigh utopian insect society—where every female possesses a vote, where the decisions are unanimous, where the majority is always correct in its judgments and where even the advertising is honest.

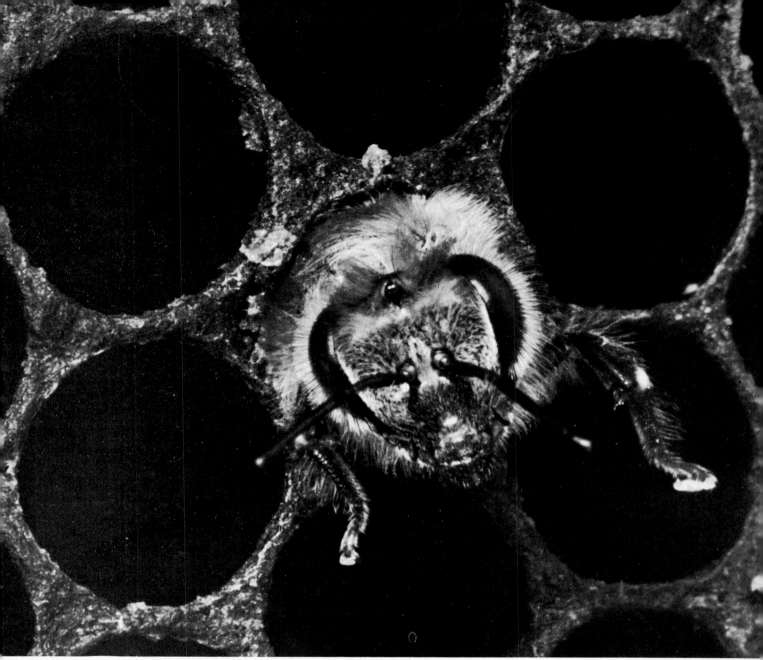

A WORKER BEE, DAMP AND DISHEVELED, STRUGGLES OUT OF THE WAXEN CELL WHERE IT HAS SPENT THE FIRST THREE WEEKS OF ITS LIFE

A Brief Life of Toil

From the moment it chews out of its hexagonal wax cradle and daintily cleans its new body, the honey-bee worker is occupied. For 10 days it acts as a foster mother, feeding younger brothers and sisters. For 10 more days it cleans the hive and builds combs. As the fourth week approaches, it leaves the hive to forage tirelessly for pollen and nectar until old age or enemies overtake it.

133

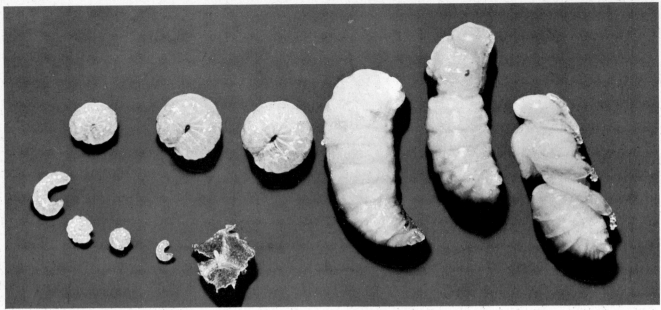

A BEE'S DEVELOPMENT BEGINS AS AN EGG LAID ON WAX (LOWER LEFT), THEN PROCEEDS THROUGH LARVAL FORMS TO PUPAL STAGES AT RIGHT

The Worker Bee: Chief Citizen of the Colony

An average-sized bee colony of 60,000 insects consists of one mature queen and perhaps 100 drones. Every other insect in the hive is a worker. No hive can exist for long without a queen and drones, and great care is lavished upon its royal members. But by far the main business of the colony is the spawn and nurture of the workers. Life for a worker bee begins as an egg, one of 3,000 a queen may lay in a single day. After three days' incubation the egg hatches and for six days more the larva, little more than a legless, living stomach, eats ravenously. During its first 24 hours the grub increases its body weight five and a half times; for as much as 30 minutes out of each hour a nurse bee stands overhead, patiently feeding and attending its charge. By the end of the sixth day, the larva has spun a silken cocoon, writhing and gyrating within the close confines of its wax cell. Then after 12 days' pupation it emerges, outfitted with the finely tooled body and complex instincts of a full-grown worker (*opposite*).

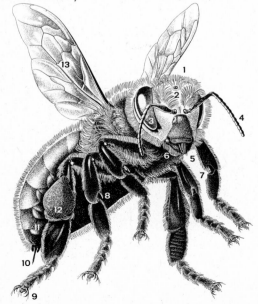

A BLUEPRINT FOR EFFICIENCY

The portrait of a worker bee opposite, painted with the aid of a microscope, shows the details of this insect's intricately efficient body. The numbers on the small drawing at left identify parts of the anatomy. The blunt triangular head (1) is studded with three simple eyes, one of them visible on the forehead (2), and two compound eyes (3). The antennae (4) are divided into 12 segments and supply the bee's sense of smell and touch. Mandibles (5) crush and shape wax for comb-building. Curling back under the head is the proboscis (6), used for sipping honey, nectar and water. The antennae are drawn through grooves in the front legs (7) to clean them. Long spines on the middle legs (8) remove wax from glands. Each foot has pronged claws (9) for clinging to flowers. A barbed sting (10) protrudes from the abdomen, and wax scales (11) are secreted along the body's rear segments. The pollen basket (12) on the rear leg is full from a collecting trip. Two separate sections of the wings are joined by marginal hooks (13) when the bee is ready for flight.

The Busy, Year-Round Life
inside a Beehive

The highly organized life of a beehive is shown in this painting, which incorporates activities that go on at different times of the year. At upper left a queen, surrounded by worker bees, lays eggs in an empty comb. At top center new workers, ending their pupation, emerge from their silk-capped incubation cells while nurse bees go headlong into the empty cells to clean

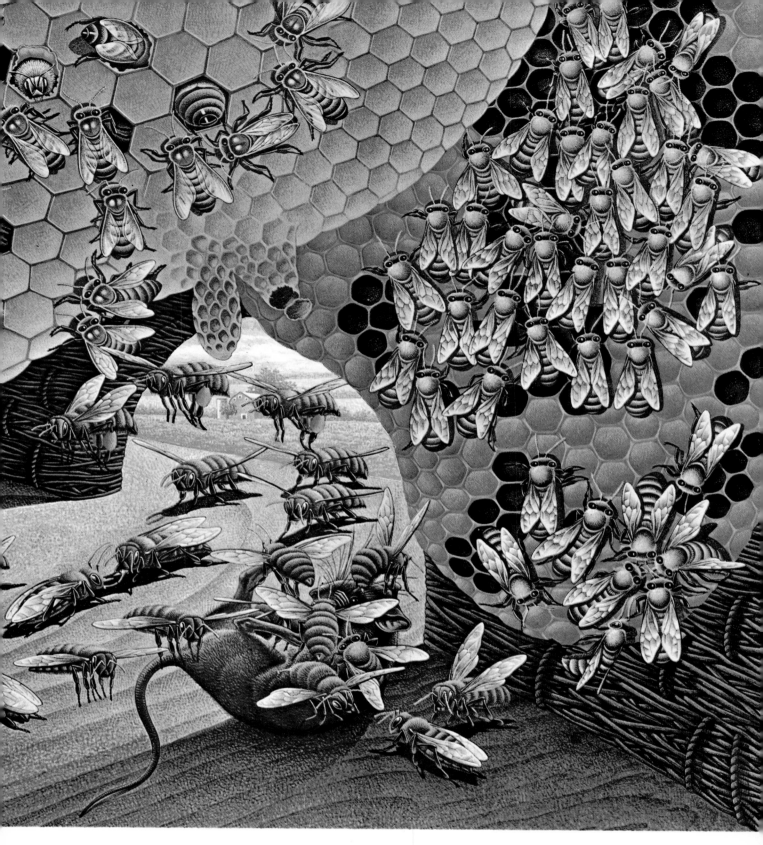

them. At the right edge of the comb two protuberances house pupae of two new queens. At bottom left two queens, encircled by watching workers, fight a battle to the death, since normally only one queen will reign in a hive. At bottom center, field workers standing head-to-head with hive workers deliver their loads of nectar, while above them other field workers carry burdens of pollen to special storage cells. At right hive workers sting an intruding mouse to death. Standing at the hive entrance facing inward, three air-conditioner bees fan air into the hive to evaporate water from the honey. At the bottom edge of the comb a cluster of engineer bees builds new wax cells. Above them is a winter scene with the bees huddling for warmth.

A Ring of Danger Circling the Safety of the Hive

All may be busy and orderly within this hive, but a host of enemies waits hungrily outside. A garden spider (*left*) spins its web between hive and flowers while a dragonfly hovers overhead, scooping up workers in flight. The bear (*background*), protected by its thick fur, will destroy an entire hive to satisfy its sweet tooth. The kingbird, or bee martin (*top right*), sucks

nectar and juices out of the bee, then discards the empty body. Below the kingbird is a robber fly, whose enormous eyes give keen sight which it uses to spot flying bees, intercepting them in mid-air with hooklike claws. At right the praying mantis lurks motionless in the foliage till a bee comes too close. The skunk, which loves both bees and honey, is seldom able to break into a hive but it will scratch outside till the bees come out, then deftly kill them with its paws. Hiding in the flowers at lower left, a toad envelops bees with its tongue, apparently immune to the sting venom. But perhaps the worst enemy is not visible in this painting. This is the wax moth larva, whose random tunneling through the bee comb can wipe out a colony.

SWOOPING KILLER, a giant water bug captures a dragonfly nymph in a murky pond. Air-breathing water dwellers, these insects attack tadpoles and fish almost twice their size. Fewer than 200 species exist.

7

The Water Dwellers

ANYONE sitting for a few moments by the side of a woodland pond cannot fail to be impressed by the sheer variety and abundance of the insect life it holds. The still surface of the water is like a sheet of transparent rubber stretched tight, and upon it numerous insects seem to defy gravity as they leap, twirl and slide across the silvery expanse. In a handful of root-laced mud from the water's edge may be found a number of oddly shaped creatures—the larvae of insects that are best known in their winged adult forms. The air seems filled with the glinting, metallic sheen of damselflies and dragonflies, the gossamer wings of mayflies, the dancing swarms of crane flies. It is this very insect abundance that helps to feed the pond's other inhabitants, the fish, the turtles and salamanders, the choirs of frogs.

A few kinds of insects spend their adult as well as their immature stages in the water, but most are aquatic only as larvae. They inhabit every kind of fresh-water environment. At least one species has managed to establish itself wherever there is water on the land: some live in cold glacial streams, others in hot springs with temperatures as high as 120° F., still others in swift rapids, in brackish shallows, and even in lakes with a salt concentration many times that of the ocean. Some

FOUR COMMON INSECTS OF THE POND

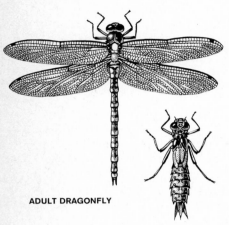

ADULT DRAGONFLY

DRAGONFLY NYMPH

The dragonfly and damselfly are similar in that both have two pairs of large, filmy wings, short antennae and long bodies. But the damselfly's body is generally thinner and it can close its wings over its back when at rest. Dragonflies invariably keep their wings out flat in the position shown above, and are stronger, faster fliers. Their bulging eyes meet each other on top of the head. The young, too, are similar, but the damselfly nymph has three finlike gills attached to its tail.

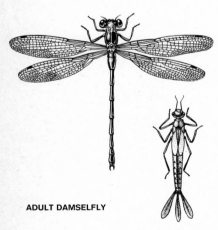

ADULT DAMSELFLY

DAMSELFLY NYMPH

species have only the most modest of water demands. Rain water in a discarded tin can is often sufficient for mosquitoes; certain tropical species even thrive in the scant moisture held between the leaves of aerial plants. The floodwater mosquito lays its eggs on the mud after a deluge; the eggs do not hatch until another flood takes place, perhaps many years later.

Aquatic insects have numerous advantages over their relatives that are confined to the land and the air. They have largely escaped competition and crowding from the hordes of land insects; they have eluded many of the usual predators, although they have exchanged these for such new enemies as fish and frogs; they are less troubled by sudden variations in temperature. Nevertheless, they have found adjustments necessary in their water world. They have had to tap new food sources and find ways of escaping from drying ponds. Many of them are presented with a serious problem: how to get out of the water when they emerge from their pupae.

But of all the challenges that beset water insects, obtaining an air supply is the most pressing. The ancestors of insects long ago lost their gills when they left the sea and developed new apparatus for breathing atmospheric rather than water-dissolved oxygen. This apparatus—common to all insects today—consists of a network of extremely small air tubes that branch through the interior tissues and open to the outer atmosphere through a row of small holes, called spiracles, on each side of the body. Air reaches the body cells by entering the spiracles, and this flow is encouraged by expansion and contraction of the insect's body, which acts like a pump. The tiny air tubes are prevented from collapsing by being wound with a spiral of hard material, much as rubber hosing is often reinforced by being wound with wire. Equipped with this breathing system, adapted for survival on land, roughly 3 per cent of all insect species have nonetheless returned to the water for part or most of their lives. In the return, the system for using atmospheric oxygen was modified in many ways. Some water-dwelling insect larvae have come upon the gill method of getting oxygen, as fish do, and are fully aquatic. Others, both larvae and adults, continue to take their oxygen from the air and have developed special ways of bringing this air beneath the water surface. The wide variety of ingenious methods of underwater living has been developed by totally unrelated species. Water insects by no means evolved from some common ancestor: instead, many different insect lineages arrived at these solutions to an aquatic livelihood independently.

The nymphs of mayflies, dragonflies and stoneflies still retain the air tubes of land insects, but to them are attached gills that can strain out the abundant oxygen dissolved in the water. These gills often look like wispy fern leaves extending outward from the abdomen or, in the case of stoneflies, from the head and thorax. The dragonflies have a somewhat different arrangement. Their gills are located on the hind end of the digestive canal; expansion and contraction of the body wall act like a pump that forces water in and out. These gills work by simple diffusion of oxygen through their surface and into the air tubes.

The nymphs of most mayflies possess seven pairs of gills, shaped like flat oval plates, that stand out along both sides of the abdomen. The forward six pairs are kept in constant vibration, while the seventh pair is stationary. The first pair begins an oarlike stroke, followed immediately by the second pair, then the third pair, and so on. In this way, a continuous flow of water is set up over the gills, flowing backward until it reaches the stationary last pair of gills. These deflect the water, from which the oxygen has now been removed, so that it will not be used again. In water abundant in oxygen the rhythm of the gill strokes is leisurely. But if there is a shortage of oxygen, they beat so rapidly as to create the appearance of a halo along each side of the nymph's body.

The mayfly nymph feeds on bits of organic matter that are too small to be of much interest to most other water dwellers. The nymph converts this flotsam into its own tissue and it, in turn, becomes an important food source for foraging fish, amphibians, turtles, birds and other water insects. The nymphs meet many hazards, and only a few out of the teeming populations that hatch from each season's eggs survive to adulthood. The survivors may live up to two years at the bottom of a lake, molting perhaps more than 30 times. But after they emerge they are children of a day, surviving sometimes only a few hours. A mayfly's wings are thin and feeble. Its legs are too weak for it to walk. The mouth parts may be useless or totally lacking, for the adult mayfly does not eat. Instead of food, the digestive system becomes filled with air like a balloon, giving the mayfly additional lift to supplement its flimsy wings. It might be thought that such fragile insects, apparently so ill-fitted to endure, are only recent additions to the insect fauna. Not at all. They are known as fossils as far back as the Lower Permian, some 250 million years ago.

The adult mayfly must stay alive only long enough to join the nuptial flight, usually held over water in the late afternoon or early evening. From a cloud of males, one darts out and seizes a female. The female is a reproductive machine, filled with eggs from the tip of its abdomen to the rear of its head. These it casts upon the water, and then drops listlessly to the surface. The morning after a nuptial flight finds the shore littered with dead mayflies. Along the Great Lakes in some years, truckloads of mayfly bodies are hauled from city streets; bridges and roads become too slippery for travel; electric signs are turned off at dusk so as not to attract the clouds of insects. The life of the adult mayfly is soon over, but the eggs possess a remarkable mechanism that aids in their survival. Each egg has attached to it fine threads that uncoil as soon as the egg touches water. Some threads are equipped with adhesive disks at their ends that serve to hold the egg fast to the lake bottom, but others merely become entangled in underwater vegetation and thus anchor the egg.

Mayfly nymphs often fall prey to one of the most voracious of aquatic insects, the dragonfly nymph. This hunter does not stalk its prey, but rather remains still, concealed by its brownish coloring. It possesses a strange, hinged structure that looks like a stout arm: it is actually a modified lower lip, with the tip converted into grappling hooks for seizing prey. When not in use, this arm folds up snugly beneath the face. But when something to eat comes within range, it is shot forward by powerful muscles and impales the prey. The arm is then folded back into place, bringing the prey within reach of the nymph's jaws. There it continues to be of use, serving as a saucer that catches bits of the victim which drop from the jaws while feeding. Dragonfly nymphs devour a wide variety of aquatic insects, including their own kind, and some are even known to seize small fish and tadpoles.

The adult dragonfly is an equally rapacious air-borne hunter. The rear of its head is hollowed out and loosely attached to the thorax, like a ball and swivel, so that the insect can turn its head in all directions to search out prey with its bulging compound eyes. The eyes of some species are so large that they meet in the middle of the head. The mandibles are toothed and ridged, and the maxillae are sharp tines that impale and turn the food as if it were on a spit. The long,

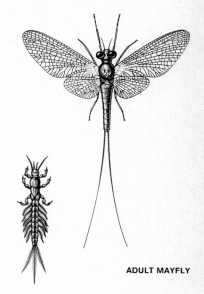

ADULT MAYFLY

MAYFLY NYMPH

The adult mayfly has a shiny body with two or three conspicuous tail filaments, often longer than its body. Its transparent, veined wings have more of a butterfly than a dragonfly shape. The mayfly young is aquatic, like the other nymphs on these pages, but is distinguished by the gills along its abdomen. The mothlike caddisfly adult has long antennae, chewing mouth parts and four wings which fold over its body. Its larval life is usually passed in a protective casing of debris.

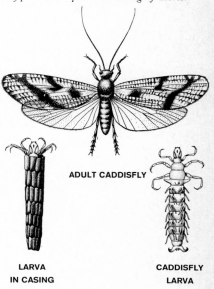

ADULT CADDISFLY

LARVA IN CASING

CADDISFLY LARVA

spiny legs are mounted far forward on the thorax; in flight they are folded into the form of a basket or net for scooping prey out of the air. The wings are very long and braced in such a way that they are strong yet pliant. Dragonflies are capable of long sustained flights, soaring, hovering and darting; speeds as high as 60 miles an hour have been clocked for some species. So wedded to the air are dragonflies that some mate on the wing and others lay their eggs while skimming the surface of the water, occasionally dipping the abdomen under the surface to deposit an egg.

LIKE mayflies and dragonflies, the larvae of caddisflies are completely aquatic. They are a widespread group, inhabiting a variety of aquatic niches in small houses, or cases, that they build themselves. The larvae are usually slender, with long legs that extend forward. Thus a caddisfly larva can protrude its thorax and legs from the case and drag its mobile home with it as it feeds. It also has a pair of hooks at the end of the abdomen with which it clings tenaciously to the case. These grappling hooks make it almost impossible to force a caddisfly from its case without damage to the insect. It can, however, be persuaded to leave by gently prodding the abdomen with a pin. If it is then transferred to clean water containing nothing but fragments of broken glass, the larva will construct a new —and transparent—case out of the glass fragments. The larva's movements then can be watched, and it will be seen to make graceful undulations with its body, driving a continuous current of water through the case and over the gills, soft white filaments along its side and back.

Each species of caddisfly constructs a characteristic kind of case. The basic plan is a tube made of silk that the larva exudes. Each tube is then adorned with the building material of ancestral choice: sticks, leaves, stones, shells or sand. Some species cut leaves into rectangular pieces and put them around the tube; others arrange the leaves in thin strips which wrap the tube in a spiral. Some use fine grains of sand to construct a tube that increases in diameter toward the front, like a trumpet. Some arrange sticks side by side, as in a log cabin. One species cements sand grains together to create an astonishingly close replica of a snail shell. The caddisfly is adaptable, however; if its traditional building materials are not available, it makes do with whatever is at hand. A good many caddisfly cases are found with bits of twig or reed trailing behind. These probably serve as buoys that lighten the weight of the case and keep it at approximately the specific gravity of water; in that way, a caddisfly larva can nimbly climb over plants and stones, unconcerned by the fact that it is transporting a case that, in the air, would probably be too heavy for it to pull.

Some species of caddisflies do not construct cases at all. These larvae usually inhabit swift streams and use grappling hooks to anchor themselves against the current. Some such larvae do not neglect their heritage as silk producers: they fashion underwater nets. The net may be tubelike, up to four inches long, buried in the bottom of a stream except for one open end that projects up into the water. Or the caddisfly larva may spin a funnel-shaped tube that has the wide end fastened and the narrow end floating downstream like a wind sock. Another larva stretches its flat net between stones. The threads of these nets are not sticky, like the threads of the spider's web; instead the caddisfly larvae depend on the force of the water to hold their prey fast. In addition to food, stream flotsam is also trapped in the nets, which must be cleaned out periodically.

The completely aquatic insects also include the caterpillars of certain moths. Some kinds bind leaves together and construct cases around themselves, while

THE SNORKEL OF THE MOSQUITO LARVA

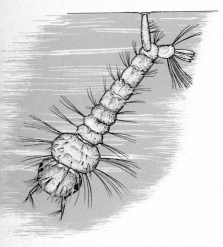

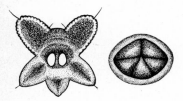

THE FLAPS: OPENED AND CLOSED

SIDE VIEW OF CLOSED FLAPS

The breathing tube of the common mosquito larva protrudes from its back near the tip of its abdomen (top). It has five flaps (center left) which open to reveal a pair of breathing pores when the insect is at the surface. These are closed (center right and bottom) when the mosquito submerges.

others build floating rafts of vegetation. One species of aquatic moth has a female that lives its adult life submerged: its wings are very small and it uses its legs to swim. The male of this species has fully functional wings and can leave the water. When it mates with the aquatic female, it does so either through the surface film or by re-entering the water.

There has been much uncertainty as to how these aquatic caterpillars obtain oxygen. It seems that aquatic plants are included in the material with which they construct their cases and these continue to carry on photosynthesis and thus liberate oxygen. This oxygen is available for use by the caterpillar, and the carbon dioxide the insect gives off can be used by the plants in photosynthesis. Thus, the plants act both as portable oxygen generators and as air purifiers.

Many of the insects that have returned to the water, however, have neither developed gills nor otherwise adapted their respiratory systems; they continue to breathe with the same equipment used by their landbound relatives. But they have developed two breathing devices that make it possible for them to live aquatic lives: these may be compared to the snorkel tube and the aqualung. The snorkelers are typified by the larvae of gnats. They renew their air supply by rising to the surface and sticking a tube located on the hind end of the body out of the water. The opening of this snorkel is equipped with a valve, which is kept tightly closed when the larva is under water. But when the tip of the snorkel breaks through into the air, the valve opens automatically. This is because the outside surfaces of the valve are attracted to water: on emergence the valve plates are drawn outward and downward, thus opening the spiracles to the air. The larva of the soldier fly varies this method somewhat by possessing a fan of hairs that form a complete circle around the end of its snorkel. When this larva rises to the surface, the hairs extend outward like the points of a starfish, anchoring the larva at the surface and opening the spiracles. When the larva dives below the surface once again, the hairs of the fan curve inward, trapping an air bubble that acts as a reserve supply.

Mosquito larvae, or wrigglers, similarly draw in air through a breathing tube. Since their snorkels break through the water surface easily and can always put them in contact with fresh air, they can live in almost any kind of water. Different species have become specialized for living in rain water collected in tree holes, in the brackish water of salt marshes, even in polluted water. Mosquitoes keep their snorkels dry with an oily secretion that repels water. Knowledge of this has allowed mosquito control by man, who spreads a thin film of petroleum over the surface of breeding ponds. Since the snorkel's oily secretion is effective only against water, this petroleum easily enters the breathing system and suffocates the larva.

Some insects have developed methods of tapping atmospheric oxygen without having to visit the surface to fetch it. The larva of the dronefly possesses a tube at the end of its abdomen that can be extended like a telescope to a length of almost six inches. It has spiracles at its tip, enabling its owner to feed on the bottom of a shallow pond and at the same time reach an air supply at the surface. The aquatic bug called the water scorpion also has a long breathing tube at the end of its abdomen, but this tube cannot be lengthened or shortened. The snorkel apparatus makes the bug look as if it were armed with a stinger and its common name comes from this fact and from the bug's clawlike front legs which resemble those of a true scorpion. The larvae of some flies and beetles also obtain their air without venturing near the surface; they get it from the air spaces between cells

FOUR COMMON INSECTS OF PONDS AND BROOKS

THE BACKSWIMMER

Propelling itself jerkily with strokes of its hair-fringed, oarlike hind legs, the backswimmer spends its life literally on its back, poking its tail above the surface at intervals to catch a breath of air. It is a voracious hunter of small insects.

THE WATER BOATMAN

This insect resembles a "right-side-up" backswimmer, having the same enlarged hind legs for rowing. It traps air under its wings and clings to underwater plants to hold its buoyant body down. Like the backswimmer, it can fly when it has to.

in submerged plants. One swampland mosquito larva has a snorkel of the usual sort, except that its breathing apparatus has been modified into a pointed instrument. The larva thrusts the point into the tissue of such water plants as sedges and cattails in order to obtain an air supply. The underwater world has its parasites also, and they not only consume the living tissues of their hosts but also tap their supply of air: many eat their way directly through the body wall of their victim.

The aqualung method is entirely different from the snorkel method. Insects who use it carry a bubble of air around with them. This bubble, which is in contact with some of the insect's spiracles, serves as a sort of gill. As the insect consumes the oxygen in the bubble, the oxygen pressure in the bubble decreases until it becomes much less than that of the oxygen dissolved in the water around it. At that point oxygen passes from the higher concentration of the water into the lower concentration of the bubble and replaces what has been used up by the insect's breathing. With the oxygen supply continually renewed in this way, the insect obtains from its bubble many times the oxygen it originally held. The amount of air that an insect can take down may be sufficient for only about 20 minutes, yet it can stay down for as much as 36 hours because the supply in the bubble is constantly renewed from the surrounding water.

Typical of the aqualungers are the large, voracious diving beetles. Their spiracles are not placed along the sides of the body, as with most land insects, but on the back, under the wing covers. When a diving beetle needs to take a breath, it breaks the surface and lowers its abdomen, trapping some air in the space under the wing covers. Water boatmen and backswimmers similarly carry air stores under their wing cases, but in addition they possess a coating of short hairs that retains a layer of air around their bodies. This explains why they often have a shimmering appearance and seem to glisten like silver. Such a coating of air renders these insects very buoyant and they must work constantly with their paddlelike legs to keep themselves submerged. When they wish to rest, they must cling to the underwater parts of plants; otherwise they would bob to the surface like corks.

In addition to the insects that live under water, other kinds have developed a surface way of life, walking or gliding along the top of the water without becoming submerged. One would think that the surface of a pond or stream was a precarious place to live, but an insect can lead an active life if it is light enough and properly supported. At the junction of air and water there exists an incredibly thin film: this surface film is not only elastic, it is also remarkably strong. Although a needle, for example, is much heavier than an equivalent amount of water, it floats if it is carefully placed on the water so as not to break the surface film. However, once an object breaks through, it becomes wetted and, if heavier than water, it sinks. There is a little springtail that holds itself on top of the surface film by means of a sucking disk on its underside. It is so small and light that the surface film supports it when it is at rest. It can even release its hold, jump into the air and land again on the surface. It always lands right side up because the sucking disk on its underside is attracted to water.

The most familiar of the surface dwellers is the pond skater, or water strider, an insect with a long narrow body, short forelegs and extremely long middle and hind legs. Its forelegs are held above the water and are used for grasping prey; the middle legs paddle and the hind legs steer. A water strider can not only glide swiftly across the surface, it can also leap and land again without getting wet. It is protected against wetting by a velvetlike pile of fine hairs; even if the strider accidentally becomes submerged, it is buoyed up and kept dry by a coat of air collected in these hairs. The strider avoids breaking through the surface film because of an adaptation of its legs. Its claws are not at the very tips of its feet, as with most insects, but a little above; the feet end in fanlike tufts of hairs that serve as "snowshoes," allowing the strider to move on top of the water while its weight causes only dimplelike depressions in the elastic surface film.

THE whirligig beetle makes its home in this meeting place of air and water, and its life is divided to take advantage of both spheres. It can be seen on the surface of ponds, often in large groups, gyrating erratically in all directions. It is a strong flier, able to migrate to another pond when the one it inhabits dries up. It can also dive beneath the surface, carrying a bubble of air on its abdomen. The structure of the whirligig's body reveals this divided life. The upper part of its body repels water, leaving this surface dry, while the underside and the legs are kept constantly wet. Its compound eyes are divided into an upper and a lower portion, so that the beetle has a separate view of what is in the air above and what is beneath in the water.

Water offers much more resistance to progress than air, and insects have developed a variety of methods for coping with the problem of underwater locomotion. If one compares the body outline of the diving beetle with that of many land beetles, the water inhabitant is seen to be considerably more streamlined. The diving beetle has a blunt front end, a smooth oval shape that is free from irregularities, and few hairs or spines. Female diving beetles are so streamlined that the males often have difficulty grasping them during mating; in many species, the front feet of the males are modified to form adhesive cups, with which they cling to the females.

Backswimmers, also considerably streamlined, swim upside down, as their name implies. Like the water boatmen and whirligig beetles, they have paddles on their legs for locomotion. Development of these flattened leg sections or of legs with rows of closely set hairs are not the only specializations of these insects. They also have had to make considerable changes in their musculature. A canoe paddle can be lifted out of the water for the recovery stroke, but an underwater insect's paddle cannot be. Therefore, backswimmers have had to develop a leg action which gets a purchase on the water when it is pushing the insect along, but offers a minimum of friction when the leg is brought forward for the next stroke. This feat is accomplished by the hairs on the legs. One way, they spread stiffly and permit a powerful stroke; the other way, the hairs hang limp. Normally the backswimmer's paddles sweep the water together, but they can often be used singly for turning, just as an oarsman uses a single oar to change a rowboat's direction.

Another method of underwater locomotion utilizes the principle of jet propulsion. The nymph of the dragonfly has gills placed in the hind end of the digestive system, where the water washes over them as the abdomen expands and contracts. By taking in water and then expelling it rapidly, the nymph can dart away suddenly from enemies. The opposite problem, that of standing still in swift water, is met by water insects in a variety of ways. Those that live in fast water are constantly threatened with being dislodged or washed away. Many seek safety in clumps of moss and water plants. Some mayfly nymphs that inhabit swift water are extremely flattened and have widely spread legs, allowing them to cling tightly to stones so that the current flows over their backs with a

THE WHIRLIGIG BEETLE

Although usually seen gyrating rapidly on the surface, this beetle is equally at home beneath it. It has one pair of eyes on top of its head and another, for underwater viewing, on the bottom side. It lives on other insects that fall in the water.

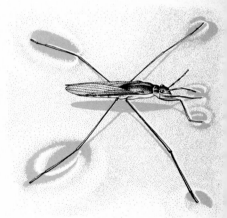

THE WATER STRIDER

With its slender legs and a light body, both covered with tiny hairs to buoy it up, this insect depends on the tensile strength of water to enable it to skate swiftly about on the still surface without falling through. It has wings but is a feeble flier.

minimum of drag. Caddisfly larvae that inhabit rapid streams build sturdy cases of pebbles that protect them against the grinding action of current-tossed stones; some even attach large stones to their cases to act as sinkers. Black fly larvae and certain aquatic caterpillars anchor themselves with silken threads as stay-lines. The larvae of the net-winged midge possess a half dozen or more sucking disks that hold them firmly to the rocks and enable them to inhabit the swiftest portions of streams. "Water pennies" are the larvae of little beetles that live in fast water. They are extremely flat and nearly circular; their entire bodies seem to act as suction cups holding them to rock surfaces.

Insects that inhabit ponds are often faced with the problem of a lessened or exhausted water supply, especially during the dry summer. The drying-up of a pond is a disaster to an aquatic insect, unless it can migrate to another pond or somehow endure the drought. The water dwellers use both methods. Some mosquitoes lay their eggs in summer when their home pond has dried up completely: somehow they are able to select hollows that will fill up with water again as soon as there is rain. As a result, these eggs hatch with the first wet weather. But some mosquito eggs possess an additional safeguard to ensure the survival of the species. These do not hatch after the first rain, but instead require a second or even a third soaking before they hatch. Without such a safety feature, all the eggs might hatch after a temporary wet spell, and the larvae would die if the pond dried up once more. Other insects escape drought by direct action. Many simply bury themselves in the mud at the pond bottom and await the return of water. Diving beetles and water bugs, powerful fliers, leave the drought-ridden area and search out new sources of water.

SINCE the insects of ponds and streams are so abundant, it is surprising to find that only a very few insect species have taken to life in the ocean. There is a midge, found in the Pacific Ocean around Samoa, that lives a completely submarine existence in all its stages. The female lacks antennae, mouth parts, wings or front legs; her mid- and hind legs are only rudimentary. The male possesses short wings, but they are useless for flight. The water strider is another insect that can live on the surface of the ocean—often several hundred miles offshore—but it is not really aquatic, since it gets its oxygen directly from the atmosphere. These marine striders need never return to land to reproduce: they attach their eggs to little rafts of seaweed floating on the ocean surface.

Insects are not prevented from inhabiting the sea because of its salinity, as many people believe. There are numerous insects that live in water that is much saltier than any ocean. The wrigglers of some mosquitoes, for example, have been reared experimentally in water three times saltier than sea water, while a fly larva in Utah's Great Salt Lake flourishes in water that is 22 per cent saline. Such insects survive because practically no part of their skeleton admits water and also because insects can usually withstand a much greater variation in the composition of their blood than can mammals.

Then why have the endlessly adaptable insects neglected the vast reaches of the ocean? The scarcity of plant life, the sea's great depth and its turbulence are all factors. But probably the main reason is that in the oceans the insects have at last found their match. A more ancient group of arthropods than insects, the crustacea, inhabited these waters first, flourished and secured a firm grasp on the niches that any ocean-dwelling insects might have filled. The crustacea now dominate their watery realm. Some, like the sowbug, have even invaded the insect's dry land domain.

A CLUTCH OF MOSQUITO EGGS DRIFTS IN A STAGNANT POOL. TRANSPARENT AIR FLOATS FRILL EACH EGG, KEEPING IT UPRIGHT FOR HATCHING

An Aquatic Existence

Of nearly one million insect species on earth, only a few thousand are water dwellers. Using an incredible variety of ingenious devices—including prototypes of the aqualung, diving bell, snorkel and jet propulsion—these have adapted themselves to every kind of liquid environment. Insects have been found living in stagnant water, brine, hot springs, cold glacial streams and even crude oil.

ABOVE THE SURFACE a Connecticut pond presents a placid aspect. The shallow water, drenched in sunlight, is a rich garden of lily pads and other water plants which provide hiding places and forage for the pond's many insect forms.

The Underwater Environment

For the average aquatic insect, survival in a watery world requires a just-right balance of water temperature, sunlight, oxygen in solution, food and living space. This balance is particularly favorable in the shallows of ponds and lakes. There the relatively few insect species that have adapted themselves to underwater life thrive in great numbers. In the view at right, for example, a small sample of pond water 8 inches deep by 10 inches wide contains only four kinds of insects but over 35 individuals.

Fresh-water shallows are rich in life for several reasons. For one thing, they usually have a high oxygen content, essential to the welfare of gill-breathers like dragonfly nymphs (*top center*). The major source of this oxygen is the rank plant life of the shallows, which releases it in the water through photosynthesis, itself abundant because of the plentiful sunlight that penetrates at these depths. The lush growth also provides an abundant larder for insect herbivores like the water boatmen. Plankton, which grows easily in the shallows, feeds tiny protozoa and crustacea which are eaten by small predatory insects like the diving beetle (*bottom center*) and backswimmers. These in turn are food for nymphs and larger carnivores. But temperature is the ultimate moderator. In summer the shallows are warm and life thrives; in winter they freeze, the delicate balance of underwater life collapses and the busy scene at right disappears until spring.

BELOW THE SURFACE is a grimly competitive world (*right*), including such predators as a diving beetle and tadpole (*bottom*), and a water tiger larva devouring a water boatman (*top center*).

The Surface Dwellers

Not all aquatic insects make their homes under water. A few—like the water strider *(left)* and the whirligig beetle *(right)*—live out their lives on its surface, submerging only occasionally. This is because they have acquired a unique adaptation: the ability to walk or maneuver on the surface of water without sinking into it. What makes this possible is the mysterious property of water called surface tension. For reasons not fully understood, water "likes" to stick to itself and strongly resists rupturing. So

THE LONG LEGS OF A WATER STRIDER DIMPLE THE SURFACE FILM BUT DO NOT PUNCTURE IT. IT PREYS ON INSECTS THAT FALL IN THE WATER

great is this resistance that very pure water—made in the laboratory—has been shown to have the tensile strength of steel. This makes a water surface act as though it were covered with a thin skin on which animals as small as water striders can stand without falling through. Occasionally, water-walking insects do pierce the surface film. When this happens, the whirligig can swim back to the surface (*right*). The water strider floats up, buoyed by a coating of air bubbles that cling to hairs on its body.

HOLDING A GLEAMING AIR BUBBLE IN THE TIP OF ITS ABDOMEN, A WHIRLIGIG BEETLE BRINGS ITS AIR SUPPLY DOWN FROM THE SURFACE

A LACEWORK OF GILLS decorates a caddisfly larva, seen outside its usual hiding place in a tubular casing. Its gills are continuously fanned through the water, absorbing oxygen from it.

A PENCIL-SHAPED NYMPH of the furtive damselfly breathes like a fish but has two sets of gills: a triple affair growing out of its abdomen and a row of small, tuftlike gills along its sides.

Gills and Snorkels

Some of the most ingenious of all insect adaptations are devoted to the problem of breathing under water. Small though they are, all insects need plenty of oxygen to support their high rates of metabolism. Aquatic species employ three methods—the breath-ing tube, the gill (both shown above) and the air bubble (*page 153*)—to supplement an air-intake system common to all insects. This is a network of branching tubes called tracheae reaching to every cell in the insect's body. Although insects are able to

HANGING HEAD DOWN, a culicine mosquito larva siphons air through two spiracle openings. The malaria mosquito larva has breathing tubes flush with its body, and lies horizontally.

A SPEARLIKE AIR LINE, actually a long double tube, attached to tracheae at the rear of its abdomen, provides the water scorpion with an air tap to the surface. The tube is unretractable.

"breathe" when they have to by muscular action of the abdomen, pushing air in and out of the tracheae, this does not penetrate the finest inner tubes, and these must get their oxygen through a process known as diffusion: the drifting of oxygen molecules into the tubes to replace those absorbed by the tissues. However, oxygen molecules diffuse very slowly in narrow tubes, and will not travel at a useful rate for more than a few millimeters. It is this that ultimately limits most insect body size to under an inch.

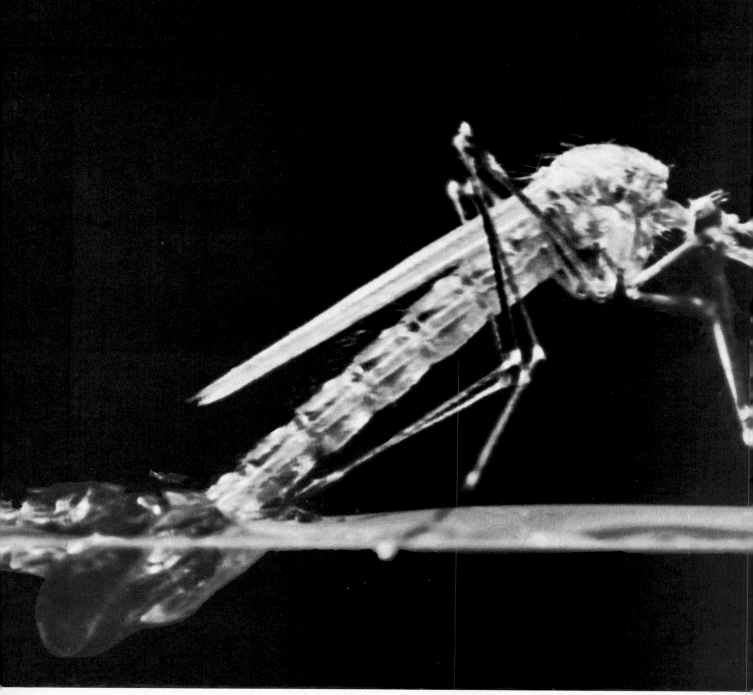

A NEW-MADE MALE CULEX MOSQUITO PULLS ITSELF ONTO THE WATER SURFACE, LEAVING ITS PUPAL CASE BEHIND. VISIBLE ON THE ANTENNAE

The Short Life of the Male Mosquito

Easily the best-known water-dwelling insect is the mosquito. Two thousand species infest the earth, breeding as numerously in chill arctic lakes as in steaming tropical pools. In summer, by the time it emerges as a winged adult (*above*), it has spent its life in water: first as an egg floating on the surface for one or two days, then one or two weeks as a larva and two or three days as a pupa, hanging head

downward from the surface. As a full-fledged mosquito it has only two or three weeks of life remaining, during which it mates.

The mating process is one of the most unusual in the insect world, being largely dependent on the male mosquito's sense of hearing. The male seems unaffected by the physical presence of the female; when she flies, however, producing her thin, high-

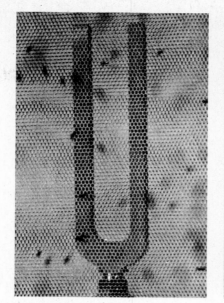

DUPED MOSQUITOES in a laboratory experiment demonstrate that males hear the hum of the females' wings and are attracted to it. At left, a tuning fork at rest gets no response. Vibrating at right, it makes a hum that draws males to it.

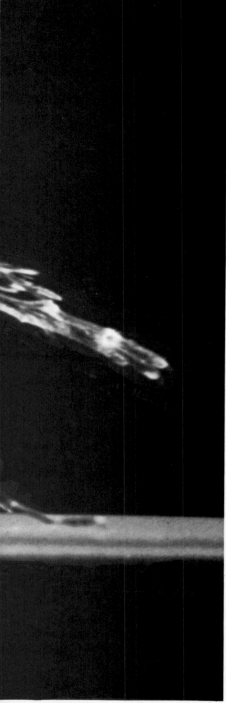

WINGS AWHIR, a female mosquito at left attempts to fly while suspended from a needle glued to her thorax in a real-life enactment of the experiment above. Hearing the sound, a male approaches at right and grips her leg, preparatory to mating.

ARE THE FIBRILLAE WHICH AID IN HEARING

pitched whine, the male becomes instantly attracted to her. Sound waves emanating from her wings impinge on the male's antennae, causing sensory cells in the antennae to vibrate and send impulses to the mosquito brain. The male responds by immediately taking flight toward the female, seizing her and mating.

How strongly the male is tied to this pattern of sexual behavior has been demonstrated by substituting the sound of a tuning fork (*above right*) for the flying female. The male is immune to the spell of the female at only one time in its adult life. During the first 24 to 48 hours after emergence it is deaf and unresponsive. This is because tiny hairs on the antennae called fibrillae, which aid in hearing, take a day or two to dry out and extend properly.

Insects That Must Leave the Water—and Return

For most water dwellers, which live half their lives in water and half in the air, making a successful transition is a crucial problem. As a nymph (*below*), an insect is equipped only for life under water. As an adult, however, it must have air to breathe and to dry its wings the instant it appears. Solutions vary. The buffalo gnat emerges from the pupa in a bubble of air, in which it rises to the surface. With precise timing the dragonfly nymph crawls out of the water shortly before its skin splits to release the adult. Later, egg-laying creates the reverse problem. Needing a liquid environment for its eggs, the damselfly (*opposite*) lays eggs by daintily lighting on the water and dipping its abdomen beneath the surface.

GRISLY NEMESIS of the pond bottom, a dragonfly nymph ambushes a small fish. Feeding voraciously, the nymph molts a dozen or more times in one year before the adult phase emerges.

GOSSAMER BEAUTIES, female damselflies light on the water to lay their eggs (*opposite*). These are deposited on the undersides of leaves to ensure that the nymphs will hatch in water.

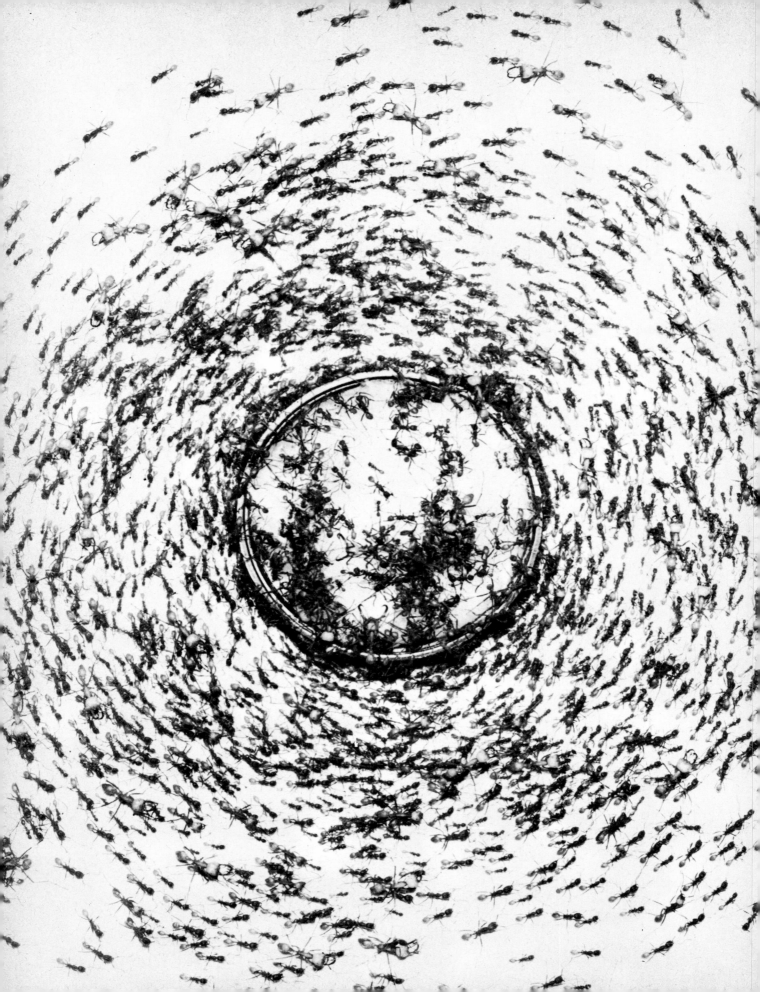

8

The Ant: Wisdom or Instinct?

NSTINCT," wrote Fabre, "is omniscient in the unchanging paths that have been laid down for it: away from these paths, it knows nothing. Sublime inspirations of science, astounding inconsequences of stupidity, are alike its portion; the animal will display the first when conditions are normal, and the second when they are governed by accident."

Typical of the numerous experiments Fabre devised to test the intelligence of insects was his interference with the life of a hunting wasp that drags grasshopper prey back to the burrow, leaves the grasshopper outside while it inspects the burrow, then drags the victim inside. The prey is always hauled by its antennae, and when Fabre snipped off the antennae level with the grasshopper's head, the wasp was not unduly disturbed; it grabbed one of the mouth palpi and continued hauling. While the wasp descended to inspect its burrow, leaving the grasshopper outside, Fabre cut off the grasshopper's palpi, too, and moved the prey farther from the nest. On emerging, the wasp soon located its mutilated victim and examined it carefully: there were no more appendages on the grasshopper's head that the wasp could seize to drag its prey the short distance to the burrow. Eventually the hunter gave up even though the prey had no shortage of appendages in plain sight that might have been used for hauling—its six slender legs and an ovipositor as well.

Fabre even went so far as to place one of the grasshopper's legs under the wasp's mandibles, but the wasp did not grab hold. "To understand that she can take a leg instead of an antenna is utterly beyond her powers," Fabre concluded. "She must have the antenna, or some other string attached to the head, such as one of the palpi. If these cords did not exist, her race would perish, for lack of the capacity to solve this trivial problem."

Much has been learned since the time of Fabre about the complex behavior of the insects. It largely confirms that what man usually regards as intelligence scarcely exists in the insect world. Some of the more advanced insects have been shown to possess remarkable memories and an ability to learn; but even so, the insect's world is one in which foresight and consequences, in the human context, do not exist. One can be sure that a caterpillar chewing on a leaf is not aware of the transformation that will someday take place in the pupa. Yet many of the remarkable things that the caterpillar does—such as finding a pupation site and spinning a cocoon with an escape hatch—are preparations for that time. Much of this mystifying behavior is the result of unreasoning response to stimulus. Generally, the response is inflexible. All hunting wasps of the same species seek the same kind of prey and dig their nests in the same sites and in the same way. So strait-jacketed are they in their innate behavior that they often become trapped by it. A fly caught in a house may spend an hour banging against the glass at the top of a window when all the time the bottom of the window is open.

Nevertheless, one family of insects—the ants—has been acclaimed for its wisdom since ancient times. Surely if intelligence exists in the insect world to any great extent it will be found here. The populous communities of ants are the nearest approach to civilization that exists in the insect world: there are undeniable resemblances between their communities and man's. Like human societies, ant communities have become expert at the three primary methods of obtaining food: gathering, hunting and growing. Ants have probably led a social life much longer than bees or wasps; the caste system was certainly developed at least 30 or 40 million years ago and examples of various castes have been found fossilized in Baltic amber. Unlike the bees and wasps, every kind of ant in the world is social. Teeming ant cities endure for immensely long periods and the longevity of individual ants is often remarkable: some workers live up to seven years and queens for 15.

Man does not have the keen sight of the hawk nor the acute hearing of the dog, but his losses in fine sensory perception are more than counterbalanced by his possession of a brain more complex than those of his fellow vertebrates. Among the insects, in turn, the ant lacks the enormous eye of the dragonfly and the special ear of the cricket. But by a curious coincidence, many ants have a nervous system that is physically different from that of their fellow insects. Most insects have two masses of fused nerve ganglia in the head: the front mass acts as a brain and the second controls the mouth parts. In a number of ant species, however, these two nerve masses have become united to form a single large organ—presumably because the ants' largely liquid diet has permitted a simpler organization of head anatomy. Whether or not this fusion actually increases these ants' capacity to learn remains a matter for future study. The most that can be said at present is that ants live long enough to learn from experience.

Many ants can learn to go through a maze that contains six false turns, and even a maze with 10. They seem to accept their lot when being kept in experimental nests: they stop trying to escape even though they easily could do so and they cease struggling when handled. They even learn to collect food that is regularly set out for them at a time when, under natural conditions, foraging would have ceased. Even among ants of the same colony, there are significant individual differences in memory and learning. However, these abilities are severely limited. An ant that has learned to run a maze leading from the nest to food, for example, must learn its lesson all over again if positions are reversed and the ant enters the maze on its way from foraging grounds to the nest instead. Apparently, what the ant learns when it is hunting for food is useful information only when it is hungry.

Indeed, investigation of many seemingly marvelous ant feats has often revealed prosaic explanations. In the tropics, when sticky ant-repelling bands were placed around the trunks of coffee trees, the ants within an hour or so had found alternate routes up high grass-blades that touched the trees' lower branches and it took only a day for them to pioneer a roundabout route that led up another tree, many yards away, and thence along an overhanging branch to a forbidden coffee tree. Yet this was probably accident rather than inspiration. Some ants were no doubt left on the trees when the sticky bands were applied; unable to return to their nest by the usual route, they eventually found another way home by trial and error. Other ants were then able to follow the scent of this new trail back to the trees. Similarly, ants have often been seen to cover sticky bands on tree trunks with bits of earth—in order, it is mistakenly believed, to gain safe passage across. But ants will usually cover up any sticky substance they find near their haunts, whether or not this act is of any practical value to them in foraging.

The individual ant is simple and uncomplicated in its behavior; yet when it exists in a community with other ants, it can carry out a remarkable repertory of activities and complex behavior patterns. The question of how ants act together—somehow getting work accomplished amid the seeming confusion of the colony—has been partially answered by "trophallaxis," literally "food exchange." Ants lick one another and exchange food and glandular secretions as well. When two ants from the same nest meet, they exchange strokes of the antennae and often pass a droplet of fluid from mouth to mouth. Eggs and larvae in the nest are constantly licked, and the queen is perpetually groomed. A common bond is thus set up in the colony that ensures the interest of the workers in the queen, the brood and one another. Most ants are dependent for their survival upon this exchange: the queens of army ants, for example, invariably sicken and die after only a few days of isolation from their battalions. It is also possible that in this way, as with termites, a social hormone is passed through the colony, regulating the proportion of soldiers and workers, and possibly even males and females.

Go to the ant, thou sluggard," advised King Solomon in Proverbs. "Consider her ways and be wise: which having no guide, overseer or ruler, provideth her meat in the summer, and gathereth her food in the harvest." One of the entomological puzzles of the last century concerned this observation by Solomon. There was no evidence that ants actually harvested grain. In 1871, however, a British naturalist showed that Solomon had been right after all, for in southern Europe he discovered ants that maintained granaries. Because these

SOME ANT OCCUPATIONS

CARPENTERS

Shown here and on the following pages are eight common American ants, each with a different way of life. Above is the carpenter ant, a large dull-black insect that tunnels in newly dead wood and lumber. It is plentiful in Canada and the eastern states. A timid insect, it forages outdoors at night, although in houses it will feed during the daylight hours.

LEGIONARIES

America has its army ants, called legionaries, which differ from true army ants in that they do not move in a mass but run rapidly in single file. They also stay in their bivouacs much longer. They live by hunting other insects, storing their meat and carrying it with them when they move—usually at night under a cover of leaves. Most legionaries are almost blind.

DAIRYMEN

One common garden ant throughout most of the northern states is a dairy ant, a herder of aphids. It builds the small sand mounds seen on paths and tennis courts. It is small, brown in color and, for an ant, good-natured. Most of its energies are taken up tending aphids, moving them around and protecting them from enemies, but it occasionally raids other ant nests.

harvester ants, as they are called, are found in Europe only on the shores of the Mediterranean, they had escaped notice for centuries.

Many ants use seeds as food, but only the harvesters have built an economy which depends largely upon seed gathering. These ants usually inhabit arid regions where food is scarce and competition is keen; they store up the seeds that they collect in the growing season for use during the dry season when this food is not available. Sometimes one of the harvesters' large mounds is surrounded by a ring of plants that are not otherwise found growing in the vicinity. It was once believed that the harvesters deliberately planted such miniature fields in order to ensure a handy supply of seeds. This, of course, is not so: what happens is that some of the seeds stored in the nest begin to germinate and the ants toss these onto the rubbish heaps surrounding the mound. A few such culls take root and grow. The ants may harvest the seeds from these plants also, but this crop is nothing more than an accident.

Even though harvesters do not plant crops, they have become expert in storing what they gather. The workers among some kinds of harvesters are unusually large: they serve not as soldiers but as threshers, using their powerful jaws to crush the hard seeds. There are special rooms in the upper part of the nest where the seeds are sorted out from other objects mistakenly brought back by foragers. Some groups of ants stay inside the nest by the hour, chewing the contents of these seeds and thus producing so-called ant-bread. It was formerly thought that the harvesters used some witting process to convert the seeds' starch into the sugar that they eat. It is now known that the process is automatic: the large amount of saliva that the ants secrete while chewing accomplishes this transformation.

ALTHOUGH it is a myth that harvester ants plant fields, there are ants that both cultivate and harvest crops. More than 100 species of related ants, all found in the New World, maintain gardens of fungus and practice a complex kind of agriculture. A study of the evolution of ant behavior makes it possible to reconstruct the steps by which this behavior may have developed. One explanation is that the fungus-growing habit arose accidentally from a peculiar activity of certain harvester ants. One advanced group of harvesters is noted for dragging bits of leaves and stems back to the nest. This debris serves no known purpose and is later thrown out: an explanation for this peculiar behavior is that the foraging ants feel compelled to bring something back from each trip and, if they cannot find seeds, they return with other small items. Whatever the reason, these harvesters' nests do contain vegetable debris that makes ideal compost for fungi. Furthermore, fungus often grows naturally on the harvesters' store of ant-bread. How—or if—the jump was made from the compulsive collecting of debris to the purposeful acquisition of compost for fungus gardening is a matter for speculation.

The ants that cultivate fungus are called leaf cutters—they are usually small and often armored with spikes. The workers march out of the nest in long files that lead to a tree or large bush. Some ants merely snip off pieces of leaves on the tree, others shear off whole leaves which drop to the ground, where they are cut into pieces small enough to be carried back to the nest. The workers then form a long line returning to the nest, holding their bits of leaf like parasols aloft. The Reverend Henry C. McCook, a pioneer observer of ants, said they looked "like Sunday-school children carrying banners." Leaf cutters can defoliate a tree in a single night and have become serious pests from South America to Louisiana. They do not feed upon the leaves, but instead chew them in the same way that harvesters chew seeds. The result is a spongy mass of compost that is kept in special chambers deep in the nest, and the fungus strands grow on this. When the ants bite off the ends of these strands, little heads form, looking like miniature cauliflowers.

A sizable leaf-cutter colony may contain multiple nest entrances covering an area more than a hundred square yards. Even in a tropical forest, these ant-made glades are devoid of plant growth—it is either choked off by the earth upflung from nest excavations or it is stripped of its leaves as soon as they appear. A thriving nest little more than three years old may have nearly a thousand entrances, although not all of them are in use at any one time. Some entrances may be used for a few days while a nearby tree is being defoliated and then abandoned until the tree puts out a new crop of leaves. The entrance passages may descend for as much as 16 feet and terminate in chambers that are a yard long and nearly a foot wide and high. On the floor of each chamber is a garden—a deep carpet of chewed leaves, entwined with strands of fungus. Small workers, restricted to indoor tasks of cultivation, crawl over the garden. The feeding of the ant brood is uncomplicated: nurse ants merely carry the larvae around and put them to browse in the luxuriant beds of fungus. Only the large workers take to the trails and bring back the harvest of leaves, and the largest of all the leaf cutters are the soldiers that guard entrance and trail. A substantial leaf-cutter colony may reach a population of several million ants. It is probable that foreign queens of the same species are accepted into the nest, thus allowing the colony to survive beyond the lifetime of a single queen.

Only the specific sort of fungus cultivated by the particular ant species will grow in these gardens, although the nests are in moist soil where fungi abound and "weed" fungi are constantly being brought into the gardens on the leaves. It was once thought that the insect farmers had an endless task of weeding such foreign fungi out of their gardens, but it is now known that such weeding is not necessary. However, action by the ants is essential to the success of a crop. If they are removed, the garden begins to deteriorate and is soon overwhelmed by weed fungi. The trick of maintaining a pure fungus culture without constant weeding seems to depend on the saliva the ants work into the compost as they chew it up. It is thought that the saliva contains an antibiotic that inhibits the growth of undesirable fungi. It probably contains a growth-promoter for the right fungus too, for neither it nor the ants can thrive without the other.

THE drudgery which one often associates with the life of the ant is nowhere better demonstrated than among the leaf cutters. Their nests reach gigantic proportions, they lead unvarying lives of endlessly stripping trees of leaves and carrying them back to the nest. Yet the fungus growers have developed a way of life that confers benefits enjoyed by few other insects. They exploit a food source for which there is little competition and they have achieved the same self-sufficiency in foodstuffs that the human farmer enjoys. They have also accomplished something few other living creatures have done: they gather a raw material available in large quantities—leaves—in order to obtain an end product—food. Thus they need harvest only the abundant leaves of the forest, neither risking a loss of population on hunting expeditions nor posing a threat to other insects. The leaf cutters never come into conflict with the army ants, the other dominant group of ants in the New World tropics and semitropics, although ants of both kinds may reside temporarily side by side.

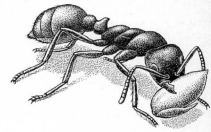

SEED COLLECTORS

Many ants, known as harvesters, live by gathering seeds. Shown above is the Texas harvester, the largest of its kind, and a hoarder of great quantities of small seeds in storerooms in its mound. If these seeds should sprout, they are dumped outside the nest, where they grow and provide more seeds for the ant. The bite of the Texas harvester is painful to humans.

FUNGUS GROWERS

A medium-sized reddish ant, the fungus grower, or leaf cutter, common from Texas to North Carolina, builds mound-like nests a foot wide. It lives by chewing up leaves into a mulch and then cultivating a kind of fungus on the mulch, eating small bulbs put out by the fungus. The fungus can be cultured but will not put out bulbs unless it is tended by the ants.

THIEVES AND BEGGARS

These are tiny yellowish ants, found in eastern and central states. They live underground, often in the nests of other ants, making small subsidiary tunnels that their larger hosts cannot enter. In many nests they are tolerated although they live by killing their hosts' helpless larvae and pupae. Today they are common scavengers for food scraps and dead insects in houses.

STORERS OF HONEY

These are ants of the Southwest desert. They have dark abdomens and yellowish or brownish heads. Because of the aridness of their environment, they have worked out a way of storing sweet juices during good times in the flexible bodies of certain young workers. These workers swell and swell, as nectar is poured into them by foragers, reaching maximum size in about a month.

SLAVE MAKERS

Slave makers live by making off with the eggs and larvae of other ants, and rearing them to do their work for them. They campaign by surrounding an anthill and making small attacks on it. The ants inside try to shore up its defenses while getting ready for a mass escape. As they come out the slavers fall on them and carry off their young, killing only when they have to.

The army ants are abundant in tropical America and Africa (where they are known as driver ants), and a few species exist as far north as Colorado and North Carolina. They are the antithesis of the leaf cutters—carnivores and nomads. They have no permanent place of residence but live off the land they ravage. Their nest, or bivouac, is a seething cluster of their own bodies, as many as 150,000 ants, with spaces between their hooked legs forming chambers for the queen and brood. The cluster may be protected inside a hollow tree or simply hang from a branch.

Some species of army ants, as they set off on a hunt, follow a close column formation, while others advance along a wide front. As the army moves out from the bivouac, it branches and rebranches, outflanking and encircling prey. The battalions may eventually cover three quarters of the territory within a radius of a hundred yards of the nest. "Wherever they pass, all the rest of the animal world is thrown into a state of alarm," wrote the naturalist Henry Walter Bates, who explored in Brazil about a hundred years ago. "They stream along the ground and climb . . . all the lower trees. . . .Where booty is plentiful, they concentrate all their forces upon it, the dense phalanx of shining and quickly moving bodies, as it spreads over the surface, looking like a flood of dark-red liquid. All soft-bodied and inactive insects fall an easy prey to them, and they tear their victims in pieces for facility in carriage. Then, gathering together again in marching order, onward they move, the margins of the phalanx spread out at times like a cloud of skirmishers from the flanks of an army."

THOSE who have watched army ants flanking and enveloping prey and organizing their forces with what appears to be insect generalship are inclined to credit these insects with an intelligence they do not possess. For example, in the vanguard of the advancing wave and deployed along the sides of the trails are the soldiers with their huge jaws; behind them are the medium-sized workers, and in the center are the smallest workers, transporting the brood. It has been claimed that this is a disciplined army, but the marshaling of the troops is more a matter of accident. The soldiers are not intentionally placed at the flanks and vanguard but arrive there because they are unable to find footing among the bustling mass of their little sisters. They are pushed to the sides and front, an action that also happens to have the advantage of putting the most formidable ants in the most useful positions.

Nor are the army ants' flanking movements, which result in the surrounding of prey, the consequence of astute leadership. The ants in the forefront of the advancing wave are often called the "skirmishers," but their behavior hardly justifies such a bellicose title. As the column starts out from the bivouac, the ants in front set up a chemical trail that is followed slavishly by the rest. However, the skirmishers never venture more than a few inches into the scent-free territory ahead. They make a brief sally ahead, thus laying down an odor trail, then rush quickly back to the column. It is this hesitant advance that results in flanking movements. As the rest of the army bunches up behind the skirmishers, the continual pressure of new arrivals pushes some of the ants in the forefront to one side. The result is a wing that moves off to the flank. This movement temporarily relieves the pressure on one side of the forefront but the pressure of the advancing column is soon felt on the other side. A wing forms there also, producing another flank. This continual branching and rebranching of forces—due more to timidity than to ferocity, if judged in human terms—sometimes results in a milling swarm 16 yards wide. Such disorderly behavior, however, confers an advantage on the ants: prey is literally engulfed by the advance and mopped up by the ants following behind.

Should some unusual event befall an army-ant legion, its capacity for response is limited. The irregular terrain in the tropical forest normally prevents the army's advance guard from making a full circle and thus accidentally hitching onto the odor trail at the rear of its own column. But on a sidewalk in Panama, where rains washed the odor trail away, a column once became separated from its main army. The column described a circle by accident and thereafter followed that circular trail. The ants continued on the march, their pace slowing down as they became weaker, until they all died.

ONE might logically think that army ants march because all the food in the vicinity of their bivouac is gone and they are forced to push on to virgin territory. But this is not so: at the same time that one army abandons its area and takes to ravaging the countryside, another army may bivouac in the abandoned territory and profitably hunt there. The fact is that army ants have a regular rhythm of marching, hunting and resting, of bivouacs made and bivouacs broken. In one South American species that has been closely studied, the rhythm consists of a 17-day nomadic phase, during which the army spends each night in a different place, and a static phase, lasting 19 or 20 days, when the ants remain in a fixed bivouac.

This rhythm coincides with the reproductive cycle of the army-ant queen. Unlike other social insects, this queen does not lay its eggs steadily, but rather in enormous batches at intervals of about a month. The army goes into bivouac when the larvae it has been transporting and feeding start to spin their cocoons. While these larvae are pupating, there are none to feed but the adult ants, and the foraging raids dwindle. After the army has bivouacked for about a week, the queen's abdomen is swollen to perhaps five times its normal size and egg-laying begins—upward of 25,000 eggs in a week. The eggs hatch in a few days, and the daily raids increase in order to feed the new batch of larvae. By about the 19th day after entering the static phase, the thousands of larvae that had entered their pupal stage at the beginning of the phase start to emerge from their cocoons as adult ants. It is then that the army breaks camp and enters its 17 days of nomadism, carrying the new brood of larvae with it.

It is no common-sense realization that more food will be needed for the new batch of young that spurs the army ants to abandon their bivouac. Instead, at about the time that the new batch of eggs hatches, the generation maturing in its cocoons starts moving inside these silken coverings. The older workers become excited by the movement and aid the new recruits in breaking out of the cocoons. They also lick the recruits and thus obtain from them some exudation that excites the colony and sets it off on its phase of restless wandering. As these new recruits mature and their skin hardens, they become less stimulating to their older sisters. At this same time, however, the army is stimulated by the young larvae, for these immature ants also exude some flavorsome secretion that excites the adults. It is this substance, rather than a knowledge of the need for more food, that keeps the ants on the move. But as soon as the larvae mature to the point of pupation and enter their cocoons, this stimulation disappears— the ants bivouac and remain until the exudations of the new recruits and the new larvae stimulate them to move once again.

"The ants' most dangerous enemies are other ants, just as man's most dangerous enemies are other men," wrote Auguste Forel, a pioneer psychiatrist who

ANT WORLD IMPERIALISTS

The voracious Argentine ant is a small, aggressive species which has developed extremely effective fighting tactics. When in combat, the ants surround their enemy—often many times their own size—keeping well out of reach of its dangerous mandibles (top). Suddenly, one ant rushes in and grabs a leg. Others quickly follow and bite off the legs (center). With the victim immobilized, the ants dismember it at once (bottom). Slowly migrating throughout the world, imperialistic Argentine ants are methodically wiping out other species of ants wherever they meet.

was also a pioneer observer of ant behavior. Ant battles, even between colonies of the same species, are carnages terrible to behold. The ants seem constantly girded for warfare, and casual observers have thought that they post sentinels to guard their nests and foraging territory. These supposed sentinels are easily recognized: their antennae are laid back, their legs drawn close, their bodies pressed tightly against the earth. They remain motionless for hours. But these are not sentries wisely posted by the nest; they are ants exhibiting a little-known characteristic of ants—their laziness. Contrary to popular belief, ants are not always hard at work. The supposed sentinel position is actually a posture of rest that ants often assume shortly after leaving the security of the nest or venturing beyond familiar foraging grounds. These loafing and probably rather timid ants are only accidentally of benefit to the community. They serve the nest simply by being dispersed widely around the territory. If foreign ants invade, the action may excite some solitary loafer enough to arouse the rest of the community.

TOGETHER with the harvesters and the fungus growers, the ants that have achieved the highest degree of social organization are those that derive the major part of their food from the little aphids that feed on the juices of plant stems, leaves and roots. Aphids are among the most defenseless of all insects. They are small, soft-bodied and weak. But they have one characteristic that has stood them in good stead for millions of years. They suck more fluid from plants than they need, and this surplus oozes out of their bodies in the form of a sweet excretion known as honeydew. This is overwhelmingly attractive to ants and over millions of years many kinds of ants and aphids have developed a sort of mutual accommodation. The ant strokes the aphid and is rewarded with a bit of honeydew, either in the form of a tiny jet or in a droplet collected at the end of the aphid's abdomen. In return, the aphid enjoys a bodyguard of attendant ants that may well keep away numerous predatory insects.

Although the evidence that an intimate bond exists between certain aphids and certain ants is fairly clear, the ants' capacity for animal husbandry has been much exaggerated. Ants do not herd the aphids like cattle. The aphids form herds of their own, sometimes numbering 80 to 100 individuals, whether or not ants are present. The ants merely locate these aggregations and take advantage of them. Nor do the ants put the aphids out to pasture, except in the case of a few ant species. Usually when an ant is observed carrying an aphid off in its jaws, the ant is not taking the aphid to greener pastures but bringing it back to the nest to be used for meat rather than sugar.

In the same way, ants are credited with building corrals of mud or plant fibers around their aphid herds and defending these enclosures from attack by other insects. This observation is correct only in part. Ants often build earthen enclosures around any food source—a dead insect or a drop of jam—and they defend such windfalls against theft by bees and flies. That they do the same thing in the case of the aphids, which are just another food source to be guarded, cannot be considered husbandry. In addition to these so-called corrals, ants are thought to build barns—shelters for their aphid cattle. The real purpose of these constructions is probably for the ants' own protection against excessive light or heat. The aphids are protected too, but the ants cannot be assumed to understand this.

The pattern of behavior that ants display in attending, caring for and protecting aphid herds is actually not so different from normal ant behavior as might be thought. Ants usually tap each other with their antennae, caress each other and exchange droplets of liquid—much as they do with aphids. They treat the aphids—a source of sweet secretions—much as they treat their own larvae and other workers that are also food sources. The aphids are thus protected and moved about in the same way that the ants protect and move about their own larvae. Even in the case of a few ant species that appear remarkable because they bring aphid eggs into their nests for the winter, the aphids are treated no differently than the ants' own broods.

Some ants carry the collection of sweet liquids a step farther than do the aphid-tenders; they bottle it. The so-called honeypot ants store in the bodies of their own workers a sugary liquid obtained from aphids and other insects and from the exudations of oak galls. The workers selected for this task become living tanks, their abdomens so swollen that they are practically globular. The inflated creatures can scarcely move; they spend their lives hanging from the roughened ceilings of their chambers. The honeypot ants have been acclaimed for their foresight in establishing reserves against seasonal droughts. Using some of their number as living storage tanks undoubtedly confers benefits upon these species, but the action did not arise from foresight on the part of the ants. They have merely perfected the common ability of all ants to carry food home in a distensible crop—the "social stomach." Even the ants that collect honeydew from aphids are often to be seen struggling homeward bloated with full loads in their social stomachs. At the nest they distribute the food to other members of the colony and their bulging abdomens return to normal size. The honeypot ants probably arose from some such ancestors.

Any young worker in the honeypot ant colony may become a storage tank: the choice is made by accident. A storage place is needed by a returning forager; it gives the liquid to any newly emerged worker nearby. The worker accepts the sweet liquid and soon it is besieged by other returning foragers, all of whom empty their crops into its. The worker's cuticle is capable of immense expansion. Load after load is poured in and the ant fattens enormously.

INSECT "FARMER" AND "COWS"

The "milk" of aphids is actually excreta in the form of sweet liquid drops called honeydew. These drawings show how an aphid responds to an ant's gentle stroking by exuding a globule of honeydew which the larger insect immediately consumes. When neglected, the aphid must excrete the honeydew anyway. It falls on a leaf or twig and is later eaten by an ant.

THERE has been a persistent notion that the society of ants is governed by some mystic laws of the community. How else, one wonders, could the ants divide their tasks and act in concert so efficiently? How do ants "know" that the brood must be cared for, that food is needed, that the queen must be attended to, that work must be done in repairing and enlarging the nest? Careful observation has shown that the ant community does possess leaders—but they are not the dictators commonly imagined. These ants do not go about giving directions or organizing work forces. Rather, they initiate work by example. In each nest, there are certain veteran ants that, even after a winter's hibernation, retain some memory of the old trails and foraging grounds. A small proportion of the workers, otherwise indistinguishable, differs from the majority by being the first to begin work; these ants have been shown by experiment to have a greater ability to learn than most of the individuals in the community. Such ants are known as the "excitement centers," or "work-starters"; they are the individuals in the nest that do their jobs a bit better and more quickly than the other ants. The examples the work-starters set act as stimuli to the other ants and they join in.

Jobs are concluded in the same way that they begin. When a work-starter has been at some task for a long time and is tiring, the ant constitutes less of a stimulus to draw other ants into the work and to keep them at it. The routine workers drift off, leaving the nearly completed task to be finished by a few remaining individuals.

Almost everyone has observed that food left on a picnic cloth is soon found by a scouting ant; in a little while this ant returns, accompanied by its nestmates. Obviously there was some way in which the scouting ant was able to communicate its discovery. It has recently been learned that several ant species possess the ability both to produce and perceive sounds. These sounds not only seem to be distinctive for each species but also for the different castes of a single species. Further study may reveal that such sounds play a part in ant communication. Even now, it is known that—regardless of sound—ants can readily communicate unspecific excitement. A scout returning to the nest will peck other ants on the thorax or abdomen, and strike them with its antennae, forelegs and head. If the find is a particularly large one, the scout may even give an ant danger signal—running about in great excitement with jaws open or abdomen held high. These actions set the other ants bustling. Proof that they do not mysteriously understand the cause of the excitement to be a discovery of food is the fact that they take up whatever tasks are at hand. Some start repairing the nest; others take care of the brood. But some of the agitated ants spurt out of the nest in all directions and, inevitably, a few of them find the food source.

Some of the more advanced ants have gone farther than this. The returning scout lays down a scent trail by pressing its abdomen to the ground. The scent lasts only a few minutes, but this is long enough for alerted ants from the nest to follow the trail and find the food source. If these ants are unable to carry all of the food home by themselves, they refresh the trail scent as they return to the nest to summon further aid.

Studies of ant behavior have made it increasingly evident that little of what these insects do can be called intelligent action when measured by human standards. At the same time, few students would agree with Mark Twain who called ants "the dumbest of all animals." Ants stand near, if not at, the pinnacle of invertebrate development. Small as they are when compared with man, they display memory, learning and the ability to correct mistakes. Yet these faint glimmers of intelligence are strait-jacketed inside stereotyped patterns of behavior that often make the ant appear inexplicably stupid. They possess no mystical abilities, as early observers of insects used to claim, nor is there any such thing as a "soul" in the nest of a social insect.

NEARLY 2,000 years ago, the Roman naturalist Pliny explained the rain of honeydew from summer trees as one of three things: the sweat of the heavens, the saliva of the stars or a liquid provided by the purgation of the air. He also believed that insects lacked blood and that a giant ant, "the color of a cat and as large as an Egyptian wolf," mined gold in the mountains north of India. Today no one believes such legends and traveler's tales about insects, but other notions that are just as foolish have persisted. The bizarre and curious insect is still often admired for the wrong reasons—the "wisdom" of the ant, the "industry" of the bee, the "angry" sting of the wasp. The insect does not become any less fascinating because it is motivated by hormone rather than foresight, and cares for its brood not for human reasons but because of the secretions it can lick from the larvae. Just as intelligence blossoms most fully in man, insects can continue to be admired for exhibiting the fullest flowering of complex stimulus-controlled activity in the animal kingdom. Even shorn of all mystery, insects continue to be an abiding source of fascination to man.

HONEYPOT ANTS, CHOSEN BY THEIR FELLOW WORKERS TO ACT AS NECTAR TANKS, SPEND LIFE HANGING HEAVY-BELLIED FROM THE NEST ROOF

The Societies of Ants

Through highly evolved nerves and chemistry, a few insects like termites, wasps and ants have come to pool their tiny brains and teeming numbers in complex societies, rivaling those of man himself. Ant communities take thought for the morrow in food stockpiles like the living honeypots above. They also hunt, herd and farm with uncanny organization, as is shown on the following pages.

A JANITOR ANT blocks the entry to its nest with its immensely enlarged, perfectly camouflaged head. When one of its worker-sisters wants to go in or out, the janitor uncorks the opening only for an instant before concealing it again. Though technically soldiers, the janitors seldom fight but use their massive mandibles mainly to dismember quarry caught by the workers.

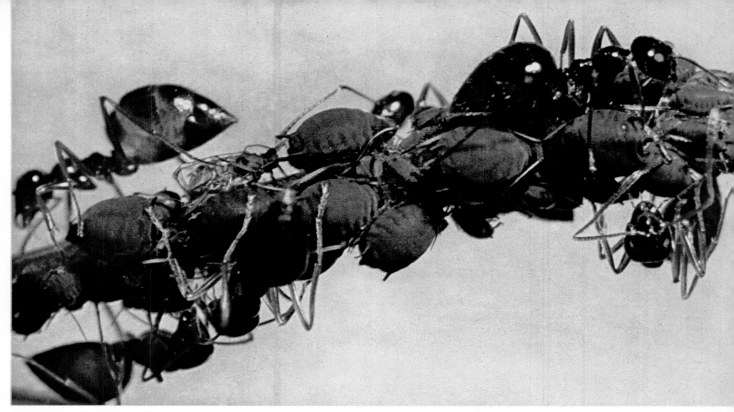

GARDEN VARIETY FORMICA ANTS TEND APHIDS ON A TWIG. THEY MILK THE APHIDS OF HONEYDEW BY STROKING THEM WITH THEIR ANTENNAE

Ants of Many Skills

All ant societies are divided into three castes: queens that found new colonies and thereafter function as egg-laying machines; winged males that take a nuptial flight once with a queen, fertilizing her for life, and thereafter die; and runt sterile females that lead tirelessly neuter lives drudging away at an amazing variety of skilled chores needed by the community. Some act as nurses, some as housekeepers, some as hunters or even soldiers. The highly specialized janitor ant worker opposite lends its head as a door to disguise and guard the home its fellows excavate in a trunk or twig.

Workers of several "dairying" species of ant like those above and at right herd and milk various small insects that pay for protection by giving off sweet honeydew. The honeypot workers on the preceding page offer themselves as community storage silos. Harvester ant workers practice an instinctive, robot agriculture by the reaping and storing of plant seeds. Weaver ants may even be said to use tools, for they wield their own silk-extruding larvae to sew together the delicate shelters that they construct from leaves.

TROPICAL DAIRY ANTS sheep-dog a herd of honey-giving tree hoppers and their white nymphs as they browse on some young red leaves in the South American rain forest.

A BRISTLING HORDE OF ARMY ANTS MARCHES ALONG A BRANCH, WORKERS CLUSTERING TO FORM A SHELTER FOR THE BROOD AND QUEEN

ARMY-ANT NURSES on the march carry larvae while soldiers and workers race about on the flanks of the column, bringing food and sharing in the larvae's much-sought-after secretions.

AN ARMY-ANT SOLDIER advances with sickle-shaped mandibles on the ready. Whatever it encounters it attacks. Whatever it kills is cut up and carried off by small, second-rank workers.

Specialists in Carnage

In tropical forests all over the world the unchallenged lord of the insect realm is the blind, carnivorous army ant. When an army-ant colony marches, 10,000 to 100,000 strong, it kills every animal that remains in its path save a few specially endowed exceptions like the stink bug. So formidable are the mandibles of its soldiers that they have been known to reduce comatose pythons and tethered horses to bare skeletons in a matter of hours.

The most common genus of army ant in the Western Hemisphere is *Eciton*, pictured here. *Eciton* colonies march by night and stop to camp and forage in daylight. Each of their rampages normally lasts for 17 days. Then they settle down and bivouac quietly for 19 or 20 days, while one generation of larvae spins cocoons and pupates and the next hatches from eggs. During marching periods, the larvae are carried and fattened up for metamorphosis by special nurse workers. The larvae, in return, secrete stimulating juices which are lapped up and stored by the nurses for later regurgitation and distribution to members of the other castes—the workers and soldiers back from foraging forays. In this way the larvae's secretions reach the entire colony and goad it on to kill more food. Then, as the larvae are ready to pupate and stop eating, the secretions dry up and the colony calms down and bivouacs.

THE ACROBATIC WORKERS of *Eciton* army ants interlock their legs during bivouac and array themselves in networks and galleries to form a living edifice around the queen and brood. This puts a tremendous strain on the legs and joints of the ants at the top, but they are built to withstand many hundred times their own weight, and support the whole colony without difficulty.

LEAF-CUTTER ANTS STRIP FOLIAGE FROM A TREE TO CARRY IT OFF IN PROCESSION AS FERTILIZER FOR THEIR SUBTERRANEAN FUNGUS GARDENS

Farmer Ants That Grow Underground Crops

Army ants hunt with spartan efficiency, dairying ants are often found living on their "herds" of other insects, but the leaf-cutting ants shown on these pages subsist entirely on vegetation and agriculture. They create their own food by cultivating mushroom gardens within subterranean nests that penetrate one to 15 feet underground and spread over many yards. By this mode of life leaf cutters avoid competition with all other kinds of ants and survive attack from predators by sheer prosperity—the numerical superiority of their farming communities.

All through the tropical forests of South and Central America they can be seen stripping the leaves from trees, dropping or carrying them to the ground and then transporting them to their nests like so many bobbing regattas of green-sailed small craft. Below ground they chew up the leaves and use the mulch to fertilize their one all-purpose crop, a nutritious fungus. The fungus has been cultivated by the ants for millions of years and it is seldom found growing wild. Each young leaf-cutter queen brings some to be planted in the first tunnel it digs for a new colony.

IN AN EXPERIMENT TO DETERMINE HOW FAST LEAF CUTTERS WORK, ONE ANT DISCOVERS A ROSE AND CARRIES A PETAL OFF TOWARD THE NEST

TEN MINUTES LATER FELLOW WORKERS OF THE ANT HAVE ARRIVED IN FORCE AND 20 MINUTES LATER (BELOW) THE ROSE HAS BEEN RAVAGED

In "Kisses" a Complex Chemical Language

All the seeming intelligence of ant society—the tactics of the fighters and husbandry of the farmers—is achieved through the social act demonstrated below: a sort of kiss called trophallaxis. During the "kiss," one or both of the ants gives the other a taste of the chemicals it has in its crop. The crop is a special community organ separate from the individual's digestive stomach. The chemicals stored in it are complex mixtures, modified by each new "kiss" but originating mainly in secretions given off by the lar-

ENGAGED IN THE PLEASURE OF TROPHALLAXIS, TWO EUROPEAN MOUND-BUILDERS SWAP SOME INFORMATION ABOUT THE REST OF THE NEST IN A

vae and eggs of the colony. The composition of the mixture constitutes a chemical message which acts on the simple hereditary nervous system of an ant to communicate the needs and excitements of its society and tell the insect what it should be doing.

MOUTH-TO-MOUTH EXCHANGE OF "MESSAGES" STORED IN THEIR CROPS

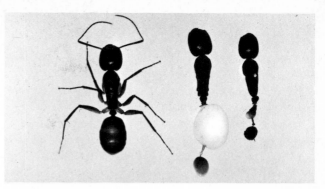

THE TWO-STOMACHED ANT stores community food in its elastic crop (distended in the dissected ant at center) and digests food for its own use in the small sac below it *(center and right)*.

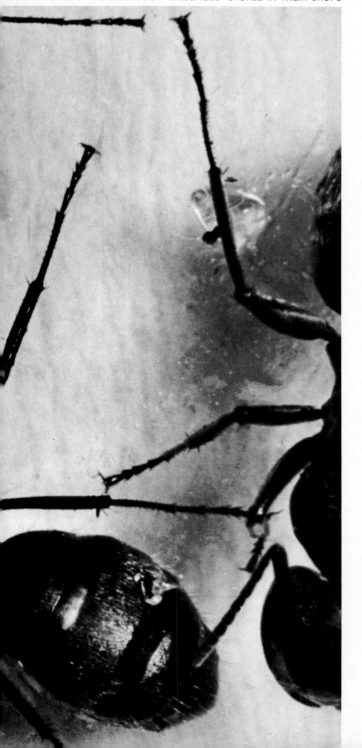

DECOCOONING A YOUNG ANT, two nurse workers rend a seam in the pupal silk. Their excited tugging began when they smelled secretions from the ant inside, signaling "I want out."

179

The Credentials of a Queen

Founding a new ant nest of any species is as arduous an act of maternal heroism as any in the animal world. Young queens, superfluous in their own parental nest, take to the air, unprotected from predators, and stay on the wing until searching males of the same species find them and fill their organs with sperm, which is stored to fertilize their future eggs. Once fertilized, a queen alights, builds a nest, lays eggs, feeds the hatched larvae with its own stored food and dwindling strength, and finally lies back while its first small, underfed worker-daughters take charge.

Thereafter the workers tend the young, enlarge the nest, fight the battles and generally keep the queen in clover. Occasionally the queen or a worker lays an unfertilized egg. This hatches into a male ant which goes forth to breed and die. A few eggs hatch out as rival queens, but they in turn leave and found their own nests. Pursuing this routine a queen may live for a dozen years or more and in many species grow until it is a two-inch matriarch.

AN EGG IS LAID by a queen of the mound-building ants. Secretions coming to the surface of the membrane from inside the egg are believed to give the worker proper instructions for rearing it.

SAFE IN THE JAWS of the waiting worker, the egg will be carefully moved from place to place to give it the best exposure to temperature and humidity. Harmful fungi will also be removed.

A Key to the Principal Orders of Insects

This key to the principal orders of insects will tell you whether an insect is one of the flies or one of the true bugs or one of the beetles, for example, but it will not tell you what particular fly or bug or beetle you have in hand. For that, you should consult one of the guides listed in the bibliography *(page 187).*

The key is based on one devised by the British entomologist Harold Oldroyd for his handbook, *Collecting, Preserving and Studying Insects,* and is reproduced here through the courtesy of his publishers, Hutchinson and Company, Ltd., London, together with some of Oldroyd's introductory remarks on insect identification. "We have an insect before us," he says, "—how do we begin to identify it? In practice, three methods are used: *general appearance, spot characters,* and *keys.*

"Identification by *general appearance* means getting to know one's insects by sight. An entomologist will look at an insect and give you a name for it. Ask him how he recognizes it, and he will recite a number of small details that you know he could not have seen with the naked eye. If he were frank, he would say: 'I know it is an *Andrena* because I know *Andrena* by sight, just as I know my uncle by sight.'

"*Spot characters* are the rough-and-ready checks we all use: 'scaly wings?—Lepidoptera; clubbed antennae?—butterfly.' There is no certainty in this method, because other insects may have scaly wings or clubbed antennae, but it gives a clue, and provides a check on memory.

"*Keys* work by a process of elimination, gradually narrowing down the number of possibilities. At each step, keys usually ask you to choose between two alternatives. Thus:

1. Two pairs of membranous wings . . . . see **2**
Only one pair of membranous wings, the other pair being either hardened into wing covers, or absent . . . . see **29**
2. Forewings and hind wings alike. . . . . see **3**
Forewings and hind wings different . . . . see **18**
3. . . . . (and so on).

"If the insect agrees with the first alternative, then read on at numeral 2; if the second alternative is correct, then jump over all the intervening numbers and read on at numeral 29. Go on like this until you come to a final choice:

35. Abdomen with forceps: **DERMAPTERA**
(Earwigs)

36. Abdomen without forceps: **COLEOPTERA**
(Beetles)

If you are lucky this will give a correct identification, but do not be surprised if it does not.

"Remember that a key does not identify the specimen: it only gives a hint of what it might be. The real identification is made by comparing the specimen with another specimen that is already named, or with a drawing, or with a good detailed description."

This key has two parts: the first for insects with wings, and the second for wingless forms.

WINGED INSECTS

1. Insects with four wings (so-called wing covers count as wings) . . . . see **2**
Insects with only two wings . . . . see **18**

2. Wings covered with scales: **LEPIDOPTERA**
(Butterflies and Moths)
Wings without scales, though they may be hairy . . . . see **3**

3. Only the hind wings used for flight; forewings partly or entirely horny or leathery, and cover hind wings . . . . see **4**
Both pairs membranous and used for flight . . . . see **7**

4. Mouth parts tubelike, adapted for piercing and sucking: **HEMIPTERA and Some HOMOPTERA**
(True Bugs)
Mouth parts adapted for biting and chewing . . . . see **5**

STINK BUG

5. Forewings with veins like hind wings, though stiffer, and covering hind wings: **ORTHOPTERA**
(Grasshoppers, Crickets, Katydids, Cockroaches, Mantids, Walking Sticks)
Forewings without veins; modified into hard, horny covers for hind wings . . . . see **6**

6. Forewings short. Tip of abdomen with characteristic pair of forceps: **DERMAPTERA**
(Earwigs)

EARWIG

Forewings nearly always long, covering abdomen and enclosing hind wings; if wings are short, no forceps: **COLEOPTERA**
(Beetles)

7. Wings narrow; without veins, but fringed with long hairs. Very small insects, less than ¼ inch long: **THYSANOPTERA**
(Thrips)

BEAN THRIPS

Wings more fully developed and with veins present . . . . . . see **8**

8. Hind wings much smaller than forewings . . . . see **9**
Hind wings similar in size to forewings . . . . see **13**

9. Forewings with a large number of cross veins, making

Insect Key, *continued*

a netlike pattern. Abdomen with two or three long "tails":
EPHEMEROPTERA
(Mayflies)

MAYFLY

Forewings with fewer veins, not forming a netlike pattern. Usually without "tails" . . . . . see **10**

10. Wings obviously hairy. Mouth parts very small, except for palps: **TRICHOPTERA**
(Caddisflies)

CADDISFLY

Wings not obviously hairy, though tiny hairs can be seen under the microscope. Mouth parts well-developed . . . . . . see **11**

11. Mouth parts tubelike, adapted for sucking: **HOMOPTERA**
(Aphids, Leafhoppers, Plant Lice, Scale Insects, Cicadas)
Mouth parts not tubelike, but adapted for chewing . . . . see **12**

12. Very small insects, soft-bodied, mostly less than ¼ inch in length. Tip of leg bearing only two or three segments:
PSOCOPTERA
(Booklice)
Often much bigger, wasp-like or beelike insects; or if very small, then hard-bodied, with the abdomen narrowed at its base into a petiole, or "waist." Tip of leg bearing four or five segments: **HYMENOPTERA**
(Bees, Wasps, Ants, Sawflies)

13. Tip of leg bearing three or four segments . . . . see **14**
Tip of leg bearing five segments . . . . see **16**

14. Wings with few cross veins, and with hind wings greatly expanded toward the wing tip:
PLECOPTERA
(Stoneflies)

Fore- and hind wings very similar in shape; or if hind wings are expanded toward the tip, cross veins are much more numerous . . . . . see **15**

15. Small insects, generally less than half an inch long, with long antennae, and with wings folded flat over the body:
ISOPTERA
(Termites)

Generally longer than an inch, with very short antennae. Wings held away from the body even at rest: **ODONATA**
(Damselflies and Dragonflies)

16. Along foremargin of wings there are very few cross veins. Mouth parts are prolonged into a beak: **MECOPTERA**
(Scorpionflies)

SCORPIONFLY

Along foremargin of wings are a number of cross veins. Mouth parts short . . . . see **17**

17. Hind wings broader than forewings, at any rate at the base. At rest, this area is folded like a fan: **MEGALOPTERA**
(Alderflies, Dobsonflies)
Hind wings similar to forewings, without this fanlike area: **NEUROPTERA**
(Lacewings, Snakeflies)

LACEWING

18. Forewings only; hind wings reduced to knoblike organs known as halteres. Mouth parts either tubelike, for piercing, or spongelike, for sucking: **DIPTERA**
(True Flies)
Hind wings entirely absent; no halteres: **EPHEMEROPTERA**
(Some Mayflies)

WINGLESS INSECTS

1. Some segments with jointed legs, which can be moved . . . . see **2**

No jointed legs; or if these are present and can be seen, they are enclosed in membrane and cannot move . . . . see **16** and after.

2. Parasites, living on warm-blooded animals or closely associated with them . . . . see **3**
Not parasitic on warm-blooded animals: either free-living, or parasitic on insects, snails, etc. . . . . see **8**

3. Body flattened from side to side, hard and bristly, with strong legs. Jumping insects; parasites found living on birds and mammals:
SIPHONAPTERA
(Fleas)

FLEA

Body either rounded or flattened from above; not jumping insects . . . . see **4**

4. Mouth parts adapted for chewing . . . . see **5**
Mouth parts adapted for sucking . . . . see **6**

5. Rear of abdomen bears forceps. Found on bats and small rodents; tropical:
DERMAPTERA
(Parasitic Earwigs)
No forceps. Found on birds or mammals. Worldwide:
MALLOPHAGA
(Chewing Lice)

6. Flattened; rather spiderlike in appearance, with head fitting into a notch on thorax, and with the antennae hidden. Claws hooked: **DIPTERA**
(Louse Flies, Sheep Ticks)

SHEEP TICK

Not spiderlike. Antennae clearly visible . . . . see **7**

7. Snout short, unjointed; body long and narrow. Tips of legs bearing one large hooked claw. Permanent parasites of mammals: **ANOPLURA**
(Sucking Lice)

BODY LOUSE

Snout longer, jointed; body more oval. Tips of legs with two small claws, not hooklike. Only temporary parasites: **HEMIPTERA**
(Wingless Bugs)

BED BUG

8. Terrestrial: living on dry land or on animals other than mammals and birds . . . . . see **9**
  Aquatic: mostly nymphal forms of land insects. . . . . . see **29**

9. Mouth parts not visible; appendages on some abdominal segments or with a forked "spring" near tip . . . . see **10**
  Mouth parts visible . . . . . . see **11**

10. Abdomen with six segments or fewer, usually with a forked "spring" near tip. No long bristles at tip: **COLLEMBOLA**
(Springtails)

SPRINGTAIL

Abdomen with nine or more segments; no spring. Several segments have simple appendages. Long, bristlelike extensions at the tip of the abdomen: **THYSANURA**
(Bristletails)

11. Sucking mouth parts . . . . see **12**
  Chewing mouth parts . . . . . see **16**

12. Body covered with scales or dense hairs: **LEPIDOPTERA**
(Wingless Moths)

FALL CANKERWORM

Body bare or with few scattered hairs . . . . see **13**

13. Almost whole of thorax visible from above is composed of the middle segments, or mesothorax. Prothorax and metathorax both small and hidden: **DIPTERA**
(Wingless Flies)
  Mesothorax and metathorax about equally developed. Prothorax also is usually visible from above . . . . see **14**

14. Snout small and cone-shaped. Body long and narrow. Claws usually absent: **THYSANOPTERA**
(Wingless Thrips)
  Snout longer, jointed. Body more or less oval. Claws present . . . . see **15**

15. Proboscis arising from front part of head. Abdomen without hornlike protrusions at or near the tip: **HEMIPTERA**
(Wingless Bugs)
  Proboscis arising from hind part of head. Abdomen often with two hornlike protrusions at or near tip: **HOMOPTERA**
(Wingless Aphids)

16. Abdomen with false legs, fleshy and different from jointed legs of the thorax; caterpillarlike forms . . . . see **17**
  Abdomen without legs . . . . see **19**

17. Five pairs of false legs or fewer, with none on the first or second abdominal segments; false legs have minute hooks on their margins: **LEPIDOPTERA**
(Caterpillars of Moths and Butterflies)
  Six to 10 pairs of false legs and always one pair on the *second* abdominal segment; no hooks present. . . . . see **18**

18. Head with a single small eye on each side: **HYMENOPTERA**
(Larvae of Sawflies)

SAWFLY LARVA

Head with several small eyes on each side: **MECOPTERA**
(Larvae of Scorpionflies)

19. Antennae short and indistinct; larvae. . . . . see **20**
  Antennae long and distinct; adult insects . . . . see **22**

20. Body caterpillarlike . . . . . see **21**
  Body not caterpillarlike:
    Larvae of Some **NEUROPTERA**
    and Many **COLEOPTERA**

21. Head with six small eyes on each side:
    Caterpillars of Some **LEPIDOPTERA**
  Head with more than six small eyes:
    Larvae of Some **MECOPTERA**

22. Abdomen with forceps at tip: **DERMAPTERA**
(Nymphs of Earwigs)
  Abdomen without such forceps . . . . see **23**

23. Abdomen strongly pinched at base into a "waist." Sometimes the antennae are bent into an elbow: **HYMENOPTERA**
(Ants and Wingless Wasps)

WINGLESS WASP

Abdomen not constricted into a waist . . . . see **24**

24. Head prolonged underneath body into a long beak, which bears mandibles at its tip: **MECOPTERA**
(Wingless Scorpionflies)
  Head not prolonged into a beak . . . . see **25**

25. Tiny, soft insects . . . . . see **26**
  Fairly small to very big, usually hard-bodied insects . . . see **27**

26. No processes at tip of abdomen: **PSOCOPTERA**
(Booklice)
  Processes at tip of abdomen: **ZORAPTERA**
(No Popular Name)

27. Hind legs enlarged for jumping: **ORTHOPTERA**
(Nymphs of Grasshoppers and Crickets)
  Hind legs not enlarged for jumping . . . . see **28**

28. Tips of legs bearing four segments. Pale, soft-bodied insects living in wood or soil:

ISOPTERA
(Termites)

TERMITE

Tips of legs bearing five segments. More highly colored insects, living in the open or domestically, but not in wood: **ORTHOPTERA**

(Nymphs of Cockroaches, Stick Insects, Leaf Insects)

29. Mouth parts adapted for piercing:

Nymphs of Water Bugs—
HEMIPTERA—
and Larvae of Some
NEUROPTERA

Mouth parts adapted for licking and chewing . . . . . . see **30**

30. Body enclosed in a case made of pebbles, sand or debris:

TRICHOPTERA
(Larvae of Caddisflies)

Not living in such a case . . . . see **31**

31. Abdomen exhibiting external gills . . . . see **32**
Abdomen without external gills . . . . see **35**

32. Two or three long processes at tip of abdomen. Trace of wing covers in older nymphs . . see **33**
Never more than two processes at tip of abdomen. No wing covers: **MEGALOPTERA**

(Larvae of Alderflies)

33. Three long processes at tip of abdomen . . . . see **34**
Two processes: **PLECOPTERA**

(Nymphs of Some Stoneflies)

34. Head with "mask" below, capable of extending forward:

ODONATA
(Nymphs of Damselflies)

Head without "mask":

EPHEMEROPTERA
(Nymphs of Mayflies)

MAYFLY NYMPH

35. Head with a "mask" below, capable of extending forward:

ODONATA
(Nymphs of Dragonflies)

Head without "mask" . . . . . . see **36**

36. With long antennae, and long filaments at tip of abdomen:

PLECOPTERA
(Nymphs of Some Stoneflies)

Without filaments: **COLEOPTERA**
(Larvae of Beetles)

Picture Credits

Credits for pictures from left to right are separated by commas, top to bottom by dashes.

Cover: Hermann Eisenbeiss from Photo Researchers, Inc. 8: Dr. Roman Vishniac. 10: Stephen Rogers Peck. 12,13: Matt Greene. 15: Enid Kotchnig, based on a drawing in *Principles of Insect Morphology*, by R. E. Snodgrass, McGraw-Hill Book Company, Inc., 1935. 17: Dr. Ralph Buchsbaum. 18,19,20: Paintings by Antonio Petruccelli. 21: David C. Stager—Dr. Roman Vishniac. 22,23: Dr. Edward S. Ross, Dr. Eliot F. Porter—Dr. Alexander B. Klots, Dr. Edward S. Ross (2), Dr. Alexander B. Klots, Dr. Edward S. Ross, S.E.F. from Photo Researchers, Inc. 24: Hermann Eisenbeiss from Photo Researchers, Inc. 25: S. Beaufoy, H. Lou Gibson—S. Beaufoy—Dr. Alexander B. Klots. 26: Dr. Alexander B. Klots. 27: Birnbach Publishing Service—Robert E. Lunt from Annan Photo Service—Rudolf Freund. 28,29: N. E. Beck Jr. from National Audubon Society, Dr. Alexander B. Klots—Andreas Feininger, Dr. Alexander B. Klots. 30: Left Marjorie Favreau—David C. Stager; right Peter Stackpole—Lee Passmore and F. E. Beck—Dr. Ralph Buchsbaum. 31: Dr. Alexander B. Klots. 32: Andreas Feininger. 34: Matt Greene. 36,37: Gaetano Di Palma. 38,39: Frances W. Zweifel. 41: George V. Kelvin. 43: Dr. William H. Amos. 44,45: Paintings by Mel Hunter. 46: Dr. Alexander B. Klots. 47: Andreas Feininger. 48: Dr. William H. Amos. 49: Stephen Collins from Photo Researchers, Inc.—Dr. William H. Amos. 50: Andreas Feininger. 51,52,53: Dr. Roman Vishniac. 54: Dr. Alexander B. Klots. 56,57: Frances W. Zweifel. 60: Su Zan Noguchi Swain. 63: Andreas Feininger. 64 through 69: Dr. Roman Vishniac. 70: Dr. Alexander B. Klots except top left Gordon F. Woods; center right Andreas Feininger. 71: Fritz Goro—Sakae Tamura. 72: D. V. from Black Star. 73: Dr. Werner Croy from Black Star. 74,75: Howard Sochurek. 76: Eric Schaal. 80,81: Lowell Hess. 83: Enid Kotschnig. 84: Matt Greene. 85: Enid Kotschnig. 87: John Markham. 88,89: Andreas Feininger, Dr. Ross E. Hutchins. 90,91: Dr. Ross E. Hutchins. 92: Stephen Collins from Photo Researchers, Inc.—Dr. Ross E. Hutchins. 93: Courtesy American Museum of Natural History. 94 through 97: Andreas Feininger. 98: Wallace Kirkland. 99: Andreas Feininger. 100: Lennart Nilsson from Black Star. 102: Frances W. Zweifel. 103: Gaetano Di Palma. 104: Stephen Rogers Peck. 105: Su Zan Noguchi Swain. 109: Andreas Feininger. 110: Dr. Alexander B. Klots, Dmitri Kessel. 111: Dr. Alexander B. Klots except bottom right Dmitri Kessel. 112. 113: Top S. Beaufoy; bottom Dr. Alexander B. Klots. 114: Dr. Alexander B. Klots except bottom Alfred Eisenstaedt. 115: Dr. Alexander B. Klots. 116,117: Andreas Feininger. 118: Brian Brake from Magnum. 119: New Zealand National Publicity Studios. 120. 121: Dr. Thomas Eisner and Dr. Charles Walcott except left Dr. Thomas Eisner. 122: Wallace Kirkland. 124,125: Matt Greene. 127: Lowell Hess. 128: Gaetano Di Palma. 130,131: Matt Greene. 133: Wallace Kirkland. 134: Wilhelm Rebhuhn—Rudolf Freund. 135 through 139: Rudolf Freund. 140: Dr. Alexander B. Klots. 142, 143: Lowell Hess. 144: Su Zan Noguchi Swain. 146,147: Lowell Hess. 149: Dr. Roman Vishniac. 150,151: Alfred Eisenstaedt. Wallace Kirkland. 152: Dr. Syd Radinovsky, Department of Entomology, Oregon State University, Corvallis, Oregon. 153,154: Dr. William H. Amos. 155: J. R. Eyerman, Laurence E. Perkins from Annan Photo Service. 156,157: Dr. Eliot F. Porter, Dr. Louis M. Roth and Dr. E. R. Willis (2)—Dr. Thomas Eisner. 158: Terry Shaw from Annan Photo Service. 159: Sakae Tamura. 160: Courtesy American Museum of Natural History. 164,165,166: Renee Martin. 168,169: Stephen Rogers Peck. 171: Dr. Thomas Eisner and George M. Happ. 172: Dr. Ross E. Hutchins. 173: Dr. Alexander B. Klots from Monkmeyer Press Photos—Alfred Eisenstaedt. 174,175,176: Rudolf Freund. 177: Fritz Goro. 178,179: Dr. Thomas Eisner except bottom right Lennart Nilsson from Black Star. 180,181: Lennart Nilsson from Black Star. 183 through 186: Stephen Rogers Peck. Back Cover: Matt Greene.

Acknowledgments

The editors of this book are particularly indebted to John B. Schmitt, Professor of Entomology, Rutgers University, who read it in its entirety. They are also indebted, for special advice and consultation, to F. M. Carpenter, Professor of Entomology, Harvard University; Elso S. Barghoorn, Professor of Botany, Harvard University; Alexander B. Klots, Professor of Biology, The City College of New York; John C. Pallister, Department of Entomology, The American Museum of Natural History; Thomas Eisner, Assistant Professor of Entomology, Cornell University; James Baird, the Massachusetts Audubon Society; Ross E. Hutchins, entomologist, Mississippi State Plant Board; Edward S. Ross, Curator of Insects, California Academy of Sciences; and William H. Amos, Chairman, Science Department, St. Andrews School, Middletown, Delaware.

The author of the text portion of the book would like to thank in particular a number of entomologists who over the years have contributed greatly to his understanding and appreciation of the insect world and some of whose investigations provided material for this book: John B. Schmitt, Rutgers University; Edward A. Steinhaus, University of California, Berkeley; Edward S. Hodgson, Columbia University; Neely Turner, Connecticut Agricultural Experiment Station; Asher Treat, The City College of New York; Clarence Hoffman, Entomology Research Branch, United States Department of Agriculture; and Roman Vishniac, Yeshiva University.

Bibliography

General Entomology

Borror, Donald J., and Dwight M. Delong, *Introduction to the Study of Insects*. Holt, Rinehart & Winston. 1954.

Comstock, John, *An Introduction to Entomology*. Cornell University Press, 1940.

Fernald, H. T., and Harold H. Shepard, *Applied Entomology*. McGraw-Hill, 1955.

*Frost, S. W., *Insect Life and Insect Natural History*. Dover, 1959.

Gaul, Albro, *Wonderful World of Insects*. Rinehart, 1953.

Imms, A. D., *General Textbook of Entomology*. E. P. Dutton, 1957. *Insect Natural History*. Collins, 1947.

Klots, Alexander B., and Elsie B. Klots, *Living Insects of the World*. Doubleday, 1959. *1001 Questions Answered About Insects*. Dodd, Mead, 1961.

Lutz, Frank E., *A Lot of Insects*. G. P. Putnam's Sons, 1941.

Pesson, Paul, *World of Insects*. McGraw-Hill, 1959.

Schmitt, John B., *General Entomology Laboratory Manual*. College of Agriculture, Rutgers University, 1957.

Anatomy and Physiology

Buchsbaum, Ralph, *Animals Without Backbones: An Introduction to Invertebrates*. University of Chicago Press, 1948.

*Buddenbrock, Wolfgang von, *Senses*. University of Michigan Press, 1958.

Carpenter, F. M., *Geological and Historical Evolution of Insects*. Smithsonian Report, Government Printing Office, 1953.

Haskell, P. T., *Insect Sounds*. Quadrangle, 1961.

*Portmann, Adolf, *Animal Camouflage*. University of Michigan Press, 1959.

Pringle, J.W.S., *Insect Flight*. Cambridge University Press, London, 1957.

Roeder, Kenneth D., ed., *Insect Physiology*. John Wiley & Sons, 1953.

Snodgrass, Robert E., *Principles of Insect Morphology*. McGraw-Hill, 1935.

Wigglesworth, Vincent B., *Insect Physiology*. John Wiley & Sons, 1956.

Social Insects

Butler, Colin G., *Honey Bee, an Introduction to Her Sense-Physiology and Behavior*. Oxford University Press, 1949.

Free, John B., and Colin G. Butler, *Bumblebees*. Macmillan. 1959.

*Frisch, Karl von, *Dancing Bees*. Methuen, 1954.

*Goetsch, Wilhelm, *Ants*. University of Michigan Press, 1957.

Haskins, Caryl P., *Of Ants and Men*. Prentice-Hall, 1945.

Lindauer, Martin, *Communication Among Social Bees*. Harvard University Press, 1961.

Maeterlinck, Maurice, *Life of the Ant*. Blue Ribbon, 1930. *Life of the Bee*. Dodd, Mead, 1928. *Life of the White Ant*. Dodd, Mead, 1939.

Michener, Charles D., and Mary H. Michener, *American Social Insect*. Van Nostrand, 1951.

†Morley, Derek Wragge, *Ant World*. Penguin, 1953.

Peckham, G. W., and E. G. Peckham, *Wasps, Social and Solitary*. Houghton Mifflin, 1905.

Plath, Otto, *Bumble Bees and Their Ways*. Macmillan, 1934.

Ribbands, C. Ronald, *Behavior and Social Life of Honeybees*. Dover, 1957.

*Richards, O. W., *Social Insects*. Macdonald, 1953.

Root, A. I., *ABC and XYZ of Bee Culture*. A. I. Root, 1947.

*Skaife, S. H., *Dwellers in Darkness*. Doubleday, 1961.

Snodgrass, R. E., *Anatomy of the Honey Bee*. Cornell University Press, 1956.

*Teale, Edwin Way, *Golden Throng*. Dodd, Mead, 1961.

Wheeler, William Morton, *Social Life Among the Insects*. Harcourt, Brace, 1923. *Ants*. Columbia University Press, 1910.

Butterflies and Moths

Ford, E. B., *Butterflies*. Macmillan, 1957. *Moths*. Macmillan, 1955.

Holland, William J., *Butterfly Book*. Doubleday, 1931. *Moth Book*. Doubleday, 1949.

Klots, Alexander B., *World of Butterflies and Moths*. McGraw-Hill, 1958.

Other Orders

Arnett, R. H. Jr., *Beetles of the United States*. Catholic University of America Press, 1960.

Bates, Marston, *Natural History of Mosquitoes*. Macmillan, 1949.

Fabre, Jean Henri, *Insect World of J. Henri Fabre*, ed., by Edwin Way Teale, Dodd, Mead, 1949.

*Frisch, Karl von, *Ten Little Housemates*. Pergamon, 1960.

Horsfall, W. P., *Mosquitoes*. Ronald, 1955.

McClintock, Theodore, *Tank Menagerie*. Abelard, 1954.

Reitter, Ewald, *Beetles*. G. P. Putnam's Sons, 1961.

Collecting, Preserving and Studying

Beirne, B. P., *Collecting, Preparing and Preserving Insects*. Canada Department of Agriculture, 1955.

Chu, Hung-fu, *How to Know the Immature Insects*. H. E. Jaques, ed., Brown, 1947.

Jaques, H. E., *How to Know the Beetles*. Brown, 1951. *How to Know the Insects*. Brown, 1947.

Klots, Alexander B., *Field Guide to the Butterflies*. Houghton Mifflin, 1951.

Lutz, Frank E., *Field Book of Insects*. G. P. Putnam's Sons, 1948.

Oldroyd, Harold, *Collecting, Preserving and Studying Insects*. Macmillan, 1959.

Ross, Edward S., *Insects Close Up*. University of California Press, 1953.

Swain, Ralph B., *Insect Guide*. Doubleday, 1952.

Usinger, Robert L., ed., *Aquatic Insects of California, with Keys to North American Genera and California Species*. University of California Press, 1956.

Miscellaneous

Bastin, Harold, *Freaks and Marvels of Insect Life*. Wyn, 1954.

Brues, Charles Thomas, *Insect Dietary: An Account of the Food Habits of Insects*. Harvard University Press, 1946.

Carson, Rachel, *Silent Spring*. Houghton Mifflin, 1962.

Clausen, Lucy W., *Insect Fact and Folklore*. Macmillan, 1954.

Curran, C. H., *Insects in Your Life*. Sheridan, 1951.

Gunther, F. A., and L. R. Jeppson, *Modern Insecticides and World Food Production*. John Wiley & Sons, 1960.

Harris, J. R., *Angler's Entomology*. Collins, 1956.

Kirkpatrick, T. W., *Insect Life in the Tropics*. Longmans, Green, 1957.

Lloyd, Francis Ernest, *Carnivorous Plants*. Ronald, 1942.

Macan, T. T., *Life in Lakes and Rivers*. Collins, 1951.

Metcalf, C. L., W. P. Flint and R. L. Metcalf, *Destructive and Useful Insects*. McGraw-Hill, 1951.

Ordish, George, *The Living House*. Lippincott, 1960.

Pennak, Robert W., *Fresh-Water Invertebrates of the United States*. Ronald, 1953.

Steinhaus, Edward A., *Principles of Insect Pathology*. McGraw-Hill, 1949.

U.S. Department of Agriculture, *Insects, Yearbook of Agriculture*. Government Printing Office, 1952.

Williams, C. B., *Insect Migration*. Macmillan, 1959.

* Also available in paperback edition.

† Only available in paperback edition.

Index

Stinger, *44*

Stink bug, 174; camouflage of, *111*; eggs of, *70*; metamorphosis of, *56*

Stonefly: ancestral, *18*; breathing system of nymph of, 142

Strength, physical, 12

Stridulation, 37. *See also* Sound, production of

Stripe-tailed scorpion, *30*

Subterranean insects, 98

Survival, capacity for, 11, 12-14, 42; unrivaled staying power, 19

Swallowtail, proboscis of, *49*

Swarming (gregarious) locusts, *60*, 61

Swarming hormone, 61, 62

Symbiosis: ants and plants, 125; aphid and ant, 38, 115, 168-169; aquatic caterpillars and plants, 145; cockroach and protozoa, *84*; leaf cutter and fungus, 165; termite and protozoa, 84; yucca moth and yucca, 126

Tachinid fly larvae, *115*

Taste: foul, as protective device, 105, 106; sense of, 38, 39-40

Temperature: insects' sense of, 34, 38, 40; survival in extreme, 11, 56. *See also* Climate control; Heat

Termites, 11, 82-83, 101; air-conditioning of nests of, *diagram* 85, 86; beneficence of, 86; castes of, *83*; nests of, 84-86, 92, *93*,

98; number of known species, 82; protective devices of, 83, 105, 120; social organization of, 10, 83-84, 86; symbiosis of, with protozoa, 84. *See also* Queen termite

Texas harvester ant, *165*

Thorax (mid-section), 14, 15, 34, 43, *45*

Ticks, 14, 30

Tiger beetle larva, *48*, 102; attack of, *102*

"Tippling Tommy," 97

Tomato sphinx moth caterpillar, *114*

Tool-using insects: *Ammophila* wasp, 82, *89*; weaver ant, 173

Tools, specialized. *See* Building tools; Feeding tools; Hunting, tools for

Tortoise beetle, *22*

Touch, sense of, 38, 40

Tracheae, 44, 154

Transportation. *See* Flight; Jumping; Locomotion

Trap-door spider, *30*

Tree cricket, 37

Tree hopper: herded by dairy ant, *173*; jump of, *diagram* 12

Triassic insects, *19*

Trophallaxis, 163, *178-179*

Tsetse fly, birth of, 56

Tuberculosis, 29

Tunnels, insect, *96-97, 99*

Twain, Mark, 170

Twig caterpillars, 106, 108, *109*

Typhoid, 29

Ultrasonic wave sensitivity, 36

Ultraviolet wave sensitivity, 36

Velvet ant, *43*, 102

Vinegar fly, 39

Vision. *See* Eyes; Sight, sense of

Waitomo Caves, New Zealand, *118-119*

Walking cycle, *41*

Walking-stick insect, 12, 56

Wasps, 16, *27*, 40; anatomy of, *44-45*; behavior patterns of, 10-11, 81-82; classification of, 27; flight of, *52-53*; heat escape of, 102; intelligence test, 161-162; nests of, 79-82, *87-89, 94-95*, 98; as parasites, *114, 115*; pollination by, 125; protective coloration of, 107; reproduction of, without fertilization, 56; social, 10, 80, 82; solitary, 10, 80-82; speed of, *table* 14; stinger of, *44*, 127; wings of, 51. *See also* Hornets

Water, metabolic, 11

Water beetles, 41, 145, *146-147*, 148

Water boatman, *146*, 147, *150-151*

Water bugs, *140*, 148

Water dwellers. *See* Aquatic insects

"Water pennies," 148

Water scorpion, 145, *155*; hunting tool of, 41

Water strider, 146, *147*, 148, *152*, 153

Water surface dwellers, 146-147, *152-153*

Water tiger larva, 150, *151*

Waterproofing of skeleton, 13

"Waves of determinism," 58-59

Wax moth larva, 139

Weaver ant, 173

Weevils, 13

Whirligig beetle, 36, *147*, 152, *153*

White Ant, The Life of the, Maeterlinck, 86

White ants. *See* Termites

White oak leaf miner, *124*

Williams, Carroll, 66, 68

Wings, 14, *44-45*, 51, 60; of bumble bee, *51*; control of, 34; development of, 15; after emergence from pupa, 60; evolution of folding mechanism of, 16; hairs on, 34; of Luna moth, *50*; membrane, 27; of mosquito, *51*; scaly, 25; sheath, 22, *23*; two-winged insects, 29. *See also* Flight

Wood-boring insects, 133; tunnels of, *96-97*. *See also* Termites

Wood louse, 14, *31*

Woods, insects of, 103, 123

Worms, evolution of insects from, 15, 17

Wrigglers, 145, 148

Xenarchus, 37

Yellow fever, 29, 42

Yellow-jacket wasp, 79

Yucca moth and yucca, 126, *127*

XXXXX